D1582303

8

Love is
a time of enchantment:
in it all days are fair and all fields
green. Youth is blest by it,
old age made benign:
the eyes of love see
roses blooming in December,
and sunshine through rain. Verily
is the time of true-love
a time of enchantment — and
Oh! how eager is woman
to be bewitched!

ALL OR NOTHING

What King Henry VIII wanted, he had to have, and nothing must stand in his way. He wanted the beautiful, proud, strong-willed Anne Boleyn, who refused to be any man's mistress. He also wanted a son. The King broke up Anne's romance with Lord Henry Percy and pursued her, without avail, for six years. Anne did not love Henry, but ambition gradually took the place of love and at last she yielded to him and became pregnant. To gain both Anne and a son, the King married her. This is her fated story.

Books by Joanna Dessau
Published by The House of Ulverscroft:

JOANNA DESSAU

ALL OR NOTHING

The Life-Story of Anne Boleyn

Complete and Unabridged

ULVERSCROFT
Leicester

First Large Print Edition
published 1998

The right of Joanna Dessau to be identified
as author of this work has been asserted
by her in accordance with the
Copyright, Designs and Patents Act 1988

British Library CIP Data

Dessau, Joanna
    All or nothing: the life story of Anne Boleyn.
    — Large print ed.—
    Ulverscroft large print series: romance
    1. Boleyn, Anne, *1507–1536* – Fiction
    2. Love stories
    3. Large type books
    I. Title
    823.9'14 [F]

    ISBN 0–7089–3964–3

To my friend
ELIZABETH RAYCROFT
and in memory of dear, beautiful
CAROLINE
who asked for the story of Anne Boleyn

1

TO FRANCE FOR A WEDDING

September–December 1514

The weather was most unseasonable for late September, all agreed upon that as the cavalcade of lords, ladies, knights, squires, men-at-arms, litters, carts and waggons wound its way along the Dover Road. Grey clouds hung low, a damp, chilly breeze whistled searchingly down necks, up skirts and round knees, causing cloaks to billow and hoods to blow back, hair to whip across eyes, litter curtains to flutter and gentlemen to curse as they clapped hands to their feathered velvet hats.

At the head of the procession rode the twenty-three year old King Henry VIII on a great white stallion, laughing and joking, as was his wont when matters went as he wished. Matters had certainly fallen out as he had desired except for the weather, which was a mere fleabite, he considered, when one thought of what was involved. It was a fine thing for his younger sister to be marrying the

King of France — no more than was due to a Tudor Princess, of course — but a fine thing, nevertheless and right useful politically. Mind, he had had a devilish hard fight to persuade Mary Rose of her duty. How she had stormed and wept! He grinned now at the memory, but he had not grinned at the time, by God! He had shouted as loud as she — louder, in fact, for he had feared she might not give in and one could hardly have a royal princess carried struggling and screaming to the altar, not his favourite sister, anyhap. That would have looked right bad in the eyes of Europe. Such doings could cause a riot at best and a war at worst and he did not wish to spend his money on a war. She had cockled under in the end, but only after wresting a promise from him, the saucy jade! Well, promises could always be forgot; the thing was to get her safe wed. *Certes*, King Louis was old. Fifty-eight was a great age and he was sick and ailing too. Ay, and 'twas said that he had bad breath, hunched shoulders, was tormented by sudden attacks of gout and . . .

". . . And has a constant drip at the end of his long, drooping, pock-pitted nose!" had screamed his sister, the outraged, eighteen year old Princess Mary Rose, her blue eyes tear-filled and flashing, red-gold hair flying, cheeks scarlet. "I will not. I will *not*! You cannot make me, brother!"

"I both can and will!" he had bawled in answer. "You are a Princess of England; it is your duty to wed where your King bids you! It is what Princesses are born to, Mary Rose, and you will do as I say!"

Then she had sobbed and cozened and persuaded until his heart had softened a trifle, for she was his favourite sister, dear, pretty little poppet.

"Well, the old fool cannot last for ever," he had said. "You will outlive him, sure, and then you will be a rich widow, will you not? What better than that, eh?"

She had paused at that, rubbing her eyes like a child. "Ay," she had replied, musingly. "Ay, 'tis like he will die long afore me. I had not thought of that. But royal widows may not wed where they will, neither. See Hal, if I marry this nasty old gowk, will you let me choose my own bridegroom when he dies?"

She would bargain with him, plucky little baggage! Such temerity as she had! Ay, she was a real Tudor, no doubt of that. Bursting into a laugh, he had slapped his crimson clad thigh. "Well, well, I will allow that," he had conceded, chuckling. "And you will wed Louis. Is it a bargain, Mary Rose?"

"It is a bargain, she had answered, full of

defiance, "and do you not forget it, brother!"

So here they were, on their way to Dover to wish her Godspeed and watch her take ship for her new country and her elderly bridegroom. King Henry was pleased at the way matters had turned out and had no intention of keeping his word to his sister. He only hoped that the child that his wife Katherine carried in her belly would be a boy that lived this time. If so, all would be perfect. He trusted that Katherine was comfortable in her litter. He would ride back and ascertain before long. Hey, but life was good, life was merry! He raised his fine baritone voice in song:

"Listen lords, both old and young,"

he carolled, smiling at Mary Rose.

"To the tale of a rose but lately sprung;
Such a rose to mine liking
In all this world I know but one . . . "

Turning in the saddle, he cried out to the company following: "Come now all of ye, join with me in the refrain to our Rose Princess!"

And they sang with him:

> *"Of a rose, a lovely rose,*
>   *Of a rose is all my song,"*

keeping up the ditty all the way to Canterbury where it was intended to spend the night.

★ ★ ★

In Their Majesties' train rode Sir Thomas Boleyn, Ambassador to the court of the Archduchess Margaret of Austria, Regent of the Netherlands, accompanied by his wife Elizabeth, his son George and his two daughters, Mary and Anne. Sir Thomas was a satisfied man this day. His rise to favour had been rapid, for he was of the type to appeal to the young King; forceful, driving, shrewd, hard-headed and ambitious, with a sharp eye for the main chance. Some there were who felt inclined to sneer at him, though surreptitiously, for his birth, although good, was not wholly noble, his paternal grandfather, Sir Geoffrey, one-time Lord Mayor of London, having been of yeoman stock, though rich as Croesus when he died, God save him. On his mother's side, Sir Thomas's blood was of the highest, she being a daughter of Thomas, the fabulously wealthy seventh Earl of Ormond.

In his marriage, Sir Thomas had wedded the dark and beautiful Lady Elizabeth Howard, daughter of the Earl of Surrey, but just lately become Duke of Norfolk, a very advantageous match, so all in all, he had little of which to complain. And although the Lady Elizabeth had borne him a child every year, a blessing it was that only three had survived, for too many children were a sore drain on the purse! Many hopeful careers had come to naught and many good men had been held back by lack of funds through the simple fact of having bred too great a family and thus having too many mouths to feed. He sent up a quick prayer that his numbers might not increase. Perhaps one more son? Ah, 'twas in God's hands, after all, and so far God had seen fit to smile upon Sir Thomas Boleyn.

Sir Thomas smiled also as he thought of his handsome manor of Blickling in Norfolk, bought by his astute grandsire, Sir Geoffrey, and that of Hever Castle in Kent, purchased by the same prudent gentleman, as well as a fine inheritance left by him in gold. Sir Thomas had the King's favour, ay, his eleven year old son George was a page at Court, his elder daughter, the ten year old Mary, had already spent a year at the court of the Archduchess Margaret and now had been released in order to accompany the Princess

Mary Rose on her wedding journey to France. As for his younger girl, Anne, she was to go too. At the age of seven years, Anne was a little young to be a Maid of Honour, but it were best to begin young, Sir Thomas believed, and no good opportunity should ever be overlooked, no hopeful chance lost. That was the way to rise in the world. And what if Anne had protested and wept at the thought of going so far from home? A few sharp buffets on the ear had settled all that. A child of so young an age to defy her father! Why, 'twas unheard of and Sir Thomas was not the man to allow the insubordination of a child, and a girl at that, to stand in the way of his plans. It would do Anne good to go, for all that her mother did not wish to part with her. She would learn courtly ways, learn to bridle her bad temper and become proficient in the French tongue. Sir Thomas was fluent in French and rightly proud of this useful accomplishment.

Mind, Anne would need plenty of accomplishments, he reflected, for she had no looks, apart from those enormous dark eyes which were too big for her small plain face. 'Goggle-eyes', he would call them mockingly, laughing derisively at the storm of fury that this always aroused in the little thing. Yes, a spell abroad should tame her well.

Now, Mary was a different proposition altogether. Though dark-complected as Anne, and therefore unfashionable, she was pretty in a smiling, soft-featured way. She was also gentle and placid, respectful, womanly and biddable — all that a daughter should be — while George was a son of whom any man would be proud. A fine lad was George and should go far. Smiling to himself, Sir Thomas spurred his mount alongside Queen Katherine's litter, inquiring solicitously after the health of the royal lady within, pleased to note that his wife was with the Queen. Ay, all ran happily indeed. He joined in the King's chorus, singing with a will:

"Of a rose, a lovely rose,
Of a rose is all my song!"

★ ★ ★

By the time that the procession reached Dover on the afternoon of the next day, the weather had so worsened as to make a crossing for the Princess impossible and all the company were forced to take up residence in the great castle until conditions should improve. Mistress Anne Boleyn, the Princess Mary Rose's youngest lady, was wide-eyed at her first glimpse of the sea, so grey and white, wild and tumbling, under a beaded silver curtain of rain that seemed to stretch from heaven to earth and beyond.

"And they call it the Narrow Sea!" she gasped in amazement to her sister. "Why, you cannot see its end!"

"Of course you cannot," replied Mary Boleyn knowledgeably. " 'Tis only called 'Narrow' because it is narrower than the others. France lies t'other side of that sea, Nan, and when the wind abates we shall set sail. You will puke your heart up, I'll wager. I did when I went to the Archduchess Margaret *and* when I came back! Everyone does when the waves go up and down. You'll be no different. Come, our lady mother beckons to us to go to the table and eat. Is this not a fine castle, Nan? King Henry likes it well, my father said so. We are to share a bed, you and I, in the South Tower Room, with the other young ladies, he says."

At dinner, King Henry, Queen Katherine and the Princess were served on the dais, in company with the highest nobles in the retinue. Sir Thomas and his lady sat in good places below the dais, their children lower down amongst the lesser knights and ladies, where the talk and jests were unrestrained, few seeming to have eyes for a small girl of seven years, whose head only was visible above the boards of the trestle table, until one young gentleman called across to her eleven year old brother.

"George! George Boleyn! See that your sister has somewhat to eat, poor miting. All I can tell of her is her head! It rests chin on platter, like that of St. John the Baptist. Have you 'headed her, George, and brought only her noddle to the feast?"

Thus reminded, George ceased to cram his mouth, nudged Mary beside him, and helped his young sister to fill her plate, feeling some remorse at her plight, for he was dearly fond of little Nan, so bright and spirited as she was. She would make a dozen of Mary, would Nan. He wished he might go oversea too; that would be an adventure, no force! But he was bound to red-headed King Henry's Court and that was merry enough, with masques and mummers, dancing and feasting every day, with knightly sports in which to take part and young lads like himself with whom to make friends. He could not repine, not he. It was a fine thing to be page to His Majesty.

"You will be a real French lady when you come home, Nan," he said encouragingly to the child. "I dare swear you will have forgotten all your English by then and will chatter foreign words like any popinjay, putting us all to shame."

"I shall *not!*" she retorted. "I had rather be English, I! Mayhap I shall not like it in France."

"Oh, you will," put in Mary confidently. "Only think, we shall be more free than at home. There is only Lady Guildford over us as Mother of the Maids and she is not near so strict as our own mother. I had a merry time at the court of the Archduchess, I tell you, Anna. And we shall be together too. I will show you how to go on, sister."

"I would rather have my own mother," answered Anne stubbornly. "I love her. I love her more than Lady Guildford." Her lip trembled. "I had rather go home."

"Well, do not weep, I beg you!" exclaimed Mary. " 'Tis only babies that weep. Are you then a baby?"

"No, I am not!" cried Anne, her little creamy-skinned face flushing a bright and angry red. "Do not you call *me* a baby! I mind how you blubbered when you had to go away last year, so now!"

Mary stuck an elbow in her ribs. "If you do not bridle that temper of yours, do you know what will happen to you? That extra nail you bear on your hand will grow and grow until it becomes a whole finger and you will have six fingers like a witch! Remember what our father says. He says that nail is your bad temper coming out. Dost want all to think you a witch, Anne? You will never grow pretty then, see'st thou."

At this, Anne subsided and finished her portion of pigeon pie. It was hard enough, she thought crossly, to have an extra nail on the little finger of her right hand, without being ugly as well. For she was ugly, of that she had no doubt. Did not her father call her Mistress Goggle-eyes, all bones and tantrums? Did he not call her a sour-faced little grimalkin? It was enough to make anyone sour-faced to be treated so. Of course, her mother always took her part and she loved her for it, but the words about the tantrums were all too true. Ay, she had a vile temper. Mayhap her father was right and the French court would cure it — who knew? She sniffed philosophically and bit into a lump of sugared marchpane passed to her by George. Opportunities should be grasped; her father had said that, too. Shrugging her shoulders, she decided to follow her fate as bravely as might be. After all, she was seven years old!

* * *

It was not until the small hours of the morning of the 2nd of October that the wind dropped. By four o'clock, the waters were calm enough to attempt the crossing and King Henry, with some of his personal attendants, came down to the quay to kiss his sister and to wish her Godspeed and a safe journey. The torches, held high by shivering pages, puffy-eyed with sleep, cast their wavering light upon the wet cobbles and sparkled in the jewels in His Majesty's plumed hat. The sky, streaked with mauve and yellow, was as dark grey as the sea that rolled beneath it, waves slapping against the stones of the jetty, causing the row-boats to bob like flotsam and the great ships anchored further out to rock gently, their tall masts swinging, pendulum-like, ink-black against the heavy sky.

In tears, the Princess parted from her brother and was assisted down the slippery stone steps into the small boat that was to take her to the ships that awaited her. The rest of her company struggled into other dinghies and the little flotilla moved out across the gleaming water as the pale moon shone out from behind the ragged black clouds that raced across the dawn sky. Handkerchiefs fluttered until the figures on the quay could be seen no more and the Princess, with her entourage, boarded the ships that lay at anchor.

Before the crossing was done, little Anne

had learned the meaning of sea-sickness, for another storm blew up off the French coast and the small fleet was scattered, some ships making for Calais or Flanders, while the vessel carrying the Princess reached Boulogne, but ran aground before arriving at the harbour. Mary and Anne hung over the rail, their stomachs heaving like the ocean below them.

"Thank heaven we are run aground, Anne!" gasped Mary. "The ship has ceased its pitching. I vow my belly is eased already! If I stare at the sky, my sickness seems to stop altogether, the Lord be praised. We shall have to be got off in boats, I think. Oh, I can see some that have put out to fetch us."

And it was not long before the wet, shivering, groaning ladies and gentlemen were being helped into the boats that were to take them ashore. Anne could never remember how she got from ship to row-boat, only that she was so terrified that she clapped her hands over her eyes and could not be induced even to peep in order to witness the Princess Mary Rose's somewhat undignified progress to the beaches of France, in spite of her sister's persuasions

"Oh, Nan, look — take your hands from your eyes, do! See, there is the Princess being carried over a gentleman's shoulder like a sack of meal! Oh, 'tis Sir Christopher Garnish who carries her and he is up to his waist in water! His fine clothes will be ruined! Oh, do pray look, Anne! Suppose she should fall, what then? Can you imagine if she should fall? Oh, Anne *do* look!"

But Anne's small hands remained tight over her eyes until land was reached and then she felt great surprise to discover that France looked very much like England.

"Well, what did you expect?" cried Mary, laughing. "Blue grass and green sky? Painted savages? Come, we must behave in a fitting manner. It will never do to appear awkward and rustic. Pull your hood forward, so, and hold up your skirts as I do and do not gawk about as though you do not know how to go on." She put a sisterly arm about the child's thin shoulders. "You will soon grow used to things, Nan, and then we shall have a merry time."

"Will there be much to learn?" queried Anne as they hurried along, shepherded by Lady Guildford, who was fussily rounding up her charges.

"Oh ay, indeed. It is all procedure and manners, see'st thou. How to carve meat, how to behave at table among grand company, how to sit up straight on a wooden bench, how to dress properly, how to manage a great household, how to read, write and cipher. And to speak French, of course. Our father sets a great store by that."

"It seems a great deal," signed Anne. "I fear I shall not enjoy it."

"Ah, but you will enjoy Princess Mary Rose's recognition procession through Abbeville! That will be wondrous fine and we are to be in it!"

"Oh, shall we wear the crimson gowns for that?" Anne's eyes brightened at the thought.

"Of a certainty we shall. Wait in patience, sister. We shall soon learn what is to befall."

The ceremonial procession through Abbeville a few days later on the 5th of October was a splendid affair. Princess Mary Rose, her lovely hair down her back, as befitted her virgin state, robed in cloth of silver and mounted upon a white palfrey bridled and caparisoned in gold with crimson fringes and hung with little gold bells, rode at the head of her company. She was followed by thirty-six ladies all in crimson velvet, among whom were Anne and Mary Boleyn, their horses decked in the same, whilst behind the ladies rolled a chariot covered in cloth of tissue, another in cloth of gold and a third in crimson velvet sewn with Tudor roses and the arms of France and England in gold. After the chariots came bands of archers followed by waggons containing tapestries, clothing, money, plate and jewels, thus to prove to the French people that the Princess Mary Rose Tudor, who was to wed their King, was no beggarly lady.

The beautiful Princess was a pale bride at her wedding the next day in the handsome, new-built church at Abbeville. No matter her golden robes trimmed with ermine, her dazzling jewels, the soaring voices of the choristers the glowing hues of the great windows, she trembled as she stood before the altar with her elderly bridegroom who was also attired in cloth of gold.

He is not so grotesque as I imagined, although far from handsome, she thought. I was wrong about his nose. It is long, but it does not drip, praise be to God, nor does he crouch or go stooping. It is certain that I please him, for his eyes light up when he looks at me. I hope he will try to make me happy. But oh, how shall I go on without my beloved Charles Brandon? I must not think of that, for it is of no use. This is my wedding day; I am to be a Queen and must behave like one and not shame my brother and England.

Steadied somewhat by these reflections, she managed to make her responses in a creditably firm voice and the long ceremony passed smoothly. After the wedding, once within the walls of the stately Hôtel de la Gruthuse, the King's residence in Abbeville, nothing went smoothly. Cries of dismay, shrieks of protestation, shouts of annoyance and temper rang loud and long, for King Louis, succumbing to a fit of irritability and pain from a sudden attack of the Flying Gout, to which he was prone, had dismissed all Mary Rose's English attendants, with the exception of a few, and with no word of forewarning.

"But Mother Guildford!" cried Mary Rose in distress. "Not Lady Guildford, Sire! She is my Lady mistress — has been with me all my life. You cannot send her away!" She burst into loud sobs.

"*Doux Jésu!*" roared the King. "She goes with all the others, Madame! You need no Lady Mistress now; you are Queen yourself and will give your own orders. No more arguments, I say!"

"I shall write to my brother, King Henry!" threatened Mary Rose through her tears. "He will not allow me to be treated so!"

"Write away, Madame!" shouted His Majesty, his face creased with pain. "It shall avail you little, for I am your husband and you, as my wife, are subject to none but me."

Mary Rose subsided. It was all too true. This man was her lord and she was his

18

possession to do with as he willed. In which case, it were better to agree, since if she were to be alone in a foreign land, it would be politic to have her husband as a friend, if friend he would be. She knew he desired her; she had seen that much in his eye. If she gave way on this, perhaps he would allow her many other things, be fond of her, make life easy for her. Her agile, compromising Tudor brain worked swiftly. She brushed her tears away, forced her lips to smile and knelt before the French King. After all, was not honey sweeter than vinegar?

"Indeed, you speak truth, sire," she said placatingly. "Would'st tell me then, which ladies you will allow to stay, if any?"

The King's brow smoothed a little and he looked down at her, an expression of surprise and pleasure on his heavy featured, middle-aged face. "*Eh bien*," said he, "this is right sensible of you, Madame. I had not hoped for such understanding in one so young." He put out a hand and she took it, rising to her feet. "Come," he went on, "we will confer together alone for a while. Sit here by me, child. Clear the chamber!" he called. "Away with all of you! I wish to be private with my Queen."

Gradually, in twos and threes, the courtiers sidled out of the large room, the angry English lords and ladies muttering darkly of "insult" and "unpardonable rudeness", the French nobles tittering behind their hands.

"The truth is this, *ma jolie*," confided Louis to Mary Rose as soon as they were alone, "the Exchequer will not support the upkeep of so great a company as yours and I am a careful man. Besides which, I suffered untold misery with my second wife, Anne of Brittany, who was a haughty shrew, devoted only to her own land, having no interest in aught of mine. I made the mistake of allowing her to keep all her Breton attendants and a fine dance I was led thereby. Money trickled away like so much water. In the end, it was as if I did not exist! I swore that never again would I suffer such a drain on my resources and nor will I, you understand. Also, my wretched gout plagues me most cruelly at this minute. 'Tis a pain worse than red-hot pincers and I pray it will depart before you and I seek our marriage-bed this night. I fear I am far too old for you, *ma chère*, but if you agree with me upon this one thing, I will do all I can to make you happy in days to come. You have my royal word on it."

She gazed at him thoughtfully. It seemed that he would indeed be her friend if she watched her words and ways. Her pretty lips parted in a charming smile, disclosing perfect, pearly teeth.

"I will agree with you, Sire," she said tactfully, "but I should be happy if you would allow me to keep one or two ladies with whom I may talk in my own tongue, for although I speak French easily, I am far from home and this would be a great comfort to me."

His face fairly beamed as he kissed her cheek. "What a dear, sweet maid you seem to be," he murmured. "If we are not to be as happy together as youth and age can be it will be none of my doing, *mignonne*. Call in your ladies and I will choose those who may remain. You will permit me to choose?"

She bowed her head submissively, feeling that she had made her way successfully through a potential battlefield. Finally the King chose Lady Elizabeth Grey, Anne Jerningham, Elizabeth Grey de Wilton, Mary Fiennes, Lady Anne Bourchier, together with Mary and Anne Boleyn to remain with his bride, while the courtiers who were dismissed received gifts and money, Lady Guildford being offered a pension to take effect on her return to England.

That night, after a long drawn out banquet, followed by a great ball that was still in progress, Mary Rose was escorted to the great nuptial bed by her giggling English ladies. She felt a good deal of apprehension, if not actual fear. Lifting her long golden hair, they removed her white satin night-robe all sewn with pale roses and helped her into bed. She lay naked on the feather mattress, her bright hair spread over the pillows as the girls pulled the linen sheet and heavy coverlet over her. The coverlet was of blue velvet and padded for warmth and patterned with silver fleur-de-lys as were the blue velvet bed-curtains. She shivered, her stomach quaking with nerves.

"Oh, do not shiver, Madame!" cried Anne Jerningham, laughing. "I'll warrant you'll be warm enough soon."

"Ay, that coverlet will be needless with His Majesty to cover you," tittered Mary Fiennes, causing a further outburst of giggles.

"Would you be in my place, then, Mary?" asked Mary Rose. "I would gladly change, believe me."

"Fear not, he will know how to pleasure you," Mary Fiennes assured her. "Well, he is old, but age carries experience and he has been wed before, so he will not be like some greedy young bull to pounce and think only of his own gratification."

Mary Rose sighed. She wished that she could be so sure. She doubted that she would enjoy the exercise. Now, if it had been her dear, lusty Charles Brandon in the old King's place — ! Big, beautiful Charles Brandon, dearest friend of King Henry, her brother, but recently made Duke of Suffolk, with whom she was so much in love. He loved her too and was desolated when she was sent off to France like so much baggage. He had said he wished to wed but before they could even speak of it to King Henry, the French marriage had been arranged and their dreams were over. Tears started to her eyes and her lips trembled.

At that moment, there came a knocking on the door and a man's voice cried loudly: "Way! Make way for His Majesty King Louis to enter the bridal chamber!"

Running to the door, all smiles, Lady Elizabeth Grey pulled it open to reveal the French King robed in flowing white velvet, accompanied by six grinning gentlemen. His attack of Flying Gout had obviously flown away.

"Come, ladies!" cried Lady Elizabeth. "It is time for us to leave and join the dancers below. Give you good-night, Majesties both!" Bursting with muffled laughter, she and her companions fluttered out, curtseying as they went, leaving their mistress to her fears and regrets.

Before the door closed, Mary Rose caught the sound of music and merry-making floating up from the Great Hall and heartily wished herself there. Eyes wide, she watched the King's gentlemen remove their royal master's white velvet nightcap; eyes wider still she watched them unfasten his robe to discover — ah, she could not watch that. He would look horrible, surely. She had never seen a man naked and this one was old. Horrible. And yet — ! Cautiously she peeped. Well, his shoulders were wide enough, his body was not yet wrinkled, his waist was not too bulging, but oh, what was that *thing*? Swallowing hard, she shut her eyes tightly and her breath caught in her throat as she turned her head away quickly.

Amid loud guffaws from his gentlemen, the King was helped into bed, where he lay quietly beside the shrinking Mary Rose. *Who would be a Princess?* she thought wildly. *Who would be a Princess to be shipped abroad like a prize cow to be serviced? Who would be the wife of a King? Not I.*

With a little start, she realised that the gentlemen were leaving the bedchamber and that His Majesty was leaning on an elbow amongst the pillows smiling and offering her a cup of wine.

"Drink, *chérie*," he said. "It will ease your fears. I promise to be kind."

Experienced he may have been, kind he

meant to be, but young and virile he was not. What followed was an undignified tumble and scramble, interspersed with curses, for His Majesty, eager at first, found it difficult to maintain the evidence of his ardour, due to a nervous desire to impress this lovely young creature with the force of his masculinity. It was managed at last, but the business was not a conspicuous success, causing some pain and more disappointment to the youthful Queen.

Would it always be like this? she wondered miserably, so clawing, so ruttish, so ridiculous? She wondered how she would endure it and for how long and what would happen to her after her husband's death, for in the natural order of things, he would surely die first? Moreover, except for chatting to her few English ladies, she would have to speak French till the end of her days, for all she knew. Blessings be that she was fluent in the tongue. Maybe she could learn to swear in French! Hey, that would be fair sport, but not enough to pass the time away. Under the bedclothes she whispered a few full-bodied English oaths, taught her in wicked fun by her loved, naughty Charles Brandon.

"Tail-piss and bum-broth!" she whispered. "I would I were not here."

She had riches, jewels, she was extremely

beautiful by any standards; she was Queen of a great country. A Queen, but without power, however praised and admired. The King was greatly attracted by her and could not keep his hands from her person, but his hands were not Charles Brandon's hands. Life was so unfair, especially to Princesses. Oh, how she wanted Charles. If he had been the King, how wonderful, how ecstatic last night would have been. She lay silent as her husband rang his handbell for his gentlemen to come and dress him and once he had left the room for his dressing chamber, she gave herself up to thought. She would not rise yet; it would not be expected after the first night of a marriage. She would consider her position.

Lying back on her soft, feather-filled pillows, frowning a little, Mary Rose drew a deep breath and made up her mind. She would make the best of it. It was useless to spoil the days of her youth by doleful glooming over something that could not be helped. She was only eighteen, she was beautiful, her health was good, she had energy in plenty and she had every material thing a woman could want or need. Except Charles Brandon.

Ay, that thought was the dagger at the feast. That thought was nothing but heartbreak and anguish. Then into the clothes-press with heartbreak and anguish; slam the lid and turn the key! She would dance and sing, flirt and play, wear new gowns, glitter with jewels and fill her days so full with pleasure that there would be no room for sad thoughts. Except at night.

Well then, she would cozen and pet and arouse her old husband, gout or no gout. Although her marriage-night had been a bumbling wrestling match, he had consummated it and, although she had felt no ardour herself, she had experienced a certain small physical pleasure at times. Tudors were well-known for their hot blood and she was true Tudor. She could urge the King on to give her enough pleasure that her nights might be bearable enough, surely! Better than repining. Much better.

Pulling back the bed-curtains, she rang her bell and shouted in English and in French for her ladies to help her rise, to dress her, for she was but eighteen and life was meant to be lived.

On the 5th of November she was crowned at St. Denis, just outside Paris, and for the next six weeks, all was gaiety. King Louis, thoroughly enamoured of his lovely young bride, loaded her with jewels, arranged masques and pretty surprises for her. She who loved to dance, would dance all night,

27

while he, watching her dotingly from his chair, would often rise and dance with her, if he felt able. She rode, she sang, she laughed, she deferred charmingly to His French Majesty who was entranced by her. She would play Tag along the stately galleries and Blind Man's Buff in the Great Hall, her husband puffing bravely among the shrieking, laughing players who did their best to avoid his gouty feet. He ate enormously in his late-come happiness, drank hugely and made love to his young wife whenever he could, feeling himself re-born.

At Christmas time, re-born or no, King Louis was forced to admit that his pursuit of youth had not been crowned with success. On the 26th of December he took to his bed; on the 31st he died, after eighty-two days of marriage and Mary Rose was a widow.

★ ★ ★

As soon as he learnt of the death of King Louis, King, Henry of England sent his friend, Charles Brandon, Duke of Suffolk to France, ostensibly to carry condolences for the demise of its monarch, but in reality to prevent his sister from being married to the Duke of Savoy, for he wished no one but himself to arrange any marriage to his favourite sister, preferring that the members of his family should remain under his own control. He had no idea of any attachment between Mary Rose and Brandon and would not have allowed it if he had.

As the funeral bells tolled for the dead King, Mary Rose's young English ladies sat, alarmed and subdued, in a small withdrawing room, occupying themslves with embroidery while they pondered their futures.

"Mary, what is to become of us?" asked the youngest lady of her elder sister. "And where is our Queen?"

"I can tell you that, little Boleyn," answered Lady Elizabeth Grey, before Anne's sister could reply. "She is but Dowager Queen now and she is in the Mourning Chamber where she must stay for six whole weeks."

"What?" cried Anne. "May she not come out?"

"No indeed," said Lady Elizabeth. "She must remain there, dressed all in white, with the curtains drawn for six weeks. It is the royal custom here in France."

Little Anne's jaw dropped. "Oh, the poor Queen! I should not like that."

"And nor should I," put in Anne Jerningham, "but what if she is pregnant? That must be discovered, you see. Six weeks should be long enough to find out."

29

"So what is to become of us?" repeated the little girl. "Does anyone know?"

"Well, I shall go home," announced Mary Fiennes with happy assurance, "and so will the rest of us, I daresay. As for you, Mary and Anne Boleyn, your father will settle what is to be done with you. It is no business of ours."

During the weeks of mourning, the future of the Boleyn girls was decided by their father and the future of Mary Rose, Dowager Queen of France, was decided by herself.

Discovering that she was not with child, Mary Rose received her dashing Duke, embracing him with delight, suggesting that they be married as soon as might be. He proved unexpectedly laggard, to her great dismay.

"Remember that although you be not pregnant, you are still in mourning, Mary," he said warningly. "We can do nothing until that is over, and even then — "

"Even then?" she echoed. "Why, what do you mean, Charles? Once I am out of this gloomy chamber and dressed as I wish, I shall be free to wed."

"But your brother, King Henry," he protested. "He will never give us permission, for he will wish you to make a state match, my love. I cannot see how we should contrive."

"What?" she cried. "How can you speak so? You swore that you loved me. You said, 'If only we could wed, Mary Rose!' You said — "

"I know," he mumbled apologetically. "But it is death for anyone to wed a royal princess without the King's consent. Of course I love you, darling. You are my life, dearest, but — "

"*But?*" she shouted. "*But?* You mean that you are afeared? Afeared, in spite of your fine words and promises? I cannot believe it! I cannot believe that you, whom I have so loved and admired, should be a faintheart!" She gave a sob of disappointment and chagrin. He had feet of clay. Well, *she* had not, as he would discover.

"Listen," she said more calmly, wiping her eyes that had filled with tears. "Listen to me. Why should we not wed in secret? It is easy enough to bribe a cleric — one only needs money enough and I have plenty, if you have not."

He flushed. "Oh, I have, darling, but — "

She flung up her hands. "Do not let me hear you prate that stupid word again! Where there's a will there's a way. I have the will, and if you have not, Charles, then you are no man for a Tudor." She tossed her bright head, her blue eyes blazing. "If we are true married, what can anyone do? I am my brother's pet, he will not kill me. You are his friend, he will

31

not hang you. If he should threaten, I shall face him out. I shall scream and yell and swear to die of sorrow. He will shout and storm, but then, if we show crawling penitence, he will forgive us. You will see."

"What if he deny us the Court, Mary Rose?"

She laughed with a touch of bitterness. "Ah, you fear for your position and hopes of power? Well, he will forgive you in the end, he is right fond of you and you are his confidante. As for me, well, Suffolk is a pretty county, Westhorpe is a pleasant house and I shall be your wife. It seems enough to me."

He gazed at her, dazzled by her beauty and decision. He did love her, he was honest with himself about that, but he was afraid of King Henry of England, as who was not? An absolute monarch could take his own way as he pleased, honour whom he pleased as he had done his friend Charles Brandon, but he disliked disobedience. He could kill for it and might well do so.

Of course, if he, Brandon, married Mary Rose, he would be the King's brother-in-law, God save us! This would be a great step up — if His Majesty be not too offended . . .

As he remained lost in thought, Mary Rose burst into passionate tears, holding her little hands out to him pleadingly. He could not resist her. At least, he thought with a certain rueful amusement, I am preventing her from marrying the Duke of Savoy!

"Ay, my love," he said firmly. "Ay, we will do it."

She flew into his arms, crying out with joy. Soon all was set in train and the secret wedding was accomplished and, after some terrific royal storms from her brother, all turned out as she had so confidently predicted.

2

MADEMOISELLE ICEBERG

1514–1522

During the young Queen Dowager's funeral seclusion Sir Thomas Boleyn had not been lazy. He had found a position at the Court of the new King François I for his elder daughter Mary. She was to be put among the ladies of the King's wife, Queen Claude, while Anne was placed in the household of a nobleman friend in the little village of Briis-sous-Forges, near Paris. This was to be temporary only, for Sir Thomas fully intended that his younger daughter should also be placed at Court. The stumbling-block was her extreme youth, for this was a Court of young people, very lively indeed, King François being of much the same age as King Henry of England and far more profligate in his ways. A young child would be nothing but a nuisance to those dashing French blades, reflected Sir Thomas, especially such an ugly, bad-tempered little thing as Anne.

He did not despair of success, however,

and after many letters and persuasive diplomatic conversations, a place was at last found for Anne Boleyn, now aged seven, under the care of Queen Claude and thus under her elder sister's eye. Not that he thought highly of Mary. She was a mere girl and in no way outstanding, to his mind, but she was pretty and pliable in her nature, as a woman should be and he trusted that she would make a good marriage. After all, this was all causing him enough trouble, and a good marriage would be some repayment for it. And then, of course, Mary might do something for that little grimalkin of an Anne. At least George was doing well as a page with King Henry who had taken a great fancy to him, praise be to God.

Anne and Mary found theirs to be a dull enough existence. Queen Claude, young and kindly, but plain, religious and ever-pregnant, had no time for licentiousness and she looked upon the lax morals of her husband's Court with much disapproval. She had no less than three hundred maidens under her patronage and saw to it that they were kept busy with their heads over their sewing, the learning of languages, religious exercises and prayers, month after quiet month and year after tedious year.

"I tell you, Nan," confided Mary to her

sister one day, "I am mighty weary of the way we live. I am fourteen now and marriage-ripe and you are nigh on eleven and for four whole years we have been stuck here, doing naught but murmur 'Yes Madame' and 'No Madame', ply our needles like seamstresses, learn our books like clerks and wear out our knees with prayers. No man is allowed next or nigh us — how shall we ever marry? It is worse than being in a nunnery!"

Anne, still small and thin, her eyes more than ever large and black in her creamy-skinned, oval face, stuck her needle in her work and gazed thoughtfully at her sister. Mary had become very pretty in a dark, slumbrous, full-lipped, pouting way. Her waist was rounded and slender, while her breasts had grown large enough to bulge enticingly over her bodice, which she wore as low as possible when the Queen was not by. Mary had changed very much lately, thought Anne. She looked quite womanly — different in a puzzling way.

"Dost wish to know men, sister?" she asked. "Do you wish to marry? Our father will arrange that, surely."

"Oh, as to marriage — ! Well, every maid must marry; it is all she can do, it is required and expected, so of course I wish to marry. Nor do I wish to hang too long on the

36

vine — that is so shaming. But as to *men* — "
Mary laughed. "Ah, that is not the same thing
at all."

"How is it not the same, Mary?"

"Oh, you are too young to understand; you
are still a baby. But to be with men, why, it is
a sort of excitement, a breathlessness — I
cannot tell, but I wish to learn more of it. I
have noticed men glance at me, Anne, and
more than glance. They stare. They stare at
my mouth, at my bosom and sometimes they
whisper pretty things to me if they pass us in
a corridor, but of course, they are careful not
to let Madame the Queen see or hear. Life is
so boring, Anne. I want to dance, flirt, touch
— *kiss*! It is always on my mind."

"Our father would not like you to flirt. He
wishes us to marry well and do honour to our
family."

"Oh pooh! You sound as holy as Queen
Claude, I swear you do. My mirror tells me
that I am good to look upon and I do not
mean to moulder away unseen, even if I do
have to wait a hundred years for a husband."

Nor did she. Within the year she had
learned so well and so eagerly that she had
become mistress, not only to King François,
but to a number of other noblemen as well,
thus earning herself a very unsavoury
reputation even in that lecherous Court,

37

becoming known as 'The King's English Mare' as a result of her many amours.

"And why not?" enquired François cynically of his intimates. "The name suits her very well. I have ridden her more times than any mount in my stable. And, so it seems, have all of you. Nor have you waited for my permission, I note!" He gave a laugh of half-annoyed amusement. "You have all enjoyed a goodly gallop upon her, yes? *Tiens*, she is almost public property! Pretty and hot for love as she is, I think that she spreads her favours too far and too free. I want her no more. She has grown to be a nuisance. She shall return to England."

And Mary was sent home, weeping, in disgrace.

After this, Anne, now twelve years old, shocked and upset for her sister, and missing her greatly, was determined to guard her virtue and her self-respect. She had heard the King's name for her sister; there had been others all too eager to tell her. She had heard the sniggers, the sly whispers, the insults disguised as compliments which Mary took as truth. She had seen the looks of amused contempt, some even directed at herself, and had hated it all. She had no intention of such indignity, nor to give herself so lightly as to be held in scorn. If folk were to whisper and mutter about her, they would do so in a very different fashion. Anne meant to be admired and respected, not to fall like a blown leaf beneath the weight of any gentleman who chose to eye her with favour. She would not make the mistake her sister had made. On her heart and her faith, she swore it.

So Mistress Anne Boleyn remained at the French Court to finish her education, moving back and forth from the palace of Les Tournelles in Paris to the various newly-built châteaux in the Touraine. There was Azay-le-Rideau, delicate as a fairy-tale, dreaming under great trees, its golden stone and blue-grey turrets reflected in the water of its moat; there was beautiful Chenonceaux set upon its arched bridge over the river Cher; Blois with its fanciful, twisting stone staircase and glowing red brick; great Chambord, as yet unfinished, but already nearing the size of a small village, with plans for it to contain an even more fanciful double staircase, upon which those ascending and descending might see one another but never meet; there was Amboise, neat, compact and charming, placed high above the little walled town that nestled by the wide, gleaming River Loire. All were monuments to the taste and wealth of King François, who spared no expense upon their beauty and comfort.

It was at Amboise, in the February of 1520, that Anne received a letter from her father, on ambassadorial duties in Paris, informing her that her sister Mary had dared to marry to disoblige her family. Not only had she made her name a spit-word in the mouth of every French noble, he had written, his pen spluttering angrily, but she had not so much as consulted her parents over her wretched match, choosing for her bridegroom a nobody in the shape of a mere Esquire to the Body at the Court of England, a man without title or nobility! This person called himself William Carey, was from some no-account Devonshire family, and Mary had had the temerity to announce that she was in love with the fellow! Was it not disgraceful? Of course, she could hope for no better, when things came down to it, scribbled Sir Thomas, having ruined her chances and made herself a talking-stock in the most vulgar way, without a care for her name or her family. He trusted that Anne was attending to her studies, minding her French governess and behaving mannerly, for he did not intend her to bring the Boleyn name to the mud. He remained her affectionate father etc. etc.

For once alone, Anne glanced round the great firelit room with flickering shadows and laid the letter down on the purple cushion of a window-seat, gazing through the tall casement across the pointed rooftops of the small town of Amboise, huddled below the château walls; across the broad, placid Loire with its wooded islets and swift undercurrents, across the arched bridge that spanned its gleaming width, to the flat, green lands on the northern side. The trees were bare and wintry and a chilly wind whistled about the round turrets and high chimneys of the château, rattling the windows in their frames.

What did she want from life, she wondered? The answer leapt to her mind. *To be noticed, to be envied, to be the centre of attraction, free, powerful, independent, with no one to say her nay.*

Shrugging her shoulders, she laughed at her ambitions, for how was she, a female, to accomplish such a dream? She was in her thirteenth year now, marriageable, and might soon be under a husband's thumb. This made her think of Mary who had spoken to her of marriage and men before her downfall. Poor, dear, too-loving Mary! Her way was not for Anne, even though she herself was becoming very attractive to men; their antics when in her presence proved that, although her appearance was quite different from her sister's.

She was as dark as Mary, perhaps darker,

with a bosom less than half the size and no hips to speak of, yet the nobles of the Court were always quick to brush against her, to stroke her cheek, or pat her bottom, even to look into her bodice. She would grin to herself at this sauciness. Not much to see there! It was quite noticeable that none of the Queen's other maidens received this treatment; so noticeable that she trusted that the preference of the gentlemen did not mean that they considered her to be an easy tumble like Mary. If so, they were in for a surprise.

She was learning how to flirt, to laugh, to be merry in the company of men, to be amused at some witticisms and not to understand others, even to show a certain sharp wit of her own, to tantalise, to entice, but to hold herself aloof. Although young, her taste in dress had become outstanding and often imitated. Anne counted herself fortunate in having a father who had money enough to keep her well in funds, so that she was enabled to buy expensive materials and employ a good dressmaker who would carry out her ideas. Not that he sent her the money out of love. She had no illusions about her father. It was to make her a good marriage prospect. A richly dressed, elegantly bejewelled daughter indicated a rich father and a large marriage settlement. It was all in the order of things.

She glanced down at the glowing garnet velvet of her skirt which opened upon a kirtle of grey satin embroidered with silver. The bodice was laced up the back with silver ribbon, whilst the wide sleeves — her own notion — were turned back with cuffs of the grey satin of her kirtle. These cuffs could be smoothed forward or turned back at the wearer's fancy. Anne wore her right sleeve turned forward to hide that detested little extra nail on her right hand, but several ladies had copied this invention and were wearing their own new-made sleeves in precisely the same way. She found this amusing and, as she smiled to herself, her eyes shifted their focus to stare at her reflection in the window-pane as the sky outside darkened as blue dusk began to fall.

There was her image, very slender, fairly tall, with a small, oval, olive-skinned face lit by a pair of huge dark eyes, a wide red mouth and pointed chin, the whole topped by a wealth of magnificent black hair that had the lustre of silk. It fell to below her knees, confined only by a delicate, curved silver hood, edged with pearls, set back on her long-necked, graceful head.

Not exactly pretty, but —

"Fascinating!" murmured an appreciative voice behind her and she turned swiftly to behold the King smiling down at her from his great height, his slanting dark eyes twinkling knowingly. "So you stare at your charming self in the window, Mistress Anne. Do you wait for your lover?"

"I have none, Sire," she answered, giving him look for look.

"None? And you Mary Boleyn's sister? *Est-il possible?*"

Anne jerked herself upright, her eyes flashing. "I am not my sister, Sire, neither in thought nor action!"

"Many men desire you, *ma belle*," said His Majesty thoughtfully, gazing at her as though he would strip the ruby velvet gown from her still immature body. "You are a flirtatious morsel and flirts are made to be caught, *hein?*"

"Not I, Sire. I give myself to no one, save in honourable wedlock."

He laughed. "*Mon Dieu*, how very prudish! I do not believe you, *ma belle*. Suppose I were to ask for your favours, would you refuse me? I think not."

"Indeed, Sire? Then try me!" she cried, challenging.

"You mean to deny me? Come, come, think what I could offer you. Jewels,

44

riches — *tiens*, you might be my *Maîtress en Titre*, much honoured at Court. What of that, *Mademoiselle Iceberg?*" He pronounced it "Eesbairg".

"Why, would you set aside Françoise de Foix, your *belle-amie*, for Mademoiselle Iceberg, Sire? I am all untried, I might not satisfy your desires — what then?"

"As to that, I could melt you, I am certain," said he, seizing her in his arms. "I could teach you delights of which your cold virgin heart has never dreamed. Come, *chérie*, will you not open yourself to me? You must not refuse a King. That is naughty treason! Ah, I will teach you many delicious, wicked — "

But Anne was not to learn what delicious wickednesses he could teach, for the door opened and footmen bearing candles entered, followed by Queen Claude, surrounded by her ladies, and Anne, wriggling from the arms that held her in a fast-slackening grasp, ran, laughing saucily, to join the group round the queen, leaving François to reflect dourly that the seductive little Boleyn was certainly less willing than her accommodating sister. He shrugged. *Hé*, but she would not hold out against him for long, the little one. No woman had ever done so. He smiled to himself, black eyebrows flying, full mouth curling cynically beneath the long Valois nose that had earned him the name of *Le Roi Grand Nez*. Rape was out of the question, for her father was a friend of the English King and such an action might cause an international incident. Nay, she must yield of her own will and he would have her yet. She would be bound to yield in time.

She never did. For two years he and his nobles pursued her, wrote poems and letters to her, offered her gifts, François himself penning some lines to her:

Vénus était blonde, l'on ma dit;
L'on voit bien qu'elle brunette . . .

Although he had been told that Venus was blonde, he could see for himself that she was brunette, he had written hopefully, thinking that this might touch her cold heart. All to no avail. He and his courtiers could not understand it. She was merry, she was young, elegant and so alluring that no man could drag his eyes from her when she was in the room; her sister was the notorious English Mare who had refused no one, yet this little, delicate, magnetic girl resisted all capture. They could not understand that this young creature possessed a will of granite; that once she had set her mind to a target, that target was usually achieved.

In the June of that year, King Henry of England and King François of France met in diplomatic friendship at a spot between the towns of Guisnes and Ardres called the field of the Cloth of Gold, so named because of the extreme richness of the costumes worn by the two rulers and their courtiers, together with their tents and pavilions all of satin, velvet and cloth of gold. The meeting was designed to put away all old enmities and to cement a friendly alliance between France and England.

Anne, being one of Queen Claude's ladies, and not present upon the first evening, did not witness the meeting of the Kings, but she had many opportunities to catch sight of King Henry during the seventeen days of feasting, jousting and wrestling that followed after. She gazed upon him with admiration, as did all the ladies, feeling sympathy with his chagrin at an unlucky fall when wrestling with King François and applauding his seemingly careless acceptance of such a mishap. As fair and rosy as François was dark; very tall, of a large, athletic frame that had not yet run to fat, he was extremely handsome, affable, gracious, ebullient and effusive, dancing and sporting as though tireless; at twenty-nine years old, a King of whom any country might be proud.

He did not notice Anne Boleyn.

★ ★ ★

At home in England, the members of the Boleyn family were engaged in a feud with their relatives, the Butlers of Ormond, one of whom, Sir Piers Butler, was laying claim to the title and lands of the old Earl who had died in 1515. Sir Thomas Boleyn, as the Earl's favourite grandson, was enraged at the presumption of Sir Piers, believing, with some justification, that the Earl had not intended Sir Piers to have all. There was no written evidence for Butler's claim, but he would not yield an inch, causing great dissension. He placed even King Henry in a dilemma by his behaviour, refusing to attend a hearing, asserting himself as too busy with the King's wars in Ireland to take time to be present at such piddling nonsense as a mere hearing.

This was awkward indeed, for Sir Piers was one of the King's few loyal supporters in Ireland and had built up a strong following of Irish chieftains. These worthies were quite as happy to fight for the English King, should their uncertain loyalty be rewarded, or against him, should their touchy sensibilities be ruffled. One would have to tread very carefully in this matter, as the Lord Deputy of Ireland realised only too well.

The Lord Deputy at this time was Anne Boleyn's maternal uncle, the Duke of Norfolk[1] and he had discovered his post to be productive of nothing but trouble. He had found Sir Piers extremely useful and hesitated to put him out in any way. He racked his brains to find a solution to this wretched family problem, fast becoming international, which exercised his mind night and day, so that he felt positively hag-ridden and looked it, his dark face creased and lined with worry.

Casting about in his mind for a solution to this seemingly intractable problem, the Duke thought of his sister the Lady Elizabeth Boleyn. Could she be of any assistance? Her husband was a wealthy man, he had the ear of King Henry and connections in France. Ah, France! Was there not a daughter in France? Not the one who had made a fool of herself, but another, an unmarried girl, surely old enough for a husband. He gave a sigh of relief; at last he had his answer. His sister's younger girl, Anne Boleyn, should wed James Butler, the son of Sir Piers! It was an

_____

[1] Then Duke of Surrey

49

excellent notion and a good marriage for the young woman who had obviously made no impact upon the French Court, or she would be married already. She would be grateful for her uncle's thought for her future, Sir Thomas would be pleased, the King reassured about Irish affairs and all would be well. For the first time in months he smiled, delighted to feel his difficulties lessen just a little.

Swiftly he wrote to King Henry outlining the proposal and the King, relieved at such an easy way out of the quandary, agreed with enthusiasm, losing no time in speaking to Anne's father of the project. The Duke followed this missive with another to the powerful Cardinal Wolsey, Archbishop of Canterbury and Lord High Chancellor of England, through whose square, capable hands most of the nation's business passed.

The Cardinal considered the marriage to be a very good notion and so, in the January of 1522, Anne Boleyn, not yet fifteen, alluring, bewitching, stylish, vivacious and French in all her ways, was recalled to home and wedlock.

3

LOVE LIES BLEEDING

Told by Lord Henry Percy

Spring 1522

I first saw her upon a Sunday in the springtime. It was at Placentia, the King's spacious and beautiful palace that lies on the wide double bend of the River Thames at Greenwich. My father, the Earl of Northumberland had obtained a post for me in the household of the great and mighty Cardinal Wolsey. Full twenty years of age was I and a real country booberkin, having never travelled far from my home in the North before this. My father felt that I needed some town-polish and that was true enough. I was open-eyed and gape-mouthed at the marvels of London; at the tall houses, so close-packed, at the great palaces with their gardens lining the river bank, at the stink of that river, at the wondrous sight of London Bridge — and at the beauty of the ladies. Their sparkling eyes, their rosy mouths, their jewels, their silks and velvets, their dashing witty talk — by the Cross, but I was all amazed.

Although I stared, round-eyed, with admiration at these fair dames, not one of them spared me more than a glance. If they had looked longer, perhaps they might have seen that I was tall and broad and not bad-looking. But I was also bashful and gawky with a hesitant manner that made no impression good or bad, save if someone should say: "That Percy boy is but a doltish rustic", or some such dismissive remark. I had little hope of ever obtaining the court manners that my father had wished for me, for words like these made me more diffident than ever and less like to put myself forward, which I found difficult enough anyway.

My health was none too robust, neither, so apart from wealth and rank, I had nothing to commend me, wealth and rank being commonplace at this Court, and this made it all the more miraculous that the most admired lady of all should have deigned to smile upon me, for she could have taken her choice from the highest and wealthiest in the land if she had not already been betrothed. Why, the King himself had remarked upon her.

She was the loveliest and most fascinating being I have ever beheld. There was a magic about her that drew all men to her side; I cannot tell what it was, but it drove us all crazy. It was some invisible emanation, some spell of nature that worked so. Old men behaved like silly youths in her presence, while the youths themselves — hey, welladay! They would prance and dance and jostle for just so much as a glance from Mistress Anne Boleyn's dark eyes.

Upon the Sunday of each week during this springtime, Cardinal Wolsey had a meeting arranged with His Majesty and would be rowed downstream in his barge from his great Thames-side house of York Place near Westminster to visit King Henry who was in residence at Placentia and I, among the Cardinal's several attendants, would be honoured to accompany His Eminence upon the journey. I had never seen such a barge. All gilded and painted it was, hung with gold and purple silk, fringed with red and blue; by Our Lady, it was a marvellous sight. The King owned no better, I swear.

At Greenwich the barge would float stately to the landing stage and the Cardinal, massive, red-robed and majestic, would alight, being greeted by Sir Thomas Boleyn, the Lord Treasurer, together with several other Court officials. Sir Thomas was my lady's father and a most important gent, very rich, well-landed and high in favour with the King.

At first, upon these visits, I could do nothing but stare and mumble — so sheepish and backward was I. But stare I did, to good purpose, for upon whom did my eyes rest? Why upon the dark and lovely Mistress Anne Boleyn and in that I was no different from any other man there, His Majesty included. She was fifteen in that year and so enchanting as a deep red rose but new-opened, the dew still upon it. My heart was hers from that first moment. I lost it and my wits together, for I feared, in my shyness to put myself forward, fearful of being scorned, she being betrothed. So I merely gazed, mum and mute as a silly statue.

Tall she was and slender, with a grace that I have seen upon no other. Her skin was of a golden, pearly pallor — no rose in her cheeks — yet with a glow of health, ah, I cannot describe. And her eyes, they were like two pools of black night, slumbrous yet sparkling, fringed with lashes dark as her wonderful hair that fell, virgin-fashion, in a silky mass to her very knees. Her high laugh, her voice, her little foreign gestures, her sprightly dancing — why, she made all other ladies, beautiful or no, look like stocks. I'll wager they did not love her for it!

So some Sundays went by, I silent and worshipping, she unnoticing, or so I fancied, laughing and graceful among her admirers, until we met, for it had amused a Court gallant to present me to her as a partner for the diversion of hearing me stammer and seeing me stumble over my feet. How I acquitted myself I do not know, so careful was I of the steps and my feet and the excitement of holding her little hand in my own. I was all awhirl in body and mind.

"What think you of the Court, Lord Henry?" she asked me sweetly, after a while.

She knew my name! I faltered in the figure, but recovered myself sufficiently to answer. "Why — why — I like it very well, lady," I stuttered foolishly enough. "It is very lively."

"But you do not join in our talk and games," she went on as I turned her under my arm, my heart beating fast enough to hear it. "Are you too learned or — " she twinkled her eyes at me, " — too bashful?"

"Oh, I am too bashful!" I blurted out, with the courage of desperation. "I know so little of Court ways and fear to show myself as yokelly and boorish. You and your friends would laugh at such as I."

"I do not laugh," she said, serious, looking at me as we stepped along, hand in hand. "I know well what it is like to be strange in a

55

strange place. No, I would not laugh."

"Would you not? I have no gift for wit and repartee. I would cut a sad figure amongst your friends, I daresay."

"Do not fear," she assured me. "I will answer for it that no one shall make a mock of you, Lord Henry. You will see."

And thanks to that sweetest, dearest lady, I was received by all in friendship thereafter, shy and dullard-seeming as I was. Ah, she was so kind to me, seeking me out every Sunday to put me at my ease, to dance, to talk, to play at chess, to walk in the galleries among a crowd of merry young men and maids, so that soon I grew in fairly good conceit of myself, able to dance well enough, to chat in conversation, even to make a jest now and then. I was accepted in the company and all because of that lovely lady.

I fell in love fathoms deep. How could I not? It would have needed a harder heart than mine to resist her; not that I tried. I was enmeshed, happily helpless in her charm from the beginning and in that I was the same as the rest, but for one thing. She loved me as I did her! At first, I could not credit this, but it was true. For sure, it was clear to all her friends, for they would move off and leave us to be alone as much as was possible.

One such Sunday afternoon while the King

and the Cardinal sat together in the Privy Chamber, discussing affairs of state, my lady and I sat alone in a small antechamber, discussing our own.

"We must wed, darling," said I, my arms tight about her, kissing her passionately. "I love you to madness. How can we be wed, though, when you are betrothed?"

"And I love you," she replied tenderly. "It is because you are so different from all the men I have ever known. You are true-hearted and sincere and you love me for myself, not from policy, or by arrangement, or for money and land, for you have riches of your own. As for my betrothal to James Butler, I do not know him and I do not wish it. I shall refuse the marriage."

"But a betrothal!" I gasped. "That is as binding as marriage! How could — "

"How could I refuse a marriage? Why, think of the King's own sister, the Princess Mary Rose! She married where she wished in the end. There are some, you know, who recommended His Majesty to take Charles Brandon's head for marrying the Princess as he did. But she braved it all out and gained her happiness in the end. As I shall do, Harry. As *we* shall do, dearest. We must have resolution, that is all."

"In that case we shall wed," I said

confidently, "for you have resolution enough for us both. Oh darling, is not the world a beautiful place? See how the sun shines in upon us as we sit here. It is a good omen, I swear."

Alas for good omens! Someone overheard us that day and carried the tale to King Henry who was much offended at our presumption, for it would chance to spoil his plans in Ireland, although we knew nothing of that at the time. Indeed, as I sat in the Cardinal's barge on the return journey to York House that evening, I was in a dream of delight, fancying love, happiness and a blissful future. A dream soon to end, for it was all too soon after this that Cardinal Wolsey sent for me to talk with him.

As I walked the length of the Tapestried Gallery, each step taking me nearer to the stout, scarlet-robed figure seated in a great carven chair at the furthest end, I could see that His Eminence was angered, though for what reason I could not tell. My heart began to misgive me, for I was always timid and easily cowed, and a sense of apprehension ran through me even before the Cardinal began to speak.

I can still quote his very words.

"Lord Henry Percy," he began, deadly quiet, "I marvel not a little of thy peevish folly that though would'st tangle and insure thyself with a foolish girl yonder in the Court. I mean Anne Boleyn!" he snapped, seeing me all astonished. "Ay, I know of your doings!" he went on, louder. "Dost thou not consider the estate that God hath called thee unto in this world? Thou art heir to one of the wealthiest earldoms in this realm. Therefore it had been meet for thee to have asked thy father's consent in the matter and also made the King's Highness privy thereto."

"But — but — I am honourable!" I cried, shocked. "I wish to marry the lady, Your Eminence."

"Then thou should'st have submitted such business unto His Highness!" rapped out Wolsey, glaring at me.

"I would have, sir, indeed I — "

Swiftly he cut across my faltering words.

"But now behold what ye have done through your wilfulness!" he roared, making me flinch and blink. "Ye have not only offended your father but also your most gracious Sovereign Lord and have matched yourself with one such as neither the King, nor yet your father will be agreeable."

"But why, my lord?" I dared to ask, being made bold through dismay. "She is of good birth, wealthy and I love — "

"Her birth is nothing to do with the matter,

boy! And as for love — that is for the low-bred. Take no doubt that I will send for your father and at his coming he will either break this unadvised contract, or *disinherit you for ever!* Ay, that touches you, I see! The King's Majesty himself will complain to thy father on thee, rest assured of that. As for the lady, His Highness intends her for another man for important reasons of policy, as you well know, sirrah: What have you to say now?"

All this in a deep, terrifying bellow, on purpose to intimidate me and I fear it did. But it had flashed through my mind as he spoke that he was hardly one to speak of being low-bred, for he was but a butcher's son himself. Yet butcher's son or no, he held power next only to the King, so I knew I had best not speak of breeding. Struggling to steady myself, I took a deep breath. "My lord," I said, my voice shaking, despite myself, "I know nothing of policy and I most humbly ask Your Grace for your favour in this and also entreat the King's most royal Majesty for his benevolence in the matter, for which," I finished, timorous, but defiant, "I cannot deny nor forsake!"

His Eminence rolled his round grey eyes to heaven as though asking the angels to witness such idiot insubordination. "By the Holy Cross!" he cried in mocking amazement. "Is it wisdom or water that ye have in your head?"

"Nay!" I cried, stung. "I am pledged and cannot honestly withdraw! Besides, I — "

"Hah!" shouted the Cardinal. "Thinkest thou that the King and I do not know what we have to do in so weighty a matter as this? Your father shall come and we shall take such order as the King thinks best. And, meantime, I charge thee, boy, that thou presumest not to seek the girl's company, or it would seem that thou dost ignore the King himself! To be sure of this thou shalt stay close here in York Place."

And these were the exact words as he spoke them.

So I could not even bid her farewell or explain. I was heartbroken and frantic and, to upset me further, I heard through friends that she was as desolated as I; white, quiet and drooping like a cut flower. As for me, my father soon arrived and in a terrible rage. I was always afeared of him and his temper and it was a truly painful interview that we had, during which, stamping, thundering and roaring, he did indeed threaten me with disinheritance — to be sent off without a servant or a penny to my name. Well, it was no threat, he meant it true, I knew my father. I knew, too, that I could not have supported such a life; my heart shook at the mere thought, so I gave in. I was craven, cowardly, poor-spirited, weak — call it what you will — I was well aware of my failings. I was bullied into hateful, cringing submission. Moreover, as a deadly finishing stroke, my father revealed to me that he had betrothed me, six years earlier, to the Lady Mary Talbot, daughter to the Earl of Shrewsbury. I had known nothing of this, for I had not been told, my father having considered it unnecessary to inform me. This betrothal, for political and dynastic reasons, could not be broken, bellowed my father at full pitch of his lungs, and I realised that now I was trapped as fast as any prisoner.

"I will set all in train at once for your marriage with the Lady Mary!" promised my father, loud and furious. "Nor will you be able to run from it, I warn you. Your idiot folly shames me so that I know not where to look!"

And so I was sent home, sick to my heart with misery, guilt and shame. I was told, later, that my lovely Anna had defied her father, crying out against Cardinal Wolsey for parting us and vowing revenge upon him.

"If ever it should be in my power, I shall do the Cardinal as much displeasure as he has done me!" she had cried to her father. "Nor will I take James Butler as husband, and so I tell you!"

Such spirit as she had. Such a brave heart. Far stronger and braver than mine, I knew, and felt the more of a weakling when I learnt of her bold words. And then I was really astonished to hear that she had not been forced to wed James Butler, but only sent home to Hever in disgrace. Was that because of her courage and determination, I wondered, or was it some deeper matter? I could not understand it . . .

Anyhap, my life was ruined from that time on. My marriage was a disaster, my ever-capricious health failed, my existence became a misery and all was calamity and trouble for me.

4

HEVER

1522–1525

It was no light matter for a lady to be sent from Court and Mistress Anne Boleyn felt the shame of it very keenly. No less so did her father, Sir Thomas. Her disgrace was his own, he ranted, and did not stint his reproaches and bewailings, these serving to render his obdurate daughter the more so.

"You are likely to wreck all I have worked for!" he fumed as they rode, she sullen, he fulminating, through the green Kentish countryside, the birds calling from every budding branch, the sun shining bright as the two Boleyns were not. "You have angered the Cardinal, infuriated your uncle Norfolk and outraged His Majesty who was disposed to look upon you with kindness! Who knows what benefits our family might have gained through obedient and seemly conduct on your part? Now all might be lost. Dear God, it makes me boil to contemplate you, by the Cross it does! When I think of the trouble I have taken and the expense I have been put to in order to give you a good upbringing, I could spit!"

He did so, causing his horse to shy, startled.

"Such daughters as I am cursed with!" he shouted. "Who would have daughters, I say? They are nothing but a wretched plague to a man!" He shook his head as if unable to believe his ill fortune and continued his tirade as their small entourage clopped along the narrow, winding, high-hedged lanes, deeply rutted, but partially dried out in a warm and sunny spring.

"Is it not enough that Mary should make her name a sluttish byword in France, only to be sent home and then contract a contemptible marriage?" he enquired loudly of the unanswering heavens. "And now this! Was ever a man so unfortunate? When I return to Court I shall wonder if I have not lost my position through your folly: I cannot imagine why the King did not insist upon your marriage to James Butler — it is beyond me." He glared at the sullen-faced Anne riding beside him. "Perhaps he eyes you with favour?" he asked hopefully, struck by a sudden thought.

"And why should he do that?" queried the young lady, scowling.

"Ha, you can speak then!" cried Sir Thomas, with a crack of bitter laughter. "I had thought you struck dumb. Ay, why indeed? Why should he seek out a bad-tempered bitch like you, indeed! Have you thought of the profit his interest could bring, what benefit to your father? No, not you, lack-wit that you are!"

"What, do you mean that he would seek to bed me?" Anne's lip curled with scorn.

"Why not, if it is the King? It is not dishonourable in such a case."

"Such doubtful honour is not for me," retorted Anne, "King or no."

"Ah, you are a numskull!" snapped her father. "Anyhap, His Majesty would need to be hard-pressed to consider *you*, stubborn and intractable and sullen as you are. Who will want you now, ha?" he shouted furiously.

His horse reared at the sudden loud sound of his voice.

"Curse the animal!" he roared, keeping his seat with difficulty. "Horses and women — they are all of a piece! Did you think to better yourself in the world by tangling with the young Percy?" he demanded, when his mount had quietened. "Was it the young fool's rank that beguiled you? It makes no sense, for I am rich, your lineage's high and a

66

good marriage was planned for you which would have pleased your uncle Norfolk and the King himself! What reason had you to provoke everyone possessing influence and power? Did you run mad?"

"I love him!" she shrilled, goaded. "Or do you not understand love?"

"Love? Pah! Childish nonsense! I never heard such pishery! You are as ridiculous as your stupid sister, upon my soul! After this, it will be impossible to get you any kind of a husband!"

Anne tossed her head angrily, giving no reply and, in mutual disharmony they came to Hever, riding through Sir Thomas's new eastern entrance in surly silence, their attendants clattering behind them, into the small courtyard with its stone flags and old-fashioned timbered walls. Lady Elizabeth, who had run out to welcome them was not reassured by the sight of the two, ill-humoured, darkly frowning countenances that confronted her.

★ ★ ★

In the days and months that followed, Anne gloomed and glowered about her home, out of temper and out of favour, blind to the pleasantness of its aspect, the beauties of its gardens and the gentle countryside. The charming manor house of castellated golden stone, encircled by a lily-laden moat, was nothing but a prison to her. In vain her pretty mother's concern, in vain her father's constant demands to show an agreeable face when, on his visits from Court, Anne's mood did not lighten, for she felt that never again would she enjoy such unclouded, innocent happiness as she had done with Lord Henry Percy, now lost to her for ever.

It is of no use for me to write to him, she thought despondently, climbing the spiral stair to her room and staring down into the orchard below the window. If I wrote, my messenger would be stopped and searched. So there is nothing for it but to remain here unwed, or to be married to another man of whom I have no knowledge and for whom I shall have no regard. Oh God, I am so unhappy! I think my heart is broken. I wish that my Harry had made a stronger stand for me. I would have done so for him, betrothal or no. They could have killed me before I'd have given in! I loved him so dear — and still do, no matter his weakness. He was sweet and kind and we would have been happy together, I am certain, certain . . .

She began to pace about the room, half-sobbing, until the door opened and her mother came in, her dark Howard eyes full of sympathy.

"Nan! Dear child, you will make yourself ill if you fret so. There are other men in the world, my love."

"Not for me, Mother — not for me! Do not shake your head, I mean it truly. Why can women have no choice in what befalls them? Why are they given brains and feelings if they are only to be treated as creatures of no account?"

"It has ever been so," replied Lady Elizabeth lamely. "I do not know how one might change it."

"Only through power," said Anne, after a thoughtful pause.

"And when have women ever had power, daughter?"

"Ah, that is it. But we do have just a little, Mother. We are able to draw men to our sides and make them pant for our favours."

Lady Elizabeth sighed. "That does us little good, for we are all wedded off so early, before we may use such power."

"I used it," said Anne. "I drew men to my side, though I did not yield to any. And Mary, she used it."

"Oh, do not speak of naughty Mary! Her behaviour has shamed us."

"Well, has not my behaviour shamed you

also? Yet mine was honourable!"

"But you offended His Majesty, dearest. He agreed to your betrothal with James Butler and thought you presumptuous and disobedient to act as you did."

"In what was was I presumptuous? The betrothal was my autocratic uncle's idea and, as to that, my lineage is good enough for me to marry with anyone of high degree. Lord Henry Percy was neither worse nor better than James Butler as to his family and far better in wealth, as you know very well."

"And you know very well, Nan, that we cannot wed where we wish, man nor woman, simply because we are of high degree."

"Yes, but it would have been an excellent match and betrothals can be broken, if necessary. My father would have been glad enough to be allied with the Percy family, you cannot deny that, can you?"

"No Anne, but the King himself wished you to marry James Butler. You cannot go against the King's own command."

"Well, I tell you this, Mother, King or no, if I cannot marry Lord Henry whom I love, I will not marry James Butler. My father may starve me, beat me, do as he likes, I shall not have Butler. No, it was fat Cardinal Wolsey's will that I crossed. It was his doing that my happiness is ruined. He looks upon me as a silly brainless puppet, a mere foolish woman — he *said* so! And as for the King — tchah! I say that the King is the Cardinal's puppet and dances to *his* tune!"

"Be silent, Anne!" cried Lady Elizabeth, now thoroughly alarmed. "Do not talk so wildly! If anyone should hear you and speak of it — dear God, such words are treason, child. Men have been 'headed for less!"

Anne sighed, sinking back upon an oaken chest cushioned in green velvet. Suddenly she flung up her head, black eyes blazing. "Even so, right or wrong, if the chance should come my way, I shall deal the Cardinal as bitter a wound as he has dealt me!" she cried. "I do not forget wrongs that are done me. Understand me, Mother, that I have sworn it. Devil or angel help me, he shall pay!"

Lady Elizabeth crossed herself, amazed at her daughter's passionate words, comforting herself that Anne would soon recover her spirits; she was only young and first love, if it came at all, came strong and hard. Anyway, what could the child do? She half-smiled to herself. Nothing, of course, nothing at all. And yet . . . She glanced at Anne, sitting hunched, fists clenched on the chest at the foot of her yellow-curtained bed. There was that about the girl that was not ordinary. There was a force in her that neither of her

71

other children possessed. Well, a union between an ambitious, driving Boleyn and a powerful Howard could never produce a complete nonentity, that was sure and Anne was certainly not that.

"Come, dearest," she said soothingly. "We shall do our sewing together in the solar and set our minds to happier matters, I think. What do you say?"

But Anne said nothing, sitting silent and unmoving, and Lady Elizabeth was forced to descend the stairs and do her sewing alone, shaking her head and wondering what daughters were coming to.

She wondered still more, a few months later, when her husband rode home in the crisp autumn sunshine, all smiles and full of praise for Mary, the daughter he had so reviled for her light behaviour and unworthy marriage.

"Such news, wife! I am a happy man this day," he chortled, swinging off his cloak and hurling it in the direction of a nearby servant. "I see you look puzzled, but only listen. Our Mary is mistress to the King, my Lady! His Majesty is mighty taken with her — and *has* taken her!" He laughed delightedly. "Why, he was pursuing her as hot as could be, and of course she knew her duty as a good daughter and a good subject should. I am glad of it, indeed, after Anna's nonsense. Where is the girl? Still in the sullens? Jesu, it is more than half a year now! What is it with her that she is so ill-content?"

"She felt much love for Lord Henry Percy," answered his wife. "Come now and eat after your journey from London. You know that Anne is not a maid of easy feelings."

"More fool she, then," retorted Sir Thomas, striding across the hall to the dining table on its raised dais at the far end and seating himself at the head, snapping his fingers and shouting for the food to be brought in. "She must learn that it is of no use to set one's face against fate, stupid wench! However, for myself, there is now no fear of my falling out of favour while the King desires our Mary. He takes to our family, does he not?" He nudged Lady Elizabeth, grinning and winking meaningly.

Lady Elizabeth drew herself up. "If you mean that the King's eye once fell upon me, husband," she said, annoyed, "I will repeat, yet again, that it was nothing. I was never his mistress. In those days he was wishful only of Queen Katherine. Certainly he thought me handsome, said as much and stole a kiss or two. And that was all. Will you never let it rest?"

"Why, it does not worry me!" he returned,

with a laugh. "No, it pleases me very well. It is no shame to be admired by the King."

"So you say," she answered repressively. "For myself, I think differently."

"Then you are foolish," he said good-humouredly, placing an arm about her waist. "You refine too much upon trifles, Eliza. Follow the prevailing wind, say I, and take care to stay among those in power who agree together. I wish for success and a high place in the world."

"But what of poor Will Carey, Mary's husband?" asked Lady Elizabeth gravely. "What does he say about his wife and the King?"

"Nary a word!" chuckled her spouse. "Not he. He knows better than to look on both sides of a pillow. I should not wonder if he gets an earldom out of this, if he keeps his eyes shut and Mary uses her wits."

"His Majesty is not noted for the length of his love affairs," ventured Lady Elizabeth doubtfully. "His heart is not constant. I fear for Mary, husband."

"Save us, but you are cow-hearted, wife! What does it matter if his love should be short lived, so long as we all benefit from it? I tell you what, I look to this affair to advance me in earnest. You will see!"

The Lady Elizabeth certainly saw, for on

the 13th of June 1523, in the Great Hall of Bridewell, the fine palace at the mouth of the River Fleet, Sir Thomas Boleyn was created Viscount Rochford by a smiling monarch. Nor was his the only creation, for as soon as the delighted new Viscount had backed away, a little red-haired, four year old boy, all dressed in crimson and cloth of gold, was led forward to be proclaimed Duke of Richmond. This child was Henry Fitzroy, the King's illegitimate son by Elizabeth Blount, maid-of-honour to the Queen, the King's only son to date, illegitimate or not. King Henry's desire for a son to succeed him was becoming obsessional after his Queen's many miscarriages, she having borne only one child that lived, and that a daughter.

This was a joyous time for Sir Thomas Boleyn, Viscount Rochford, and it was made still more joyous by the award of a pension to him of a thousand crowns a year from the great and powerful Holy Roman Emperor, nephew to Queen Katherine of England, who had made the award in the hope of the new Viscount's continued services as Ambassador, considering him a highly able and influential man.

More benefits followed. In the summer of the next year Anne's brother the dark, handsome, witty twenty-one year old George, was given the grant of a manor in Norfolk, so pleased was King Henry with the Boleyn family. When the Viscount, with his favoured son and now-favoured daughter, Mary, rode home to Hever to see the progress of the alterations to the house as befitting a nobleman, they were laughing and merry, hand-in-hand with fickle Fortune, happy with themselves and the world. Anne, still at home, felt sadly dull and overlooked.

She was glad to see Mary, of whom much fuss was being made by their father. In contrast to Anne, Mary looked happy and radiant, her dark eyes sparkling, her full, red mouth smiling. She and Anne were delighted to meet again and talk, although Anne's feelings did not match her sister's as they walked in the gardens, their bright silken skirts whispering over the grass.

"Are you as cheerful as you seem, Mary?" asked Anne. "You look it, but are you?"

Her sister's full lips twisted in a slight grimace. "Well — yes and no," she said deprecatingly. "I am past happiness in the King's love for me, Anne, for I have fallen in love with him myself, but I feel very guilty about Will, my husband. After all, we married for love."

Anne frowned. "And do you still love him?"

"Yes, I do," answered Mary. "It is strange,

76

but I do, truly. But the King — oh, the King, Anne! He is wonderful. He is like a god and I am quite overwhelmed, for he makes love to me so often and desires me so much. It makes me feel dizzy."

"Dizzy?" queried Anne. "Is that how you feel for Will?"

"Oh no," replied Mary. "I feel differently for Will. A glow in the heart is what I feel for my Will. Oh, it is all so difficult! Besides, how can one refuse the King? As my father says, one must think of the family. But I do feel guilty." She smoothed her dark brown hair back under the green pearled caul that confined it. "Yes, I do feel guilty, Anne."

"So should I," spoke up Anne. "I should feel very guilty if I slept with the King while loving my husband."

"But I told you I love the King as well!" protested Mary. "I do, indeed, sister. I would do anything for him."

"You have," said Anne tersely. "More than I would do."

"Ah, you do not understand," said Mary. "Come, sit with me here on this bench. It is so good to talk with you, dearest, after such a long while. I am so sorry that you were sent from the Court. It was a shame."

Anne shrugged her shoulders, her face expressionless, and the two girls sank down, side by side, on to a wooden, straight-backed bench set overlooking the moat, their colourful skirts, Mary's green and rose and Anne's black and gold, billowing about them. The sun shone down, glittering on the waters of the moat and casting shadows from the apple trees nearby.

"What is it that I do not understand?" demanded Anne after a short silence.

"You do not understand the magic of the King and how one can love two men at once, Anna. Besides — " Mary paused, staring across the moat, her pretty face unusually thoughtful.

"Besides what? Come, tell me!"

"Well, it is this. I am with child."

Anne stared at her sister. "Oh . . . Is it Will's child?"

"How can I tell?" Mary drew a deep breath. "It could be. On the other hand — "

"Oh," said Anne again, rather nonplussed. "What does our father say?"

"He is delighted, of course, and is urging me to take jewels and land and as much as I can, but so far His Majesty has offered me very little."

"Well, do not let our father hear *that*," remarked Anne shrewdly. "That would not do at all."

Both girls laughed rather ruefully, then

Anne snapped her fingers. "I have it!" she cried. "You will know who is the father well enough if the child should have red hair!"

This time Mary laughed in genuine amusement. "Anne, sad and sorrowful you may be, but you can still make me laugh. I wish I had your wit. But as to the child's father, one cannot tell for true. The child could be dark, like me. After all, our father has a dark red beard and reddish lights in his brown hair, yet we three are swarthy dark like our mother and all the Howards. And what I do, I do for love, Anne, not for gifts."

"Oh, do take care, Mary. Such a philosophy can be a terrible mistake. Be a little worldly-wise, dear sister. Our mother tells me that the King is not a faithful man and his love is light. She says his real love is still the Queen."

"Never!" cried Mary, jumping to her feet. "The Queen is a failure and she has let herself grow fat. Besides, he loves *me*. He has said so, time and again. He loves *me*!"

"I agree that the Queen is a failure," said Anne. "What a man like His Majesty can be thinking of to stay with her, I do not know. She is always praying — or was when I was at Court." At the thought, her face grew sullen again. "Anyway," she went on, after a moment, "what about that little Henry

Fitzroy? The King loved his mother, did he not?"

"Oh, he never really loved her," replied Mary carelessly. "She was just a passing fancy. He has cast her off." She grasped Anne's arm quite fiercely: "I tell you, he loves me!"

Anne hoped very much that Mary would not be yet another passing fancy, but forebore to say any more upon the subject, and soon the two young women returned to the house, where their father made much of Mary and George while ignoring Anne completely.

George Boleyn, who was very fond of his sister Anne, tried his best to cheer her. She loved him in return, for he understood her better than Mary, or either of their parents. Her love for him was mixed with hero-worship, for he was four years older than she, good-looking, intelligent, witty and charming. He was sorry for the seventeen year old girl in her disgrace and depression and tried, as well as he knew how, to cheer her.

"Come, little one," he said to her kindly, one day during this visit, "do not show me so downcast a face, sweeting! Your time will come. You have only to wait; the cloud upon you cannot last for ever. Once you are back at Court you will light a flame there, I know it. Let us go riding together and we can talk our

80

hearts out amongst the fields with no one to hear our scandals, what do you say?. Would you like to go beside the river Eden, or shall we take our way to Allington Castle and visit the Wyatts? You shall choose, lovedy."

"I care not," said Anne indifferently. "It is all one to me, dear George, but it is good of you to offer."

"Well, our cousin, Tom Wyatt is at Allington now — home from Court," said George, grinning suggestively. "You know how he used to sigh for a mere glance from your big dark eyes. He has had a fancy for you ever since he saw you when you were also at Court and never ceases to ask me about you."

"He is already wed," said Anne flatly. "I am no man's plaything."

"Oh Nan, you sound like a Lutheran, I swear you do! How desperately prudish you have grown! Can you not play and flirt as you used to do? Why, I myself shall marry soon, I am sure, but I shall not let that restrain me. Life is to be enjoyed, poppet. It is time you cast your miseries aside. Shall it be Allington?"

Smiling, in spite of herself, Anne shook her head. "Do you not realise, George, that it is all so different for a man? If a man marries and plays, he is a fine fellow. If a woman does

81

so, she is a slut. If she should lose her virginity before she weds, why, she is also a slut. There is no winning for a woman, George."

His smile faded. "Ay, you are right," he said. "I had never really thought. It is hard on a woman, especially if she is beautiful and brilliant. Ay, you are right, dearest. But will you not come with me to Allington?" He laughed. "I will make sure that Tom behaves himself and you might enjoy the trip."

She shook her head. "No, brother, Allington is too far off, besides I have no heart for it, nor for Tom Wyatt. To see him would only remind me of all I have lost."

★   ★   ★

So time went by and Anne became eighteen and still at Hever. Her brother George was married, at the King's wish, to Mistress Jane Parker, daughter to Lord Morley and Mounteagle, a thin, excitable young woman for whom he had no love and little affection, but it pleased the King and that was good for Viscount Rochford.

Then, at the end of 1525, Lord Rochford came home to Hever with the news that his youngest daughter was to be recalled to Court as lady-in-waiting to Queen Katherine.

Anne received these tidings with a face blank of all expression, unable, at first, to believe her father's words.

"Well?" he barked impatiently. "Well? Have you nothing to say, girl? Are you voiceless?"

"She is bewildered, husband," put in Lady Elizabeth, smiling. "She cannot believe her good fortune after waiting so long."

"Ay, and she had best not make a botch of her opportunities this time," snapped her father, wagging an admonishing finger. "There is to be no more foolery, mind! You have a duty to your family to do well and to advance yourself in every possible way; to win praise and approbation and to make a good marriage. Keep it in your head that you are now over eighteen and no longer very young, so waste no time, you understand?"

Anne nodded, a slow smile breaking over her face, bringing the sparkle back to her beautiful eyes. At last, at last! Back to the life for which she yearned. And marriage? She almost laughed aloud at the thought. That would come in her own good time, maybe. But first she intended to make up for all those years of retirement, misery and, eventually, boredom. And as for love — ah, she would never fall in love again, she promised herself.

Love brought vulnerability; it made one soft, it gave others the power to deal mortal wounds, sweet though gentle love might be. No, she was done with love! Also, she had some scores to pay off, if she were able. Her smile broadened. Ay, life bade fair to be full of interest and excitement from now on. She would make no mistake this time.

5

WILD FOR TO HOLD

1526–1527

Thomas Wyatt had not known true love until he saw Anne again. The Wyatts and the Boleyns were relatives and the children of the two families had often played together, Thomas being of an age with George Boleyn and four years older than Anne.

He had been very taken with her dark, frenchified sprightliness when she had been at Court in 1522, but she had been so young then and had had no eyes for Thomas, being deeply in love with Lord Henry Percy. Thomas had been greatly put to the puzzle as to what such a brilliantly attractive maid could have seen in the great stammering gowk of a lad and so had everyone else, including His Majesty and Cardinal Wolsey. At any rate, the romance had been swiftly concluded, by King and Cardinal, Lord Henry being sent back to his northern wilderness, while Anne had been banished to Hever. Sweet love had no defence against the power of the mighty, reflected Thomas, and now he himself was in love, bewitched by lovely Anne Boleyn who had been recalled to Court by King Henry's expressed wish.

The tall, handsome, blue-eyed Thomas sighed as he wandered between the dark green box hedges in the garden at Richmond Palace, quill pen tucked into the blond curls behind his ear, a roll of parchment under his yellow-clad arm, a small silver inkpot in his hand, seating himself at last upon a bank of aromatic camomile under a lime tree in small leaf, the sky as blue as an angel's robe above him, speedwells like tiny sapphires in the grass beneath his feet.

"What do ye there, Tom?" cried a merry voice and, glancing up, Thomas beheld the athletic, rangy form of another of Anne's cousins, Sir Francis Bryan, coming towards him through an arch in the hedge.

"Why, I am thinking of a poesy," answered Thomas, smiling, "and it floweth not."

"Of what do you write? Of love?"

"Ever of love," confessed Thomas, "and sometimes of a lady."

Sir Francis laughed. "Ah, I can guess which lady, I'll be bound! You scribble of our cousin, the beauteous Anne, I make no doubt. She is the bright star of our Court, is she not? I tell you, Tom, I would she were mine."

"And I," agreed Thomas, heartfelt, "but she will not be captured, try as I will."

"Try as we all will," said Sir Francis, seating himself beside Wyatt on the bank. "You are not the only one, Tom. But she will have none of us, not even the King."

"The King?" cried Thomas, all but dropping his pen. "What mean you — the King? Does he also desire her?"

Again Sir Francis laughed, throwing his dark head back to the danger of losing his red-feathered cap. "Oh, Tom, you are such a dreamer! Have you not noticed His Majesty's behaviour to the lady? Why, he cannot take his eyes from her and treats her every word as some heavenly dictum. He is as far gone as you or I, my lad."

"Oh Jesu, then all hope is at an end," said Thomas despairingly, "for the King must win, no matter who fails."

"Well, he has not won yet," remarked Sir Francis, "for I have heard him endeavouring to persuade her to his bed."

"And what said she? Did she consent?"

"By no means. She did but laugh — you know her saucy way — and fob him off with excuses."

"My oath, she is a bold one! But she must yield in the end. No one gainsays His Grace, Frank."

"No one has yet, certainly."

"Nay, nor ever will. Decidedly no woman will, or dare. I hope she will not gainsay me, for I long for her. Mayhap I could storm her fortress before the King?" mused Thomas optimistically.

"As to that, may the best man win," replied Sir Francis cheerfully. "We are all in the race."

"But I love her, Frank! 'Tis not only of the body with me! I love her for her sweet self. If I were not already wed, I would offer her my hand as well as my heart. As matters stand, she has my heart already, though she wants it not."

"I am sorry for Queen Katherine," said Sir Francis suddenly. "It must be very unpleasant for her to see her husband casting sheep's eyes at one of her ladies-in-waiting before us all. He has had his fancies, as well we know, but never has he made a preference so plain. The Queen says nothing, but her looks are sad indeed, for she loves him true."

"She is a most good and sweet lady," answered Thomas, nodding in agreement. "It is unfortunate that she is losing her looks, for she was really pretty once, I believe."

"You have only to study the portrait of her as a young woman to realise that," responded Sir Francis. "But she is six years older than

His Grace and worn by so much child-bearing, poor lady, and so her husband's glances wander — well, they do not *wander*," he amended, "for they remain fixed upon Mistress Anna. And I will tell you this, Tom. Although we men cluster round Anne like bees round the comb, the ladies like her not at all. They call her wanton and lustful."

"Lustful?" cried Thomas. "Lustful is she never! I have not so much as kissed her cheek in all the time she has been at Court. Her hand is all I have been allowed. I would she *were* lustful, then I might be eased of my pain."

"Well, I have not been allowed even her hand to kiss," complained Sir Francis ruefully, "so you have beat me there. I think she has ice in her veins instead of blood."

"Heyday, the King will stand the victor, surely," sighed Thomas. "It is no contest."

"Ay, he will go far to kiss more than her cheek, more than her mouth, more than her — "

"Have done!" snapped Thomas. "You jest of what is no jest to me."

★ ★ ★

The subject of these repining, Mistress Anne Boleyn, found herself to be in a rare quandary. Seated, alone for once, upon a blue satin cushion in the window of a small antechamber overlooking the formal garden, she picked restlessly at the tiny extra nail on the little finger of her right hand, as was her unconscious habit when worried or upset. Suddenly aware of what she did, she snatched her other hand away, hiding them both in the long wide sleeves she had made so fashionable. Staring abstractedly across the gardens, she did not notice the figures of Tom Wyatt and Francis Bryan pointing her out to one another, then waving to her as she sat. Her thoughts were upon another matter that was growing to be a problem.

All unwitting, she had ensnared King Henry. A bitter triumph, for she wanted him not. She had meant no more than to laugh and play; to flirt, to tease — and that only. She had treated him as she had treated all her admirers, with sparkling glances, a flood of saucy witticisms, tantalising laughter, perhaps a kiss or two, no more. She had no plan to catch a man; she suffered no desires, no longings, save only one, and that was to see the downfall of Cardinal Wolsey, whom she held responsible for breaking her heart.

And I have no heart left, there is no softness in me, she thought, gazing over the neat parterres of the formal garden to the great trees of the park, now showing softly leafy in the late April sunshine, the grass beneath them lush and green, jewelled with the tiny purple of dog-violets, called blue mice, the pinkish-mauve of the tall bell-like fritillaries, the gold of cowslips and the starry shapes of daisies, shining bright. She saw none of Nature's beauties, her mind bent on her dilemma.

My blood is cold, her musing ran. I love no one save my sister, my mother and George, and he is but a brother, dear though he is and so comforting to me in the way he watches over me. Mayhap I have a certain fondness for Cousin Tom Wyatt, but it is fondness only, no more than that. And love without marriage I will not consider. I will have all or nothing.

But what to do about the King? Anne frowned in perplexity. He desired her intensely and had said as much. He expected to have her, too. He had given her some handsome jewellery as a token of his intent and had insisted upon her keeping these gifts under pain of his great displeasure. It would be an honour, he said, for her to be taken as his mistress. Well, she did not wish that kind of honour. She saw it as no honour to be captured, forced to yield and then be deserted when he was weary of her, as a child wearies of a plaything, as he had tired of her sister Mary among others.

Mary had been cast speedily aside for Anne. Poor soft-hearted Mary had felt great tenderness for the King, had been delighted to be so singled out as his mistress. She had come to Anne, heartsick and sobbing.

"But I do not want him, sister!" Anne had said, dismayed. "Do believe me."

"Nay, but he wants you!" had wept Mary, her pretty gentle face all blubbered with tears. "He has thrown me off and will not even speak to me! What shall I do, Anne? I am so unhappy and so shamed?"

"I do not know," confessed Anne. "I cannot tell how to re-awaken a man's heart. I have not tried to take him from you, I swear, Mary. He is not of the sort to attract me, if anyone could. But he must have given you some goodly jewels and a pension, surely, and you have your husband and two dear little children."

"He has given me nothing!" Mary had cried. "I wanted nothing but his love — I told him so. Only his love."

Anne had stared at her sister aghast. "He has given you *nothing*?" she repeated, shocked. "*Rien du tout* — nothing at all?"

"Not a penny, Anne. But I did not do it for money. How could he be so unkind, so uncaring?" And she burst into renewed sobs.

"But the children?" asked Anne at last. "Surely he has settled something on them?"

"Nothing!" whimpered Mary. "But I care not for that, except — except — that my young Henry and now little Katherine may well be his own."

"Oh Mary!" Anne was at a loss. "And well they may be. He has a heart of stone. It is too cruel. What does Will, your husband, say?"

"He says to guard your own heart well, Anne, for it is plain that the King means to have you."

"My heart is well guarded," said Anne, "and he will not have me if I can do aught to prevent it."

"But how shall you, sister? You cannot refuse the King."

"Can I not? I refused the King of France."

Mary's olive cheek flushed. "And I did not. Well, so be it. I am easy swayed."

Anne took her hand. "We are as we are, dear Mary. I do not mean to judge, believe me."

"There are many who do, Anna. It is hard for a woman at Court, whether she be wed or no. I am lucky in my husband, for he understands and still loves me."

"You are fortunate in him," replied her sister. "As to King Henry, all I can do is to run away."

"To run away? Where shall you run?"

"Back to Hever. 'Tis all I can do if His Grace grows too pressing."

Sitting there, in the window-seat at Richmond Palace, fingering the diamond necklace the King had fairly forced upon her, Anne remembered that conversation with her sister. She would run back to Hever, she had said. Easy to say. But what of her family? Her father depended upon the King's continual goodwill for all he had of status and high position, while George, though well-regarded, still had his own way to make. Once again she picked at her finger.

Indeed, the King had been mighty open-handed to dear George in the matter of his marriage to Jane Parker, for he had favoured the union. Anne's father had demanded a goodly dowry with Jane and Jane's father had been unable to provide the last three hundred pounds of the sum. Would Thomas Boleyn, Viscount Rochford, forgo that last amount, had asked Jane's father, Lord Morley, hopefully? No, Thomas Boleyn would not. So King Henry had given it, which was a great favour and right generous, and George's marriage had gone forward as His Majesty had wished. Anne dared do nothing to imperil her beloved brother's chances, even though she disliked his bride and feared for George's happiness.

She sighed. It was a predicament indeed. At that moment, the door opened stealthily and Anne turned her head to perceive Thomas Wyatt peering into the room, an eager look upon his handsome, merry face.

"Why, Tom!" she said, smiling, glad for her troublesome thoughts to be dispelled. "What would you?"

"What a question!" he rallied her, advancing further into the room. "I would be with you, sweetheart." He came to join her in the window-seat, moving her bronze satin skirts aside in order not to crush them. "What do you here, all alone?"

"I meditate," said she, "for I have much to think on."

"Are you not in attendance upon the Queen this day?"

"Ay, but later. She is at prayer, as usual, and would rather I were elsewhere. She does not like me."

"I do not wonder at that," said Thomas, "since the King eyes you with such favour." His face grew serious. "And what favours have you given him, Anne?"

Anne glanced at him indignantly. "You are insolent, Tom! What business is it of yours, pray?"

"Only that I love you," he said. "I cannot

endure to think of you as anyone's but mine."

She shrugged her elegant shoulders. "You are wed. I have no interest in married men, as well you know."

"What of the King, then?" His voice rose accusingly. "You will be his leman soon enough, by all accounts — or so I hear."

"Then accounts are wrong. I want him not."

"Heyday, what disdain is here!" Thomas's laugh was scornful. "You will fall on your back for him like all the others have done, I'll wager."

"Then you will lose your wager!" she flashed, eyes blazing. "I bed with no man save in marriage only."

He stared at her. "Do you know what you say?" he said, low, after a long silence. "I spoke of the King, Anne."

She was quiet. Then she lifted her chin. "Well?" she challenged him.

"But Anne!" He swallowed. "The King — you cannot — Anne, you jest!"

She gasped and shook her head, as if to clear it and gave a high, breathless laugh. "But of a certainty I jest, Tom!" She laughed again, more naturally and seized his hand. "*Certainement*, I jest. *Eh bien*, you know my way."

Relieved, he laughed with her. "Ah, you are a desperate tease, wicked one! You bemuse us all. There is not a man at Court who is not at your feet."

"My uncle Norfolk is not," she observed shrewdly, "and Cardinal Wolsey is not. Wolsey wishes me further, I can tell you. And I wish the same for him."

"You meddle with the mighty, do you not?" said Thomas. "Have a care, sweeting, that your daring spirit does not make you too bold." He slid an arm about her slender waist. "See, I have made a poesy for you. It is not finished as yet, but I would like you to read what I have written so far." He handed her a paper.

. . . Who list her hunt, I put him out of doubt,

she read.

As well as I may spend his time in vain!
And graven with diamonds in letters plain
There is written her fair neck about:
"Noli me tangere", for I Caesar's am
And wild for to hold, though I seem tame.

"Do you like it," he asked anxiously, seeing her black winged brows draw together in a frown.

"No, I do not!" she exclaimed. "I am *not* Caesar's, for all he did give me this necklace! I wear it in secret only, you must understand, to keep him quiet. No matter how he tries to capture me, I am *not* his!"

"I would capture you," said he, drawing her closer. "I love you, Anne; my heart is entirely yours. I think you have bewitched me as well as His Grace."

She leant her head against his broad, yellow velvet clad shoulder. "Oh, *mon cher*, it is all a confusion. I would we were little ones again, when all was plain and simple."

"If only I were not wed!" he sighed.

She echoed his sigh before pulling herself upright. "Ah, that is fantasy and will not resolve my problem," she said firmly. "And I must not dally here with you, Tom Wyatt! I must go to the Queen; it is time for me to attend her. Let me go."

He did not release her. "Nay, before I do, I demand a forfeit, a keepsake. Come, a kiss!" Laughing, she ducked, seeking to avoid him, but he managed to kiss her cheek, nevertheless. "Now for a keepsake!" he cried excitedly as they struggled together upon the window-seat, he grabbing at a little jewelled tablet that

98

she wore on a chain round her waist. The chain snapped, to a cry of annoyance from Anne and a shout of triumph from Thomas. As she looked up to protest, he kissed her mouth, a kiss of passion and longing that left them both shaken. She tore herself free and ran from the room.

★ ★ ★

It was not long before King Henry's desire grew obvious to all, his ardent behaviour causing Mistress Anne much worry and embarrassment. At last, greatly daring, fearful of his displeasure that might bring trouble to her family, she betook herself to Hever in June, upon a plea of exhaustion and weariness, to her father's furious amazement.

"Stupid bitch, you go to wreck all! You cast us down the wind! To treat His Grace with such disdain is madness! My faith, you rate your power crazy-high, my girl, and we shall suffer for it. Good God, when I think of how I have worked, how striven, and now am like to lose all, I could run witless!"

Thus raged Viscount Rochford, stamping up and down the raw oaken boards of his new Long Gallery, dark hair bouncing under his jaunty feathered cap, reddish beard wagging as he ranted.

His daughter, resentful of his noisy recriminations, said nothing, for until the King showed his hand there was nothing to say. She had played all her cards. But the King showed his hand to great effect and very soon, for letter after letter found its way down to Hever, brought by puffing, sweating messengers, galloping hard upon the King's business. Pleading letters, formal at first, then glowing with ardour later, they arrived in a steady stream. Gifts followed letters and finally the King himself, under the pretext of a hunting visit to the home of his good friend Viscount Rochford of Hever. Viscount Rochford expressed himself as delighted to play host, even though it would cost him a ransom in gold with small chance of reimbursement, should that want-wit of an Anna ruin her chances and his. But he kept his doubts to himself and returned in haste to London to escort His Majesty.

Still, a visit from the King, vile costly though it would be, showed that His Grace was not weary of the girl's antics as yet, reflected Thomas Boleyn as he rode down from London at the King's side in the small procession, pointing out the beauties of the Kentish countryside, though what kind of a game she could be playing, God or the devil only knew. She cannot hope to keep him on a string for ever! thought Thomas. She must yield to him soon and then, hey nonny-no and happy days! More steps up for Viscount Rochford! I pray she does not hold out too long, or all will be at salt and sand. Sweet Christ, what a thing that he, Boleyn of Rochford, with all his talents, should be hanging on the whims of his own daughter, the lack-brained, prideful wench! It was insupportable, by the Cross it was! Grinding his teeth, he heard the King address him and turned, his expression of fury swiftly replaced by a broad sycophantic smile as he answered his royal master's query.

"Ay, indeed, Sire, my poor Hever is a pretty enough place. I think you will find it so, though the hunting is unremarkable, I fear."

"Ah, my Lord Rochford, the quarry I hunt is most remarkable," boomed the red-headed royal giant, all clothed in mulberry and silver astride his great white horse, trotting easily beside Thomas's chestnut down the dusty lane. " 'Tis a bird not easy caught and nests at Hever." He burst into a great roar of laughter, echoed slavishly by his companions. "Think you I shall snare this bird, good Thomas?"

"I shall make it my business to see that you do, Your Grace," replied Thomas instantly. By God, she had best submit this time, he thought, or I shall thrash the life out of her!

But the bird would not be caught, nor would she surrender, taking care never to be left alone with the King, despite all her father's efforts. She had the headache; she had a cold; she was at prayer; she had twisted her ankle and was not able to walk in the garden; she was even visiting the poor, an uncommon occurrence for Mistress Anne, but what would you? Oh, she would sing gladly enough, but was unable to do so at this time, her cold having given her a sore throat. Meekly and prettily she begged His Majesty's pardon for her many shortcomings, but she was only a maid and shy. She trusted that he would understand.

After a week of astonished frustration, His Majesty was forced to understand and returned to Westminster a very puzzled man, Lord Rochford at his side apologising for his daughter's obduracy all the way back to London.

"Have done, Tom," said the King at last. "I am not angered with the lass. Bewildered, yes, but I think I can comprehend her behaviour and I respect her for it. She is true to herself. Believe me, I have met none like her in all my life; so beautiful, so virtuous, so careful of her chastity. She draws me like a lodestone, I swear!"

At this speech, Lord Rochford began to take heart and realise that all was not yet lost. Ceasing his protestations, he began to ponder the matter of his daughter and the King. Was Anne cleverer than he had supposed? Was she leading His Majesty on for gain and advancement? Ay, that must be it! She would have to throw her dice careful then, and yield at exactly the right moment. By sweet St. Prisca, he thought exultantly, I may yet get an earldom after all! Pray the Lord she does not make a pig's ear of the business. His little Anne — well, well! Smiling, he rode on.

* * *

Some weeks later, on a fine summer morning after Anne had rejoined the Court at Placentia, that beautiful turreted residence covering many acres of land beside the River Thames at Greenwich, the King's birthplace and favourite palace, His Majesty suggested a game of bowls to seek diversion. At this pastime, as with all sports, he was highly skilled and took great pride in his prowess. Amidst good-tempered laughter, sides were drawn and play began.

"Ha, see that!" cried the King, straightening up from a cast as the game progressed. "Mine there is well thrown. I play to win, you see, gentlemen!"

"By your leave, Sire," spoke up Thomas Wyatt, stepping forward boldly, " 'tis not your cast, I fear. It was mine."

"What?" His Majesty turned, astonished, quite unused to being given in error. "Why, what mean you, Tom? It was mine! Did you not see, Francis? Charles, did you not observe it?"

But Sir Francis Bryan and the Duke of Suffolk found themselves suddenly afflicted by diplomatic blindness and could not say, for Tom Wyatt was indeed in the right of it and neither gentleman felt equal to the task of contradicting His Majesty who burst into a loud laugh.

"Heyday, Tom, you do but jest with me, saucy fellow. The cast is mine!" He pointed with his little finger at the round black wood, lying so innocently upon the smoothly shaven green, wagging his hand to emphasis his statement. Upon that finger flashed a diamond ring that Wyatt recognised only too well. It had once belonged to Anne. For a moment his spirits took a swift downward plunge, then his natural impudence asserted itself and he resolved to challenge his royal master, come what might.

"Now, come, Tom, admit it," laughed the King. "Thou'rt wrong, man. The cast is mine — I tell thee it is mine!"

"Well then," said Wyatt, smiling, "if Your Grace will give me leave to measure it, I may prove the cast to be mine."

And, greatly daring, he drew from the open neck of his velvet doublet the little jewelled tablet he had seized from Anne, which he wore on a chain round his neck, pulled the chain over his head and affected to measure the cast with it, ignoring the frantic frowns and headshakings of his companions, who stood watching in dismay. The King recognised the tablet at once, as Thomas had known he would, his smile darkening to a glare of displeasure, while his cheeks flushed and his lower lip jutted out ominously. With a quick angry gesture, he strode forward and kicked the wood away.

"The cast may be as you say, but I see I am deceived!" he snapped, glowering at the tablet dangling from Wyatt's hand and, without another word, he swung round and marched off, confused and upset, followed at a run by his brother-in-law, the Duke of Suffolk, who was always anxious to remain in good odour with his royal relative after his hasty and ill-judged marriage to His Majesty's sister, the Princess Mary Rose.

"Tom, have you run mad?" cried Sir Francis Bryan, starting forward once the infuriated monarch was fairly out of earshot. "What comes to you so to taunt the King? Have you no care for our cousin Anne whom you profess to love? Already he thinks that she has deceived him. You will do no good to her, nor to yourself by such rash behaviour. We must not linger here. Come, let us walk back to the palace and pray that all will be well."

The two young men hurried along the alley of pleached limes, the leafy shadows dappling their faces as they went. "I love her dearly, Frank," said Thomas. " 'Tis no light thing with me."

" 'Tis no light thing to defy the King, neither," retorted Sir Francis. "If he wants her, he will have her and will brook no interference, mark my word."

"Ay," grumbled Wyatt. "He thinks he may order all."

"And so he may," answered Sir Francis. "He is the highest in the land, as you seem to forget. You will get yourself sent from Court yet, Tom. The royal displeasure falls very heavy and so I warn you. You should take care it do not fall on you."

"I care not!" sighed the poet. "I cannot endure to witness the way he dotes on her, as if she were his already."

"Well, and is she not?"

"Nay, she is not. She swore to me that she was not. And besides, she does not want the man himself — that is, she is not one for light bedding — oh, I pray that no one overheard me!" he finished apprehensively.

"No, we are quite alone," replied Sir Francis. "Oh!" he went on, enlightened. "Is that why she ran off to Hever?"

"Ay, that is why."

"Ha, she plays with fire, then. 'Tis a dangerous game."

"But play it she will, I fear," said Thomas ruefully. "I cannot tell what may become of it."

"Ah, she will give in soon enough," responded Sir Francis comfortably. "They all do in the end."

"Well, if she do I must leave the Court, Frank. I could not answer for my actions else."

"In which case, it were better you went. Anyhap, so crack-skulled over her as you are, His Majesty will be glad to see the back of you."

"Ay, but it will not be yet, for I cannot tear myself away."

"Sure, it has gone deep with you, Tom," sympathised Sir Francis. "Our cousin is fascinating and lovely enough to turn any man's head, I agree. I would I might be vouchsafed a kiss, let alone a jewelled tablet!"

★ ★ ★

Meanwhile, in a small parlour of the palace, away from curious eyes and ears, the former owner of the jewelled tablet was endeavouring to explain to England's aggrieved ruler the presence of that jewel round Thomas Wyatt's neck.

"Nay, Sire, be not angered," she pleaded. "The little tablet was but a gift from my aunt and I did not give it to Wyatt. He took it from me."

The King, who had burst into the Maids' Gallery and called her forth, halted in his indignant pacing of the floor. "He took it? How so? Were you private with him that he did this?"

"Oh, Your Grace," begged Anne, "do pray recall that he and I were children together and have been friends all our lives. He is my cousin. 'Tis not a question of being *private* with Tom Wyatt. It was but a silly jest."

"I like not such jests!" snapped His Majesty, frowning and staring hard at his love. "What was the jest?"

"The other maids laid a wager," said Anne, improvising rapidly and thanking God for her quick wits. "They wagered him that he could not snatch the tablet." She watched the King and saw his face soften slightly.

"H'm!" said he. "And how did Wyatt accomplish the theft?"

She achieved a laugh that sounded completely natural. "Why, he did but pull the chain from my waist as I danced so fast with you in the Galliard. 'Twas simple enough, for the chain was so fine that I was quite unaware of its loss, Sire. Then, because he had won the wager, he would not return the tablet and because it meant so little to me, I thought of it no more."

A relieved smile broke over Henry Tudor's handsome, red-bearded face. "Is it even so?" he cried. "Is it even so, sweetheart? Come, let's kiss and make our peace!" He caught her in his long arms. "'Fore God, my Nan, how I love you! I burn for you, little witch that you are! My heart is yours, know you that? When will you come to me, my darling?"

"I cannot tell," she said primly. "My conscience forbids it."

"Ah, you are wonderful!" He shook his head in admiration. "So chaste, so pure! One cannot go against one's conscience, as well I know, for mine troubles me sore in the matter of my marriage. You are surprised, ay, but 'tis fact. How alike we are, dear heart! We both have a good Christian conscience to keep us from wrongdoing — though sometimes wrongdoing is easier, thinkest thou not so?" he added hopefully.

"The Devil's path is wide and easy," observed Anne piously, feeling herself on dangerous ground and well aware of His Grace's capacity for self-deception.

"Indeed, you are very right!" agreed the King, much struck by this appeal to his religious principles. "You are very right, certainly. Do you not feel also that the harder the struggle, the greater the prize?"

"Only if God so wills," returned his beloved, neatly forestalling another argument in favour of her yielding to his wishes.

"Quite so," replied the God-fearing monarch with a sigh, conscious that by referring to the Almighty, Mistress Anne had bested him yet again. "Oh, ay, certainly if only God wills . . . What is it?" he rapped out, suddenly noticing a third presence in the room. Turning, he beheld one of his wife's ladies curtseying apologetically.

She explained meekly that Queen Katherine needed Mistress Boleyn upon her duties and would she please go to the Queen at once. For answer, the King took Anne's hand and marched with her to the Queen's chamber, where he discovered his wife and her attendants at their embroidery.

"I bring you the lady, Madam," he said loudly and unsmilingly. "Is it necessary that she be hounded in this fashion?"

Queen Katherine, small and stout, clad in a gown of dull purple silk that took every vestige of colour from her sweet, sad face, looked up with a nervous, propitiatory smile. "Hounded, husband? Oh no! I did but fear that she had forgot the time," she said placatingly, her Spanish accent always more marked when she was startled or upset. "Mistress Boleyn is to take Lady d'Eresby's place, you see, and Lady d'Eresby had the headache and wished greatly to rest."

"Oh, very well," growled the King, "but I will not have this lady put upon. Go, then, Nan," he said to Anne, "yet stay a moment — will you dance with me tonight?"

Anne curtseyed, smiling demurely. "As your Majesty commands."

"Then I command it!" he laughed, once again restored to good humour, and strode out of the room humming merrily.

★　★　★

After the Christmas revels, through which Tom Wyatt slouched glum and moody, glared

111

upon balefully by his royal master and mocked in friendly fashion by his intimates, it was clear to all the Court that King Henry was madly in love with Viscount Rochford's younger daughter and meant to have her by any means he could. Wyatt's heart was heavy in his breast; he knew that he was torturing himself by staying to watch the King's pursuit of Anne, but where should he go, what should he do?

His answer came soon after Twelfth Night, when the holly branches were taken down, the garlands put away and the Court had returned to ordinary living once more. Having nothing better to do, he was wandering gloomily along the riverside at Westminster, huddled in a hooded, fur-lined, red velvet cloak against the cold, when turning his head to look out over the water, he spied his friend, John Russell of Bedford, stepping hurriedly ashore from a boat moored at the landing stage.

"Ho, Jack!" he called, waving. "Where are you bound, so earnest and busy?"

Russell halted, waiting for Wyatt to come up with him. "Well met, Tom," he said, smiling, "for I come to finish some business and to bid you farewell."

"Farewell?" echoed Wyatt. "Why so?"

"I am bound to Italy on embassy to the

Pope," replied Russell. "I am sent thither by the King."

"Are you indeed?" Thomas frowned and took a sudden decision. "Then, if you please, I will ask leave, get money and go with you, Jack. Can you bide awhile to let me do all this?"

"Ay, right gladly," answered Russell. "I am well beforehand with time. Indeed, it will be right pleasurable for us to go together. We shall make merry, I doubt not."

The two young men hastened into the palace and soon Thomas had set all in train for his leaving. Before he left he wrote another rhyme for Anne in the form of a riddle.

> *What word is that that changeth not,*
> *Though it be turned and made in*
>   *twain?*
> *It is mine answer, God it wot,*
> *And eke the cause of all my pain.*
> *A love rewarded with disdain,*
> *Yet it is love. What would ye more?*
> *It is my health eke and my sore.*

"Oh, very knacky, upon my word!" cried George Boleyn admiringly upon reading it. "The answer is 'Anna', of course. Do you mean to give it her, Tom?"

"I shall give it to her when I leave," replied Thomas. "She understands why I can remain here no longer."

"Ay, the pace grows too hot to hold both you and His Majesty! Anyhap, I hope you may find the Italian maidens beautiful and willing."

Wyatt put the folded paper containing his riddle into Anne's hand when he took his departure. She looked regretful, but made no remark other than the conventional wishes for his safe journey, while the King fairly beamed with delight to see him go. Now that Wyatt was out of the way, he had the field to himself.

6

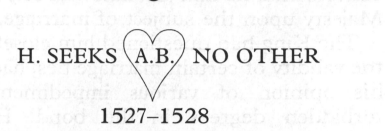

H. SEEKS A.B. NO OTHER

1527–1528

It was early spring and King Henry and his Court were residing at Placentia, as was usual at that time of the year. The weather was wild and windy, the sky grey and full of racing clouds, the river water restless as the sky above and of the colour of polished pewter. Gabriel de Grammont, Bishop of Tarbes, gazed without pleasure upon the prospect afforded him from the window of the chamber that had been assigned to him. England in the month of March held few delights for him. *Mais, tiens, Gabriel!* he reminded himself with a mental shake, he was not in England for pleasure, but to discuss the possible marriage of King Henry's daughter, the eleven year old Princess Mary, to the Duc d'Orléans, second son of King François. The little girl was soon to arrive from Ludlow where she had been living for some time as Princess of Wales. The Bishop supposed that the wedding could take place; it seemed feasible enough and yet — ! His thoughts roved back over the extraordinary conversation he had just had with His English Majesty upon the subject of marriage.

The King had questioned him closely upon the validity of certain marriage ties, had asked his opinion of various impediments and forbidden degrees in the bond. He had intimated a doubt of the legality of marriage with a brother's wife or, in the case of a female, a sister's brother. It was a fascinating discussion and the Bishop had been led on to utter his thoughts on the subject.

"*C'est bien sûr, Sire,*" he had said to the King. "If a marriage between the parties has been consummated, then for a brother to marry a brother's widow, or a sister to wed her sister's widower is illegal. Holy Church considers that no marriage."

"Indeed?" The King had appeared much impressed. "And if so be such a wedding has taken place — in all innocence, mark you, Bishop — what then of the children of the union?"

"They would be bastards, Sire," had replied the Bishop instantly and with total conviction. "You have to consult the eighteenth and twentieth chapters of Leviticus to discover that God looks with disfavour upon

116

such a union." And the King had nodded, allowing the talk to turn to other matters.

The good Bishop, gazing from his window, frowned, puzzled. Could King Henry have been referring to his own marital situation? *Mais jamais!* It could not be so! The Bishop knew of nothing that could have led to such speculations, unless . . . He bit his lip. Certainly Queen Katherine had been wed for a short time to King Henry's dead brother, but that marriage was never consummated — was it? *Hé mon Dieu, quelle idée! C'était ridicule, stupide! Non, non,* he must put the thought from his mind *immédiatement!* Thus Gabriel de Grammont, startled and shocked.

But King Henry could not put the thought from his own mind. It had settled and taken root there sometime earlier. His wife had forty-two years to his thirty-six and in all the eighteen years of their marriage she had borne one living child, and that a girl, out of a succession of stillbirths and miscarriages. There had been a little prince, but he had died after only a few weeks. King Henry was a King with no male heir and not for want of trying, neither. By God, it was a slur on his masculinity! He felt it deeply, so deeply indeed, that it was beginning to plague him night and day.

At one time he had toyed with the idea of

entailing the Crown upon his illegitimate son, the little Duke of Richmond, but the Council would have none of it and, come to that, nor would England, he dared say. The doctors had told him that Katherine would bear no more children now, so what was he to do, God damn it? Ay, God *had* damned it, surely, by giving him no sons! It was a judgment upon his unrighteous marriage, for who could prove that Katherine's union with his brother was unconsummated? He had only her word for it. He would have to rid himself of her somehow, though exactly how was hard to make out as yet. It required much thought.

Within a week or two, the young Princess Mary had come to Placentia from Ludlow to meet the French Ambassadors and Mistress Anne Boleyn had left for Hever to recruit her strength, or so she said. King Henry missed her very badly indeed. He felt lost without her dark and laughing presence, her gaiety, the excitement she engendered about her, as he endeavoured to give all his attention to the negotiations for his daughter's marriage. But he wrote to Anne. He wrote letters from the heart, fairly blazing with love and willingness to serve her in any way he could.

. . . *Beseeching you with all my heart to let me know definitely your whole intent touching the love between us; for necessity constrains me to pester you for a reply, having been for more than a year struck by the dart of love, being uncertain either of failure or of finding a place in your heart and affection . . . If it pleases you to do the duty of a true, loyal mistress and friend, and give yourself body and heart to me who will be (and have been) your very loyal servant (if your strictness does not forbid me), I promise . . . to take you for my sole mistress, rejecting all others except yourself out of mind and affection, and to serve you alone; begging you to make me a complete answer to this my rude letter . . . No more for fear of boring you. Written by the hand of him who would willingly remain your H.R.*

Anne read this letter in the privacy of her room at Hever. *Sainte Marie*, but Henry Tudor was fairly grovelling to her and in writing, too! The King himself was pleading with her, he who had never had to plead for anything in all his life! She felt quite sorry for him. Nevertheless, she would not grant him his wish. She had sworn never to bed with any man, King or no, outside marriage. Her mind was set; she would not yield. If she did so, she would lose the self respect that meant so much to her, and yet, if she continued to refuse him he might weary of her, in which case her father and brother could hope for no more advancement. Indeed, they might lose all they had gained hitherto. It was a dilemma in which she was stuck fast, unable to go forward or back. What had begun as nothing but a light-hearted flirtation on her part had become a tense and highly-charged contest of wills on the part of Henry Tudor and herself, the outcome of which she could not forsee, unless . . . She chewed feverishly at that little extra finger-nail . . . Unless he might marry her! It seemed an impossible notion, but she had held it in the back of her mind for some time. Could she make him do it? Was it crazy? Did she possess such power? She had best continue to play a waiting game and see how events would fall out.

Her answering letter to the King was sweetness itself and contained a charmingly worded refusal which threw His Majesty into a ferment. He wrote again, desiring her to return to Court, for he had something he wished to discuss with her and he longed for her presence above all things.

Delighted to comply with this request, for she was thoroughly bored with country life, Anne returned to Court early in the morning of the 5th of May 1527. This was the day upon which a great state banquet was to be held for the French Ambassadors, followed by a ball. The King was overjoyed to see her, clasping her in his arms and kissing her passionately when they were in his Privy Chamber.

"My own darling, my beautiful love!" There were tears of emotion in his eyes. "Say you did not mean what you wrote in your letter. I adore you, Nan. Do not deny me — do not, sweetheart!"

She pulled away from him, staring up at him, her great dark eyes unreadable. "Hearken to me, Sire," she said, "hearken to me and mark me well." She took a deep breath, feeling her heart begin to hammer in her breast. "Your mistress I cannot be. I have told you this many times. My conscience will not allow it."

There was a silence. What would he say next, she wondered. Would he take the bait? Did he love enough to take the astonishing step of divorce and re-marriage? Would he ask her? She held her breath.

"Never?" suddenly demanded King Henry. "You will *never* consent to be my mistress? You mean it?"

"Unalterably," she replied, digging her nails into her palms as she watched him nervously.

He sighed. "Ah, I would you were my

wife," he said slowly at last, thoughtfully, turning the matter over in his mind.

"Your wife I cannot be."

It was a statement, flat and bald. Their eyes, one pair round and blue, the other long and velvet black, met in a long, meaningful gaze. At length he spoke, the words measured and deliberate.

"Although I am already wed, my Anne, if it were possible, if it were truly possible, would you wed me if I were free?"

She could not speak at first. She swallowed, her lips trembling. "Yes," she said softly, at last. "If it were possible and you were free, I would."

He gave a great shout. "Then I shall *make* it possible!" he cried. "We *shall* wed, you and I. We shall wed if I have to move mountains to accomplish it!"

Her knees gave way and she staggered, leaning against his broad chest, limp and dizzy with relief and amazement. He had said it! He would do it!

"How shall you bring it about?" she asked breathlessly, when she had recovered a little.

"Leave it to me!" he laughed triumphantly. "Oh, my sweeting — my jewel — we shall do it! Am I not the King?" He kissed her rapturously. "Listen, darling, I have been considering putting the Queen aside for some little time. She can bear me no more children and I must have a son. So I have been thinking of suitable princesses, but right half-heartedly, see'st thou. Why did I never think of wedding you, whom I adore to madness? I have been so blind! Ah, what a Queen you will make!" He kissed her again. "As soon as these stupid revels be done I will take the matter up with Wolsey."

She drew back. "With the Cardinal? He likes me not, Sire. He will not deem me fit for Queenship. I am but a subject."

"*He* will not deem you fit? He will have no choice! But you are right, Nan, we do not want him putting difficulties in our way. I may have to deceive him a little."

She laughed on a high, excited note. "And what a rude awakening he will have! I long to see his face when he learns the truth."

"I know that you do not like him," said the King, "but try not to show your dislike too openly, dearest, for we wish him to aid us, remember. And as for me, I could not do without him; he takes so many cares off my back." He stroked her cheek, smiling lovingly. "You must be off now, my love, for I have to attend to the Ambassadors and be ready to greet my daughter when she arrives from Ludlow. She is expected at any minute. Be sure to wear your finest gown for the dancing tonight — my wife-to-be!"

They kissed again and she ran off to the room which she shared with her friend and cousin, Margaret, Lady Lee, sister to Thomas Wyatt. Bursting open the door, she threw herself upon her bed, laughing and weeping together until Lady Lee feared she would make herself ill.

"Nay, Marget, I am not ill — I am so happy, so happy and so relieved that I am nigh crazy. But I cannot tell you why yet. You will find out soon enough. Now, bear with me, my dear, for I must write a note to the King and put in it all the words I should have said awhile ago."

Jumping to her feet, she ran to a table on which stood her little desk. Opening it, she snatched up a pen, its yellow quill feather quivering in her hand as she scribbled.

. . . *My love for you is as great as thine for me,*

she wrote hurriedly.

As to our bedding, for that we must wait 'til our marriage to which I look forward for happiness therein. My virtue doth prevent my body being thine before wedding, but after that I am all your own.

As token of my love I send you this jewel as symbol of myself and the perils I am ready to undertake for your sake . . .

The jewel was a good thought, she congratulated herself, and just right, though she regretted parting with it, for it was one of the best she had. It was of coloured enamel, representing a lady in a storm-tossed ship, dependent from a large diamond brooch, with the motto inscribed upon it *Aut illic, aut nullibit* — 'There or nowhere'. Could anything be more apt? Taking the brooch from her jewel-box, she held it in her hand a moment. It was a lovely and costly bauble and she was fain to keep it, yet what was one jewel against such a marriage? Good God, she would be Queen of England! Now it was no dream. Countless jewels awaited her, boundless wealth — 'twas dizzying thought. *Sainte Marie,* it were worth all the waiting and worrying she had made herself endure and what prospects it opened for her family! God be thanked that she possessed the will to enforce patience in herself and had used it to good advantage, for see where it had brought her! A King who could not live without her as his wife. Oh, her stars were fortunate indeed! And when she was Queen, why then she could be her true self; no more dissimulation, no more demureness, no more steely patience, no more retirement, no more hanging upon the whispers of others — no more Wolsey, neither, if she could accomplish his downfall. A dazzling future appeared before her. True, and her mouth twisted, she would have to bed with the King. 'Twas pity that wedding included bedding, but one must take the rough with the smooth in this life and how smooth her life was to be henceforth! And His Majesty was not unattractive in his way. She could bear with him, for would he not make her a queen? What better than that? She laughed to herself, her eyes dancing with excitement.

The King was enraptured with Anne's note and the gift that accompanied it. His answer reached her, brought by a page to her room that May evening as she and Margaret Lee were dressing for the State banquet and ball.

"See who is at the door, girl," Anne bade her tirewoman, "and do not linger or I shall never be ready. The sleeves of this gown are difficult enough to pin on as it is."

" 'Tis a message for you from His Majesty, Mistress Anne," said the maid, big-eyed with wonder, handing over the note with a respectful bob.

"*Eh bien?* So? are you struck to stone then? Come, pin these sleeves of mine and hasten about it." Seated on her dressing stool while her sleeves were pinned into place with gold-headed pins, Anne opened her letter and began to read.

. . . For a gift so beautiful that nothing could be more, I thank you very cordially, not only for the fine diamond and the ship in which the damsel is tossed about, but chiefly for the beautiful interpretation and humble submission for which your kindness has used it . . . I will outdo you in loyalty of heart and desire to please . . . assuring you that henceforth my heart be so dedicated to you alone, wishing strongly that my body could also be so dedicated, as God can do if He pleases. This I pray Him daily to do, hoping that finally my prayers will be heard, wishing the time brief and thinking it long till we two meet again.

Written by the hand of the one who in heart, body and will is your loyal and most assured servant.

H. seeks A.B. no other.

"Marget, he says he thinks the time long till we meet again!" said Anne, laughing, to Lady

127

Lee. "Why, 'tis but a mere hour or two."

"Ah, he is mad for you," replied her cousin, combing her long fair hair. "Some say you have bewitched him."

"Well, to be sure, I cannot tell how, for I have set out no lures for him, as you know well."

"Oh, come, Nan!" Margaret burst into giggles. "No lures? Your avoidance of him was lure enough, as you know well! There is scarce a soul who does not consider you his mistress. What will come of it, say I?"

"I care naught for gossip. I am virgin still. And as to what will come of it, you will see and that soon, I hope." Anne threw back her head, shaking her mass of hair free of its net. She turned to her maid. "Now that you have finished with my sleeves, you must brush my hair. I will wear it loose tonight under my new French coif — the one with the pearls and rubies. Fetch it, girl — do not stand goggling there! I wish to try it." As the maid brushed the glossy mane of black hair, Anne set the coif upon her head, tying the ribbons under her chin. "There now, Marget, how does it look?"

"Beautiful," answered Margaret Lee with sincere admiration. "You make us all seem dowds, cousin. Indeed, you look like a queen for you stand out so greatly from all the rest."

"Do I so?" Anne rose from the stool and pranced across the room, snapping her fingers and humming a catchy tune, her golden silk skirts swaying over a black kirtle heavily worked in gold thread sewn with brilliants. The sleeves, over which such care had been taken, were of black and amber silk, slashed and puffed with white and sewn with rubies and pearls; the bodice of the gown was of gold velvet laced with black, while round the small waist was a girdle of rubies, a gift from the King. About Anne's long neck shone yet another royal gift; a collar of large pearls with a pendent letter B in gold, from which hung three pearls, oval in shape. "So I look like a queen," said Anne, with a secret smile. "Would I make a good one, think you?"

"Why yes," answered Margaret, amused at what she thought a joke. "Why yes, if there were not one already."

"*Hé, cela va sans dire* — that goes without saying." Anne moved to the door. "Now we must go and wait upon her, *n'est-ce-pas?* Come, Marget, our present Queen awaits us!" And, laughing together, the two young women hurried along the galleries to Queen Katherine's apartments to assist her at her dressing and to escort her to the new-built banqueting hall, a spacious wooden structure overlooking the Privy Garden.

★ ★ ★

The Queen and the young Princess Mary took their places beside the King on the dais raised at one end of the hall, while long trestle tables covered with fair white cloths, soon to be dirtied by splashes of gravy, sauce, custard, crumbs of bread and broken pieces of marzipan that had not been gobbled up, ran the length of the hall, seating those of less than royal degree in order of rank. Servitors scurried in and out, bearing huge, steaming joints of beef and pork, sucking pig, haunches of lamb. Golden bowls came filled with neats' tongues, carp, pigeon and quail; there were pies, both open and closed, containing mixtures of meat or fish, while platters of the finest white manchet bread were placed about the table within reach of every hungry hand. Branches of candles, as well as torches in wall-sconces, afforded a bright, warm light which glowed and flickered on each smiling face, over each jewelled headdress and feathered cap, while everyone ate and drank mightily.

When all could stuff themselves no more, the whole company, led by Their Majesties,

130

repaired to the Queen's apartments to witness a masque in which the little Princess Mary was to perform. There they saw a cunningly constructed cave fashioned of cloth of gold, guarded by tall gentlemen as torch-bearers, each one clad in gold velvet, wearing a plumed hat. At the sound of trumpets, the Princess appeared in the cave, hand in hand with the Marchioness of Exeter, to hear handclaps and cries of admiration. The little girl wore a gown of shimmering cloth of gold; her curling red hair was confined in a golden net bound round with a jewelled garland surmounted by a crimson velvet cap. Stepping forward with great composure, she spoke some verses in French and English, her voice surprisingly deep in one so young, receiving ecstatic applause.

"She is pretty enough," whispered Margaret Lee to Anne Boleyn, "but so thin and small, is she not?"

"Ay, she looks to me to be unripe for marriage as yet," returned Anne, but that would not hinder the signing of the treaty. "Oh, I would the dancing might begin, do you not, Marget? My feet itch to trip a measure, I have had enough of ceremonial."

As if in answer to her words, the masque came to an end and the courtiers and guests, with the King and Queen in their midst, a rainbow medley of jewels, silks and velvets, trooped, laughing and chattering, into the Great Hall where musicians in their gallery were already tuning their instruments for dancing. Fresh rushes mixed with lavender, rosemary, thyme, sage and lemon balm, had been spread upon the floor, branches of flowering lilac and laburnum filled the great hearths and torches blazed from the walls, their glittering reflections flashing and wavering in the diamond panes of the long windows. The company ranged itself about the walls as the King, Queen and finally the Princess, surrounded by their attendants took their places on the dais at the head of the hall.

At last, King Henry gave the sign for music to begin and, as the first notes sounded, he stood up, as custom demanded, to lead out the Queen. Katherine put out her hand and half-rose in anticipation of this, only to fall back into her chair in shock and amazement as her husband passed her by, marched up to Mistress Anne Boleyn, took the young lady's hand and led her forward to the centre of the hall under the stupefied gaze of his beholders, who were momentarily struck dumb at such a breach of protocol.

"Come, what ails you all?" shouted His Majesty, affecting careless unconsciousness of the enormity of his action. "Why do you not dance, my lords and ladies? Have I not given the office for you to begin? I *command* you all to join us at once. Be not laggard, I say!"

Soon the hall was filled with dancers prancing busily to the strains of 'Barnaby-Hey-Go-Well', laughter and conversation filled the air, while the Queen sat in her chair, a set smile upon her white face, her hands trembling, her heart beating agitatedly. Her husband had slighted her publicly upon an international State occasion! Never before had he behaved to her so and it was all she could do to control her consternation and remain quiet.

For sure, he thinks himself in love with that girl, she reasoned, her mind in a turmoil but, love apart, I am Queen of England and a Princess of Spain! Why should Henry insult me so, treat me with contempt for everyone to witness? What could he mean by it? And before the French Ambassadors, too! Why, all Europe would learn of it and begin to speculate! She sat unmoving, feeling as though she had stepped off a precipice into a cold chasm of hitherto unknown terrors. She was aware of concerned and puzzled glances turned her way and strove to ignore them. She was aware of the delicate and slender form of Anne Boleyn, her hand in the King's, a look of barely concealed triumph upon her lively face as she tripped and turned vivaciously in the dance, black eyes sparkling, long hair swinging out behind her. Katherine was aware of all this as she sat rigid and still, although she seemed to notice nothing.

At least the little Princess Mary was happy, she comforted herself, for there was her beloved daughter dancing merrily and laughing with an elegant French gentleman. May she make the most of it, poor child, for I fear her happiness will not last long, thought Katherine fearfully. If I am to be cast off, what of Mary? Oh, I run moon-mad! 'Tis the shock. It will pass. All this will be resolved — it *must* be resolved! Katherine was glad, as she was glad of nothing else that night, that Mary had been too excited to notice her father's sudden scorn for her mother. As the music throbbed in her dully aching head, the Queen began to entertain the inescapable conviction that nothing would ever be the same again, that a heavy cloud had descended upon her life which from now on, would be filled with foreboding and dark dismay.

She was right.

She was right for, a few weeks later, on the 22nd of June, King Henry sought out his worried, grieving wife, for he wished to converse with her upon a subject of grave and desperate import to them both, he said, staring at her, his expression strained. Her face was pale, her eyes red from much weeping, her shoulders sagging in a hopeless fashion as she watched her husband pace up and down the room, kicking the rushes as he strode about.

"Katherine!" he burst out suddenly. "Katherine, I must tell you — I am constrained to tell you — that although you and I have been wed these nineteen years, we have been living in mortal sin. Nay, do not speak — I have not done," he hurried on, eager to have the wretched business over. "'Tis not only I who realise this," he continued, without looking at his wife's stricken countenance, "but churchmen and respected theologians have confirmed it. My conscience is sorely troubled by this, you having been my brother's wife."

"But Henry, I was a virgin when I came to you!" she cried. "You cannot — "

"Katherine, it is of no use. I am resolved to live with you no longer and I desire that you will choose a suitable house to which you may retire."

At this, Katherine gave a great gasp, buried her face in her hands and gave way to floods of tears. Her husband put out a hand as if to pat her shoulder, then drew it back, confused and embarrassed.

"Now, now, do not weep," he mumbled. "All will be done for the best, I do assure you. Meanwhile, you must keep this matter secret and speak of it to no one. You understand?" Without waiting for her answer, he marched rapidly from the room, pausing outside to mop his brow and sigh with relief at a bad job badly done.

As for Mistress Anne, she was no less anxious and uneasy, for she realised only too well that the major part of the King's divorce would lie in the hands of Cardinal Wolsey who considered her as nothing more than a harlot. What would he do when he discovered that she, and not some foreign princess, was his royal master's choice for a second wife? He would be furious, of course, and do all in his power to bring her down. She was greatly relieved that the Cardinal was soon to journey to France in order to set matters in train for the King's marriage to a French princess — or so he thought. She resolved to put the time of his absence to good use in consolidating her position, for the Lords of the Privy Council loathed Wolsey, seeing him as a power-mad upstart, and their enmity toward him, skilfully fostered, might assist her aim.

Although no actual word had been uttered of the King's intention toward her, those at

Court had begun to mutter and wonder, for Anne's whole demeanour had changed, and not for the better. There was a certain pride and arrogance in her bearing and speech; she had become subtly unapproachable, while her gowns — for she wore a different one each day — were the envy of every lady who beheld her. As well as this, she blazed with wonderful jewels; diamonds, pearls, rubies, emeralds, sapphires gleamed on her fingers, round her neck and arms, on her beautiful gowns and in her black hair.

"Hey-day, my Anna," remarked Thomas Wyatt, with a certain regretful joviality, upon a sunny afternoon after his return from Italy, "how fine you look! How rich, how haughty! So you have given in at last, I see, and are now Caesar's in very truth. Dost recall my poor verse?"

She smiled, shrugging her shoulders. "I recall it," she said carelessly. "Come, sit here by me on this settle and let us talk." She patted the blue cushions invitingly. "I recall your verse well enough, Tom, and although it may look so, I am *not* Caesar's! You are wrong, you see, for my body is still my own." She burst into a laugh at his stare of amazement. "Oh, it is indeed so."

"Can I believe this?" he queried incredulously. "Why, the King has been chasing you these three years! The whole Court considers you his mistress and speculates upon what he means to do touching yourself and the Queen."

"*Quant à ça* — as to that," she said, "that is His Majesty's business, but I assure you that I am not his mistress, nor will be. Nay, nor any man's."

"What is your meaning, Anne? There is much here that I do not understand.

She laughed. "Of a surety there is, and I do not mean to explain it to you. You will discover in time. Anyhap, I leave for Hever tomorrow in order to quieten gossip. Do you go with the King to Beaulieu[1] in Essex, Tom? My father is to accompany him thither, together with my uncle of Norfolk, the Duke of Suffolk, the Marquis of Exeter and other lords of his select circle. What do you make of that, my inquisitive poet?"

"What?" Wyatt was astounded. "Your father so close to the King? Why so? What has he done to merit such distinguishing attention?"

She laughed again. "He sired *me*," she said and left him to conjecture.

When the news that Mistress Boleyn's father had been included as one of the King's

---

[1] Newhall Boreham, near Chelmsford, Essex

company of intimates at Beaulieu reached Cardinal Wolsey in France, he realised the incredible, the unheard-of truth that his master had deceived him over the matter of a second marriage. That, far from choosing a French princess, King Henry had decided upon Anne Boleyn — a girl without royal blood, who was, in his opinion, a whore. Wolsey found this wellnigh impossible to believe. This girl to marry the King? It was beyond all! And for His Majesty to deceive him thus, to make him a laughing stock, here in France, in such fashion, after all his years of faithful, loving service! How could such a thing be? Why, Wolsey had been the King's closest and most trusted advisor since 1509, when he had been made Royal Almoner — full nineteen years! And for fourteen of those years he had virtually ruled the country! He had been the King's dear friend, and was still — was *still* — he thought, panic-stricken, if that black-avised bitch of a Boleyn did not ruin his life, as she seemed all too willing to do. She hated him, the strumpet. Ay, that were fair enough name for such as she. She was naught but the King's doxy, just as had been her sister Mary, and he would show her his might when he returned to England!

Yet stay — and his heart thumped

unpleasantly — if the King truly meant to wed the jade, a thing he could hardly credit, then it would not be politic to treat her with disrespect, for this would surely anger His Majesty. He would write to the King at once and inform him that he intended to pay a secret visit to the Pope — easy enough for a man of his great influence — ask His Holiness to make him the King's Vicar, with full powers to act as the King desired. This should please His Grace and do somewhat to retrieve the situation, decided Wolsey, with a sigh of relief.

But the King's answering letter gave the Cardinal a severe shock, for His Grace, all impatience, had chosen a man of his own to visit the Pope, a Dr. William Knight, an old fool and thoroughly incompetent in Wolsey's opinion. How can the King deal me such a slight? wondered the Cardinal, dismayed. 'Tis the fault of that witch! he raged. I do not move quick enough for her and nor do I mean to, by God! Why, what chance would His Grace ever hope to get to wed her? Sure, the Pope would never agree and he, Wolsey, did not intend to do aught to hurry the stupid business on. A pox on all thoughts of the King's Vicar! Let things drag on and His Grace would tire of her as he had tired of all the others. And, if the royal conscience was so tender at the thought of sleeping with his brother's wife, it should be twice as tender over the Boleyn, for the King had slept with her sister, had he not? Therefore he was related to Mary Boleyn in exactly the same degree as he was to Queen Katherine, wedded or no. Nay, the Pope would never countenance it. What a diabolical situation! How in the world was he to untangle it? He had best return straight to England and endeavour to set matters right.

How that bitch had managed to gain such ascendancy over the King he could not imagine, but it seemed that she was a bad enemy. And all because he had been instrumental in forbidding her marriage to the Percy boy six years ago! And that had been done by royal command. The girl had hated him ever since, to judge by her glares and scowls whenever she set eyes on him. But the King had bidden him break that betrothal because the wench had been pre-contracted and had had no business to form another attachment.

The Cardinal bit his thumb. And what of that pre-contract? It had never been honoured and the pest of a girl was still unwed! Good God had His Majesty had an eye to her even then? Good God! Wolsey stared into space, his mind in a whirl. He

141

would have to be very careful; more circumspect than he had ever been, for it began to dawn upon him that his career, perhaps his very life might hang upon how he handled this disgraceful affair.

Once back in England, after an exhausting Channel crossing, he rode at once to Richmond Palace. He had no eye for the beauty of the scene, the charm of the great building, its sunlit rosy brick, its turrets and towers, its golden domes and spires all reflected; jewel-like in a lovely curve of the Thames. Upset and agitated, he sent his messenger on ahead to discover where the King would be pleased to see him for a private discussion. The messenger found His Grace in his Privy Chamber, seated on a cushioned settle with Mistress Anna, his arm round her waist, her head on his shoulder. Startled, the young man made to retreat, stumbling back apologetic and embarrassed.

"Nay, nay, come forward, lad, and state your business. What would you, fellow?" enquired His Grace briskly. "Where is His Eminence, the Cardinal?"

"He sent me to ask of Your Majesty whether Your Majesty wishes to have privy converse with him," answered the messenger, falling to his knees.

Before the King could reply, Mistress Anne struck in with a haughty toss of the head. "Why, where else but here, where the King is?" she cried loftily.

The astonished messenger glanced from the King to the lady, amazed to hear this bold, imperious young woman speak so casually for His Grace, before whom strong men quaked. But King Henry merely patted her knee, smiling at her in doting fashion. "Ay, she is right," he said fondly. "There is naught that need be private from Mistress Anne and so you may tell your master. He may come to me here."

Anne did not trouble to hide a broad smile of triumph. Wolsey must dance to her bidding now. She would wager a groat to a noble that his days of power were numbered and serve him right! Now he would see for himself who had the power. Ay, 'that foolish girl yonder in the Court', as he had once termed her — she had the power now and would use it! She still had no notion that Cardinal Wolsey had acted only as bidden by his royal master when he had come between herself and Henry Percy and the King had no intention that she should find it out. Also, he still hoped, though vainly, to keep his Secret Matter secret, although everyone at Court had their suspicions that Anne Boleyn

143

might well become Queen if His Grace could succeed in divorcing his wife.

★ ★ ★

Queen Katherine conducted herself with great dignity at this sad time in her life. She had sent a message to her nephew, the Emperor Charles, begging him to persuade the Pope to judge the case himself, saying firmly that since she had never had sexual relations with her first husband, the King's dead brother, Prince Arthur, King Henry had no grounds upon which to divorce her. For the rest, she did her best to behave normally, even endeavouring to be extra pleasant to Anne.

"But why, dearest? The girl is arrogant, so haughty, so insolent these days! She means to show to the full her influence over His Grace. It is an impossible situation for you and the King does nothing to improve it. I wonder you can bear to look at the wretched girl, let alone speak to her!" Maria de Salinas, who had married Lord Willoughby d'Eresby, was indignant on behalf of her beloved mistress whom she had accompanied from Spain so many years ago.

"Well, Maria," said Katherine gently, "since my husband is so fond of her, I must hold her in more estimation, for his sake, than I did before."

Lady d'Eresby gave an exasperated sigh. "But that is foolish, my love! You are too submissive, too patient. Will you not fight this?"

"Nay," replied Katherine, "for I love my husband. He is all the world to me. When I give my heart it is for ever. I must bow to his wishes, Maria. Is that not the way of a true wife?"

"Certainly," answered Maria, "if the husband is a true husband. But he is not. He — "

"Hush!" reproved Katherine. "You must not speak against him to me. Besides, I have invited Mistress Anne herself to play cards with us. I do not wish to show enmity or spite."

"*You* do not wish? Well, *she* has no such scruples!" cried Maria furiously. "She cares not whom she offends, whom she slights, that one! I will not play cards with her, I! You go too far in your gentleness!"

"Maria, you forget to whom you speak, my dear," remonstrated Katherine kindly. "Nay, I must have my way. Do not forget that if Mistress Anne plays cards with us, she cannot be alone with the King, can she? And, when playing cards, one's hands are on view for all

145

to see, are they not? If the King should follow her here as we play, he will see that *my* hands, at least are fair and unblemished."

"So you are human, my dear," murmured Maria. "I am glad of it, though to my mind the King would not care if she had waffle eyes and a wooden leg! Ah, here she comes. See how she walks as though she owns the world, so prideful and head-in-air. I hate her!"

"And she brings Lady Lee with her to make a fourth," observed Katherine. "Deal out the cards, Maria. We shall play at Primero, I think." She turned to the two young women. "Come, Mistress Anne and Lady Lee, pray take your seats with us and we can begin. The rules are that whoever deals a king wins a point."

As the game progressed, Anne won steadily. When she dealt her fourth king, Queen Katherine could not contain her feelings, which broke through her mask of restraint with a flash of rancour. "Another king! she exclaimed sharply. "Why, Mistress Anne, you have good hap to stop at a king, but you are not like the others. You will have all or none!"

At this, Anne's smooth olive cheek flushed and she was greatly embarrassed. What could one say? Who would have thought the dull, fat Queen to be so observant and so knowing? She makes a fool of me, thought

Anne, shrugging her shoulders and raising her brows in an affectation of indifference, but she was very shaken and very relieved when, shortly after, the game broke up, Lady d'Eresby having tactfully dropped her hand of cards, making further play impossible.

★ ★ ★

So matters went on with increasing awkwardness until after Christmas. The revels were over, the Twelfth Night Mass a memory only, and life had settled down to its daily ways as the dark month of February progressed. King Henry felt that the time would never pass, that it would never be spring, that his Secret Matter would never be resolved, that the longed-for dispensation from the Pope would never arrive and he would never get his divorce.

Glumly impatient, he tramped up and down the Long Gallery at Placentia, waving his friends and attendant aside. If he could but go a-hunting, that would raise his dumps for sure, he thought, but it was snowing, curse it! Pausing, he gazed resentfully from the window at a prospect of feathery white flakes flying and spiralling against a background of sullen grey. God's nails, but it was set in for days, no force! Hearing the sound of a bustle behind him, he swung round irritably to see a messenger making his way toward him along the gallery.

"Your Majesty," said the man, kneeling before the King, travel-stained and weary, "I bring you a message from His Holiness the Pope. May it please you to — "

"What!" shouted His Grace. "Here, give it to me!"

Snatching the roll of parchment, unrolling it and glancing swiftly over its contents, he was overjoyed to read that the dispensation had been granted. Ill-humour forgotten, he left the gallery at a run to find Anne. He discovered her sitting by the fire in a small parlour, talking and laughing with her much-loved brother George, who resembled her so greatly. As the King burst in, they sprang to their feet, he bowing, she curtseying a questioning look upon her face.

"Anne, dear one! Darling! Come, rise up!" cried His Majesty excitedly, careless of George's presence. "See what I have here. 'Tis the dispensation! Nay, George, you may remain, dear lad, and join with us in our joy. Let us read the document together, for we three are soon to be related!"

By the time that they had perused the document in detail, the King's smiles had changed to frowns and his expressions of pleasure to exclamations of rage. "By God, we have been duped!" he roared, clapping his hand upon the parchment. "This dispensation is worthless!"

"*Ah, mon Dieu*, Sire, but how?" queried Anne, puzzled by the legal wording of the document. "Pray explain to me."

"Why, there was to be a clause in it that would have allowed Wolsey to hold a court in England and pronounce judgement himself. But the wording has been altered! Dr. Knight had writ me before Christmas, setting out the terms of the dispensation and telling me that the Pope had asked Cardinal Pucci to word it for him. Word it, be damned! The misbegotten Pucci has changed the whole substance of it."

"But would the Pope allow that to happen, Sire," asked George, frowning.

"Jesu, it must have been done at the Pope's own command, George! His Holiness does not wish to commit himself in such a matter, 'tis plain. Now we are back where we began! Was ever anything so maddening, so wretched? Well, Dr. Knight is useless, that is for sure. I must have Wolsey do it, after all. He is the only man who can unravel this tangle."

"He will not like that," observed Anne. "He thinks me unsuitable, as you know, Sire."

"I care not what he thinks!" snapped the King. "What he thinks is of no moment. His work is to obey me and that he will do, no matter what."

And so, Cardinal Thomas Wolsey, brilliant son of an Ipswich butcher, Chancellor of England, who had held the country's foreign affairs in his hand for so many years, found himself an extremely worried man. His royal master, once his dear friend, seemed friendly no longer and was pestering him to perform what seemed to be an impossibility. There was only one thing for it, he decided. He must continue to pursue a policy of appeasement toward the Boleyn girl despite his disinclination to do so. If she were against him, so would the King be; and then what for Thomas Wolsey? Loss of place? Imprisonment? The block? Heaven forbid! So, to begin, he would resolve the feud between the Boleyns and their Irish relatives, the Butlers of Ormond. That should prove a great sweetener. It was a pity that Sir Piers Butler, who had given him such useful support in Ireland should come poorly out of it, but expedience was the way of the world and he who would survive must employ every means to do so. Therefore, Wolsey would court Mistress Anne and lay himself out to please her.

He began his plan of appeasement in that February. Anne was delighted at his action over the Boleyn-Butler quarrel, the more so when she learned that the rents of the Ormond lands were to be paid to her family by Wolsey's express order and her feelings toward him altered considerably. After all, she reasoned, he was the only man who could bring about the change that would make her Queen and it would be foolish to continue to treat him as an enemy, especially now that he appeared to be working in her favour.

Therefore, she was pleased to attend the revels and entertainments he staged for her at York Place and Hampton Court. Dining in the magnificent rooms hung with gold and silver tapestries, performing in masques, dancing and singing the night away, she began to see Wolsey as a friend. When the Court was too far from London or Hampton for her to visit Wolsey, she would write him pleasant notes and even send him small gifts and tokens.

"You are all amity with Wolsey now, sweetheart, are you not?" said the King on a bright late April day as he walked with his beloved in the gardens of Windsor Castle. "I am glad of it, for if he cannot manage this matter, I misdoubt me if anyone can."

She gave her high trill of laughter and

skipped ahead of him down a green alley, looking back over her shoulder to reply. "Oh, one must settle old scores at some time, Sire, and I have done so. What happened long ago is old tales."

She beckoned and he started toward her, but she ran from him as he pursued her along the alley and round the box hedge. Fleet of foot though she was, he caught her and kissed her soundly, bearing her down upon the grass, despite her struggles and protests. As he tried to tear open her bodice, there came a sudden call from close at hand.

"Nan! Nan! Where are you, daughter? Where is His Majesty? Nan!"

"By Christ!" growled His Grace, releasing her. "Am I never to have my way with you? Was ever a man so thwarted?"

"Oh, oh!" Anne's relief showed itself in ill-suppressed mirth. "Tis my mother. She comes a-seeking me, for sure. But I did not bid her to, Sire, I swear!"

He began to laugh, though wryly, in his turn. "Is it so? Ah, you have all the luck, little wretch! Why, given a moment more, I would have overborne you."

"Nay," she said, serious. "For then you would have lost me. You know that, my Lord King."

He knew it well. His Anna was like no

other woman. Here they were at Windsor, alone, but for his friend, Sir Henry Norreys, and Gentleman of the Bedchamber Thomas Heneage, a page or two and Nan's mother, yet still his darling held him off. Her virtue was impregnable and he loved, admired and respected her more than words could say. She was a nonsuch, a paragon, and she would be his Queen if he had to stand England on end to do it. It was amazing to reflect upon the fact that even here, in this romantic situation, still he slept alone. Sure, he found it hard to believe himself!

He pondered this yet again next morning while lying in his great bed watching the early light filter through the gaps between the crimson velvet bed-curtains. What a case he was in! A King with no son to follow him and no woman, as yet, to bear him one. Well, he had marked out the woman, but what difficulties lay in his way! And he must have a legitimate son. It was not that he was unable to father a boy, no indeed. Nay, he had a beautiful, manly lad now nine years old, by Elizabeth Blount, a boy of whom to be proud — but a bastard. It was astonishing that he, a God-fearing Christian man and a King withal, should have no legitimate son when even peasants seemed to be able to father boys a-plenty. It was

Katherine's fault, for certain.

He raised his strong, shapely arms, furred with golden-reddish hair, crossing them on the embroidered pillow behind his red head. Anne would surely bring him a prince, a prince at whom to marvel, of such superlative beauty and intelligence, cast in his own image, with Anne's dark eyes, mayhap. But how long must he wait? He was thirty-seven now, in his prime, handsome, magnificently healthy, wealthy beyond compare — and frustrated beyond bearing! The wretched Secret Matter had been plodding on for a year now and still was no nearer resolution. It was enough to drive a man mad.

He kicked his long legs fretfully under the silken sheets. Wherever I turn I meet with rebuffs, he thought resentfully. It is insupportable! I have laid the matter before Thomas Wolsey and, for all his words and seeming compliance, he appears to do but little to further my aim, while to deal with that old noodle of a Pope Clement is like trying to hold water in the hand — he runs in all directions and all away from me! So mayhap it *is* difficult for Wolsey; he has ever done his best to aid me, while Katherine impedes me at every turn. Why cannot she see reason? I wish her no ill, merely that she will agree to a divorce. Is that so dire? Should not a wife be subject to her husband? Yet she contests me in every way. Always meek, always patient, but damned obdurate. I explained my wishes to her in words that even a half-wit could have understood and she dares to oppose me! I have no son, nor will have one now, and she refuses to consent to our parting. If she really loves me, as she says, she would not deny me. And, as well as all this, Anne that gorgeous girl, will not give in to me!

He frowned, breathing hard through his nose. Why did he not take her then, whether she would or no? He had never hesitated with a woman before. He chewed his lip, for he knew the answer. He wished her to be the mother of the son she would undoubtedly bear him and that son must be legitimate. Jesu, what a coil he was in! Let him take her and impregnate her now, ay, and then find himself unable to wed her by reason of the poxy old Pope who would not pronounce him divorced from Katherine and he would be quite undone. A pretty basket of eels, indeed!

Why was he so thwarted, for God's sake? Why were his dearest wishes so obstructed? Was he not the King? He moved his head restlessly. Holy Christ, but the damned pillow was hot! And so was his temper. Such obstacles were enough to inflame any man's temper. By the Virgin, he would not suffer such denial! He would take her today, no matter how she resisted, no matter how her mother peered and spied. Let her spy! He sighed. Oh, curse it, it was all of no use, for he loved Anne, he adored her, and that was the stumbling block. If he took her he would lose her, whether there were a child or no. And if there *were* a child and it was a son, what then? Ah, St. Michael and all angels, it was enough to turn a man's brain!

Oh, but the delicate and fascinating Anne Boleyn, how lovely she was, how utterly desirable! He sighed again as he imagined her standing before him. Those eyes! Like sloes washed in wine were those wonderful eyes. And her skin — why it was of the colour of ivory or cream and of a texture like velvet, with dusky shadows where the sweet flesh curved. He thought of her mouth, so richly red, lifting so tantalisingly at the corners as if she were ever on the edge of a smile. That mouth, it was made for kisses — *his* kisses. He could never tire of kissing that ripe mouth. Oh, dear God, how he wanted her! Suppose she were leaning over him now, her beautiful hair like black silk, brushing his face, those masses of hair that seemed too heavy for the small, shapely head and the long, slender, elegant neck that supported it. Suppose — Jesu, how long could he live on hope and frustrated desire?

A small, cold fancy stole into his brain. Could he fail? Might his plans all come to naught? He stared up into the tester of his great bed, at the forms of Cupid and Psyche painted thereon, dimly visible in the curtained gloom. Sweet Christ, could he fail? Dear God above! ... He gave himself a mental shake. He, the King, fail? Never!

Never, for I will have my way, he reassured himself. I will have my way, no matter how long it take. I shall wed her, I shall bed her, and when I do and she is mine — oh, what joy, what bliss! At the exciting images conjured up by these dreams, he felt his manhood rise in readiness to act upon them and thrilled with desire. Ay, he would strip her of her garments, one by one . . . ay . . . he would hold her, stroke her, kiss her, lay her upon the bed, all sweet passionate submission, and then —

A loud snore from the page sleeping on a truckle-bed at the foot of the King's four-poster broke in upon Henry's erotic musings. With a muttered curse, he seized a silver candlestick from his bed-table and hurled it though the curtains, hearing with a satisfied grin, the sleepy sounds change from comfortable gruntings to a choking cry of surprise and pain as the candlestick found its mark.

"Cease your swinish snortings, Will!" shouted His Majesty, wide awake. "Fetch me a piss-pot! Move yourself, or must I drag you from your pit?"

7

MY TIME AND YOUTH
SPENT TO NO PURPOSE

Told by Mistress Anne Boleyn

1528–1532

Who would have thought the plaguey business of divorce would take so long? It seemed to stumble on for ever. During the same February in which the Cardinal settled our family feud, my Lord King sent two visitors to Hever where I was residing for a space. They were his second cousin Dr. Stephen Gardiner, secretary to the Cardinal, and his own almoner, Dr. Edward Fox. They calmed my fears of never being able to wed His Grace and I imagined that all would be well henceforth. These two, on their way to the coast to sail for Italy, had brought a letter for me from the King, full of reassurance.

Darling, it read, these shall be only to advertise you that this bearer and his fellow be desperate with many things to compass

Our Matter and to bring it to pass as our will could imagine or devise; which brought to pass, as I trust their diligence it shall shortly, you and I shall have our desired end, which should be more to my heart's ease and more quietness to my mind than any other thing in the world . . .

This was comfort, but even so, it was not until April that we heard from Italy and then surely things seemed more hopeful. Gardiner and Fox had been invited into the Pope's very bedchamber — 'a poor enough room', they wrote disparagingly — and now felt that very few obstacles lay in their way. I was enraptured at the vision these tidings conjured up for me. I would have power and prestige above all women and most men. I would be Queen Anne, a dizzying realisation! For mark, I was detested by old Katherine's ladies who spared me no pains to show their dislike and make my life a misery, stupid, fussy old besoms that they were. *Mon Dieu,* they would sneer t'other side of their crabbed, disapproving faces when I would be Queen! I would send the lot packing, and right swift, I promised myself.

Then, on the 3rd of May, a beautiful sunny Sunday afternoon, Dr. Fox arrived at Placentia. I was in my chamber by the open lattice, seated in my special chair given me by the King, a magnificent chair with carven arms and blue silk cushions, setting some stitches in a white lawn shift I was making, when, sensing a presence, I glanced up to behold Dr. Fox standing in the doorway. Jumping to my feet, sewing on the floor forgot, I rushed across the room and seized his hands. "Oh, what now?" I cried, breathless with excitement. "Is it good news? Is it in our favour? *Dites-moi, dites-moi vite, m'sieur!*"

"His Majesty has sent me straight to you, Lady," replied Dr. Fox, "for he wished you to be first to hear the news. The Pope has submitted to Dr. Gardiner's strong and reasoned arguments and has agreed to grant a general commission for his Cardinal Campeggio and our Cardinal Wolsey to judge the case in England exactly as we wish."

I could scarce speak, my heart beat so high. "Oh, when I am Queen, you shall both have a great reward!" I cried. "I shall see to it in person and — "

The door burst open and His Grace ran into the room, his face all smiles, his eyes a-dance with happiness, but after we had kissed I withdrew, leaving him to talk the matter over with Dr. Fox. That night the King and I were filled with hope as we sat together in the small chamber hard by the tilt-yard, listening to Dr. Fox as he described the Pope's capitulation. All would be well now, for sure, for sure!

But it was not to be. Nothing was sure, for Cardinal Wolsey reposed no trust in the crafty Pope's word. His Holiness had tricked us before, said Wolsey. He could change his mind and all would be at naught again. There must be another commission, he said; one that, when granted, would be law and the Pope must be forced to agree to it.

"Ay, and agree to it he must!" snapped the King to Wolsey, who had come to Placentia to inform the King of his feelings in the matter. "If he do not I may leave the Roman Catholic Church altogether, and so you may tell him, Thomas!"

The Cardinal threw up his hands and turned pale at these words, but His Majesty was in earnest and I knew it, for he had spoke of it with me. It would be no bad thing if he did leave the Church, I thought, for I considered the Roman religion to be old-fangled and behind the times, unaware of the feelings and longings of real, living people. For my choice, I inclined toward the doctrines of the German monk, Martin Luther, who spoke sense, to my mind. If the King foreswore Rome, what then would become of Cardinal Wolsey? No wonder he had turned pale! Anyhap, the fear of it would make him work the harder for us, so that we might gain our dear desire.

Our dear desire. Well, the King's desire was for me. Mine was for Queenship and power. At first I had not believed that His Grace would take my challenge of marriage seriously. It was more to keep his interest and to play a little with fire, for to be so noticed by a man so all-powerful was a great honour. Now, here he was, actually begging me to marry him! Indeed, I had always longed for some kind of power, as did most women, for we ladies had none at all, being rated by men as low as household animals and this I hated with all my being. But I did not love King Henry, for I was not one to love easy, nor to lose my self-respect. Admire him, I did. Who did not? He was handsome, gifted, learned and the common people adored him. Also he held the power of life and death in his hand. One could not argue with that.

If I refused him now, my family would suffer, maybe even to death. And what then of me? Cast off, humiliated, perhaps hated by him. Oh, I was hated already, I knew that, but not by the King. For good or ill, my course was set, for he would not let me go, even if I wished. So I hardened my heart and grew ever more determined to reach my goal and, in so doing, grew arrogant and uncaring.

My nerves suffered badly from the strain of it and brought out the worst in my nature as my father was ever quick to point out. I was not happy in this game of chance with life. Oft it drained me, but it had closed around me like a velvet-lined trap. So I would go on to the end, whatever it might be; loved, desired, reviled, misjudged and hated, to be Queen I could hate too. I was a good hater.

On the 11th of June 1528, we heard at last from Pope Clement, who had surely taken his time. In order to save the Roman Church in England, he promised to send Cardinal Campeggio to London with the precious document that would set the King free to marry me. It was to be kept a vital secret, so I had to hug my excitement to myself and share it with none but the King.

"Ah, *Ma'mselle Anne*, how pleased you look!" exclaimed my friend Jean du Bellay, the French Ambassador, when I encountered him in the pleached alley while shading myself from the sun. "You have not a care in the world, no?"

I laughed. "Oh, indeed I look upon the world with pleasure, *mon ami*."

"You are not then afraid of the *malaise* that creeps about London?"

"What, the Sweat?" Still smiling, I shrugged. "What would you? A plague comes to London every summer — 'tis nothing new. Besides, we are out of the City, here at Greenwich."

"*Hé*, but I have heard that the Sweat is the easiest thing in the world to die of, *ma chère*. One suffers a small pain in the head or the heart, one sweats and *voilà*! In two, three, four hours, all is over. One is dead, *Ma'mselle*."

"That is so, I believe," I replied, "but I have been told that it attacks the people only, so we here at Court, are safe, I hope."

Vain hope! A mere three days later, on the very morning that we were all to move to Waltham, one of my maids was struck and despite my tears and protests, I was sent off to my parents at Hever in order to prevent the spread of infection.

"No, no, Mistress Anne, you cannot stay at Court," said Dr. Chambers firmly to me. " 'Tis of no use to weep; to Hever you must go. What if you should catch the sickness from your maid and give it to His Majesty? What a terrible thought! You cannot be allowed to remain."

My father, who was on leave, was no more pleased to see me and my baggage-carts at Hever, than I was to see him, although my mother welcomed me.

"What if you are coddling the disease in your body after being with that maid of yours?" he yelled. "Then we shall all catch it and maybe die of it!" A sweet greeting, no force.

" 'Tis no fault of mine!" I cried. "Did I ask the wretched girl to take the woundy sickness? The King's own doctor insisted I leave and come home, for fear His Majesty should catch it."

"So! It matters naught about us here, then! So long as the King take it not, who cares for Thomas Boleyn and his household? No one! Therefore, you are sent home to pass the infection all about. Very pretty, upon my soul!"

"Oh ay!" I shouted, loud as he. "And where would *you* be, dearest father, without the King and me, if he and I should die of the Sweat? Where would your precious, so-longed-for and not-yet-realised earldom be then? Think about *that*, sir!"

He stamped from the room, muttering, but moderated his tone to me somewhat during the days after that exchange. But I was deadly feared. Feared to contract the disease and feared to lose the King's love. There were other young and pretty damsels at Court — younger than I, too, for I was nearing twenty-one, and he had never been faithful to any lady for very long. Also, there was the Queen, ever-patient, ever-loving, always eager to forgive; a constant threat to me. He could change, he might well have changed! I could not endure the thought, so wrote to tell him of my fears. His answer was immediate and heartening.

Sweetheart . . . as you have not yet felt anything I hope and believe it will pass you by as I hope it has with us . . . A thing may comfort you that it is true, as they say, that few women or none have this malady and moreover none of our Court and few elsewhere have died of it. I beg of you my wholly beloved, to have no fear nor to be too uneasy at our absence; for wherever I may be I am yours . . . I wish you between my arms that I might a little dispel your unreasonable thoughts. Written by the hand of him who is, and will always be, your Un — H. REX — changeable.

So I was comforted for a little, but for a little only. My future lay on the razor's edge of the King's fancy. There was a mountain of difficulty to scale before the summit were reached and he and I could wed, and he had not been to visit me as he always did when I

167

rested at Hever. Nay, his love and longing did not surmount the Sweat, that was plain!

I walked solitary in the rose-garden, my gown of tawny silk vying with the pink blooms, my former confidence gone, fretting myself to fiddle-strings, dreading the Sweat, dreading what would become of me if His Grace should repudiate me. What should I do? What was I doing? My mouth grew dry and I drew deep breaths, clasping my hands tight, wringing them together as I dwelt upon possible misfortune. The sun was hot on my head and it began to ache. I would have to go withindoors and rest. Sure, it was uncomfortable warm; so warm that I felt a trickle of damp run down my back and little beads burst out on my forehead. As I walked into the Great Hall I felt myself to be near soaked in moisture, while the room seemed to rock round me. Clapping my hands to my temples, I uttered a wild shriek. *Dieu me sauve*, I had the Sweat!

★ ★ ★

Ah, but I was grievous sick! I would have died, sure, had it not been for Dr. Butts. He arrived early one morning, after galloping a night and a day from Hunsdon, whither the Court had removed after Waltham. All I knew at the time was that the pains in my shoulders, back, belly and head were like to kill me with agony and after that, no more but fever-dreams and darkness.

By some miracle, Dr. Butts recovered me, weak, white and thin, only for me to learn that my father had taken the sickness but a day or two after I had succumbed. His attack was light only and his recovery swifter then mine. I was told, too, that George, my dear brother, who was at Court, had also caught the disease a few days after my departure for Hever.

"Oh, Dr. Butts!" I gasped, heart-struck, grasping at his full, black sleeve. "Is George — ? Did he — ? Oh, say he is well again!"

Dr. Butts smiled at me, his round, rosy face reassuring. "He is well, Mistress Anne. The Boleyns are a hardy race, it seems."

"And my mother? She is well?"

"She is well, God be thanked, Mistress. She has not taken the Sweat."

"*Alors*, I need fret myself no more," I said, full of relief and thankfulness, until I saw a shadow pass over Dr. Butt's face. "What is it?" I queried faintly. "Someone is dead, I can tell. Who is it? I must know."

"It is your sister's husband," he replied sorrowfully. "William Carey died on the twenty-second day of June, I fear. There was no hope for him. Your poor sister is desperate with grief."

"*Doux Jésu*," I whispered. "Poor Mary. She loved Will. We must do what we can to aid her." I sighed, thinking of Mary and Will Carey. "Who else is gone?" I asked fearfully.

"Zouche is dead," said Dr. Butts sadly.

"What, he who would ride to me with letters from His Grace?"

"Even so. And Sir William Compton. Indeed, all but one of the Gentlemen of the Bedchamber are sped."

"*Ma foi, c'est terrible!*" I fell silent once more, my head throbbing, my eyes dizzy with weakness as I lay in my cushioned chair. "Oh, but what of His Grace?" I asked, shocked that I had not enquired before. Sure, I was sick.

"His Grace's health is good," answered Dr. Butts. "He is now at Tittenhanger Park and here are the letters he has sent you. Dost feel strong enough to read them?" And he handed me a bundle of letters from the King, all breathing love in every line, which was great comfort. With them was the copy of a letter from the King of France, full of support for the divorce. I was right pleased at this, for had King Henry cast me off, I would have fared ill enough at the hands of mine enemies, and it was good to know that King François stood my friend.

Gifts arrived from His Grace almost every day; a pretty little red leather toilet case containing ivory combs, a scent bottle, a powder brush, a golden ear-spoon and nail-shaper. Next came a diamond filigree locket shaped like a book, enamelled in black, with a scent-soaked sponge inside, together with a jewelled chain, while in his letters, the King continued to plead with me to return to Court. This I would not do, for I was still wretchedly weak and languid, my looks being far from their best; while, for another thing, Cardinal Lorenzo Campeggio, purportedly on his way from Italy for the trial of the Secret Matter, was expected in England soon and I feared that my presence at Court would go against me in his mind. He was not to be allowed to discover the King's passion for me; he was to believe that the whole affair was caused by nothing but His Grace's tender conscience and the lack of a male heir. If he were to witness the King's behaviour with me, he would learn more of the truth than would be advisable and this would prejudice his verdict.

I could not afford to wait for ever, for fear His Majesty might tire of me. If he did, I could expect nothing from him, having my unfortunate sister before me as example, so I was right eager that the business be concluded quick.

As for Mary, she was wellnigh destitute. Her husband, Will Carey, had been Steward of the Duchy of Lancaster, Constable of Pleashey Castle and Keeper of two royal parks. These offices and their revenues reverted to the Crown immediately upon Will's death. Without a thought of my sister, the King distributed these amongst his friends, no matter that Mary had been Will's own wife and His Grace's mistress for several years. Upset by his action, I wrote to him, begging him to help poor Mary, receiving in answer a passionate love-letter, which had at the end a few indifferent words writ touching my sister's affairs in which, 'twas all too obvious, he had no interest at all. He wrote that he had commanded his secretary, Walter Walshe, to write to our father, telling him to look after Mary, since she was his daughter. I could imagine my father's reception of Master Walshe's letter! He would be enraged and swearing at the charge put upon him, but only before his family, mark you; before the King, never. Nay, 'twould be a smiling, obedient countenance that he would show His Majesty.

And, thinking thus of His Majesty, I was forced to ponder upon the coldness he showed to those of whom he had tired. It was an inimical coldness, icy and uncaring, as though the subject of his former affection had never existed. It caused me much unease and more yet, for another letter followed, informing me that the King had given me the wardship of Henry, my sister's son, and the custody of Will Carey's lands until young Henry should come of age. I did not want this charge, for little Henry was Mary's son and, for all we knew, the King's son too, and 'twas Mary who should govern him and receive the rents from her husband's lands. I tried to refuse this awkward governance, but His Grace would in no wise allow it. One does not refuse a royal command, he said simply. I suppose he thought that I would do my best for Mary and thus absolve him from all responsibility and he was right, of course. It was plain that he wished to have no more at all to do with her.

I felt somewhat alarmed when reflecting upon this, but managed to put my doubts from me, telling myself that I was vastly different from poor Mary and would fight for my aim to the end.

In July there came another setback, as if there were not enough already to fret me. It was discovered that Cardinal Campeggio had not yet left Italy, but was abed with the gout and thus once again the divorce was delayed! It was incredible that the matter should take so long and suffer so many checks. I wrote a letter to Cardinal Wolsey, entreating him to write to old Campeggio, to spur the ancient wittol on, to force him to climb from his gouty bed, but in spite of all Wolsey's efforts, the old dotard would not move, as though his stupid gout were more important than King Henry's divorce! I was sure that the Pope must have chosen such a doddering grey-beard a-purpose to hinder us.

So put about was I over this that I paid a fleeting visit to His Majesty at Ampthill, where the Court lay at the end of July, and persuaded him to write a letter, with me, to Wolsey, trusting that a missive from the two of us might assist the business. The King was overjoyed to see me, while I was relieved to find him as hot for me as ever, even though I still allowed him no intimate caresses of my person. Yet, to keep him thus hot, I reasoned that the time had come to relax my rule a little, but a little only, for I wished to keep my virginity and thus my hold on him.

"You understand, Sire, that I cannot stay here, at Ampthill," I said as we sat, embraced, in a rose-covered arbour one warm evening a few days later. "When Cardinal Campeggio arrives in England — if he ever does — I must not be at your side, remember. It is necessary, therefore, that I return to Hever."

"But hearken, sweetheart! The old man has at last taken ship for Provence and even now begins his journey through France!" cried the King, kissing me passionately. "I received the tidings but an hour ago. It should not be long now, my love."

"All the more reason for me to go home again," I said. "It must be done, but, *mon Dieu*, it is dull there! It fills me with *ennui* even to think of such tedium. I am so weary of this waiting, Sire. Indeed, I have been thinking that you and I — that we *might* anyhap — " I gave him a languishing look and left the end of the sentence unfinished, the better to watch his reaction. I was not disappointed.

"We might — we might what, darling? Christ, do you mean that I might play and toy with you — bed you? Oh, Nan, beloved — "

"Not so!" I laughed. "Nay, of course not to bed me, Sire. I am no light woman. But I thought that I might not be so cold to you; that perhaps I should permit a little more intimacy."

His face flushed excitedly, then paled. "Anne!" he breathed. "Dost mean it? Oh, lovedy, dearest one, dost mean now, darling?"

"Ay, now," I whispered, sinking back into his arms and trusting that I could control him.

I need not have worried, as it turned out, for he trembled and shook so much in his passion and seemed so feared that I would break, as would some precious piece of glass, that all he did was to stroke and kiss my breasts as gently as the touch of thistledown. As soon as he showed the slightest disposition to pursue his advantage, I gave a not entirely assumed cry of alarm and he desisted at once.

"I have frightened you, my rose," he murmured penitently. "If you could but understand how a man feels — "

I understood very well, but showed it not, my expression indicative only of alarm and dismay. "Oh, Sire!" I gasped. "It is well that I return to Hever tomorrow! I am feared of what you might do to me."

"Nothing that you do not permit, my love," he answered earnestly, his eyes gazing ardently into mine. "I shall visit you at Hever, rest assured."

★   ★   ★

I had been back at Hever no more than a day or two, when a messenger galloped into the courtyard bearing a letter from His Grace.

Mine own sweetheart, I read, *these shall be to advise you of the great loneliness that I find here since your departure, for I assure you methinketh the time longer since your departing than I was wont to do . . . I think your kindness and my fervencies of love causeth it, for otherwise I had not thought it possible . . . but now that I was coming toward you methinketh my pains have been half relieved. Wishing myself (especially of an evening) in my sweetheart's arms, whose pretty duckies[1] I hope shortly to kiss; written by the hand of him that was, is, and shall be by his will H.R.*

Surely, surely, I thought, he cannot change! Surely such feelings must continue! I could not envisage his heart turning from me, nor his eyes to seek another. And yet, and yet . . . He had wed Queen Katherine for love, had stayed in her bed and at her side for full sixteen years and even so had tired of her, treating her now with coldness and contempt. Could this happen to Anne Boleyn? My heart seemed to lurch in my breast and a mist to swim before mine eyes. Nay, but sixteen years! Time enough for a man to tire. He had wearied of Mary — nay that were doleful thought, that were dark and silly fantasy to think that he could ever treat me so. He

---

[1] breasts

177

adored me; he would do anything to please me! I must not give way to foolish fears that could weaken me and cause my resolution to falter. I was young, beautiful, and desired as a wife by no less a man than the King of England, a man of absolute power! Of what use to repine over what might never happen? So, casting dull care aside, I held to my resolve, come what might, trusting in Almighty God to assist me. I saw no reason why He should not do so.

* * *

Very soon, His Majesty joined me at Hever and while he was there he pleaded with me to return to Court, using many arguments to persuade me, the chiefest of which was his promise to remove me from the Queen's Household and give me an establishment of my own. I was to be lodged in Durham House, a handsome palace in the Strand, gracious and stately, with fine orchards and gardens that ran down to the riverside. Campeggio and discretion or no, I could not refuse such an exciting offer and agreed to go back to London as soon as arrangements for Durham House could be made.

"This must be kept secret for the nonce," quoth His Grace, "for we want no gossip raised before your arrival. There will be enough when you take up residence, I'll wager. But, oh, darling, what joy in the world can be so great as to have the company of you who are the most loved? I long for the day!"

He kissed me, then rose and walked upon the grass for a space, a huge, handsome figure, more than two yards high, bright in tawny silk and white velvet, his red hair brilliant beneath the jewelled brim of his black feathered hat. I rose too and walked beside him, my murrey silk skirts rustling, a pleased smile upon my face as I recollected that Durham House had been Queen Katherine's lodging before she wed the King and, as such, seeming like a good omen to me.

I was to reside there with my father and mother, a short distance from His Majesty's palace of Bridewell, which was situated on the City side of the mouth of the river Fleet where it ran in to the Thames. What could be more luxurious and convenient? Delighted, I moved there at the end of August, but to my chagrin, was back at Hever after only two weeks! Well, in justice, the King and I had been somewhat indiscreet in our behaviour, for he would set me on his knee and fondle me right lovingly before all the Court, being pleased to grant my every whim, whilst I did not attempt to restrain the pride and haughtiness of my demeanour, conducting myself as though I were indeed a Queen, caring naught for chatter and gossip.

"*Ciel, Ma'mselle Anne!*" had exclaimed Jean du Bellay, laughing. "*Le Roi* he is so *affolé* — so maddened by you — that *le bon Dieu* alone can save him!"

"*Merci, m'sieur!*" I had replied, laughing also. "And I trust that *le bon Dieu* may keep him so!"

And so, as I had warned the King, because of his open infatuation, his advisors had counselled him to send me back to Hever, so that I was not present to see my cousin Francis Bryan welcome old Campeggio when he landed at Dover on the 29th of September, nor was I in London when he arrived there on the 7th of October. It had been a mistake to be persuaded to Durham House

As it turned out, London greeted the old man not, despite all the plans made for his coming. Processions had been expected, cheering crowds, glitter and grandeur, with every bell pealing, every gun booming, but Campeggio had a fresh attack of gout and could not endure such jollification, so slid into Town by boat and went at once to bed at Bath Place, near Bridewell Palace. There never was so much cry for so little wool! I was pleased, because I had thus missed nothing, and excited because I had thought we had come to the last move in the game. Queen Katherine would retire to a nunnery on the order of Pope Clemant and old Campeggio, leaving my Lord King and I free to wed. My fears and worries were over.

But no indeed. No and no! Queen Katherine, stubborn old dame, would not hear of it. Why would she not be reasonable and see sense? Infuriated, I screamed out at George when he rode to Hever with the news.

"But what did she *say?* What did the stupid old gowk say? *Why* did she refuse? The King wants her not! Does she not realise? Tell me!"

"Why, she said that she meant to live and die in the state of matrimony to which God had called her," said George ruefully. "Let her be torn limb from limb, she would not change her mind, she said."

"Pah, she would change it soon enough if torture *were* applied, I'll wager! I wish they would do it! Is there more? *Tell* me!"

"Pray be calm, Nan. It is none of me; I do but report what took place at the hearing, remember. It does no good to yell at me."

"Ah, I am sorry, dearest!" I patted his arm repentantly. "But such obstinacy drives me frantic. Does she truly mean it, think you?"

"Oh, for sure she does. She said that if,

after death, she should return to life, she would sooner die over again than change her mind. And she said it not once, but many times."

"And what of Campeggio?" My voice was harsh with strain. "Could he not persuade her?"

"In no wise. Nay, he sat rubbing his gouty knees, rolling his watery eyes and wagging his grey head — '*I am convinced she will act accordingly*,' quavered he," replied George, giving a spirited imitation of the aged Cardinal which, although right comical, did not amuse me one jot.

"Never mind that! You see what it is?" I cried. "It is all a plot to delay me — I know it! Campeggio but feigns his gout, I swear. He sympathises with Katherine and the Emperor Charles. George, you must see it is so. If I am not right, why has not Campeggio visited me here? Answer me that! His Grace *promised* me that he should do so! Am I not Queen-to-be?" I shouted, beside myself with anxiety and rage, stamping about the parlour, kicking at everything that stood in my way.

"Nan, Nan, I beg you to be quiet!" beseeched George, coming to me, his hands out. I pushed him aside.

"Quiet!" I screamed. "Why should I be quiet? I am betrayed — 'tis a plot to bring me

182

down! What is the King about to allow it? Mayhap 'tis he who is at the head of it! Mayhap he tires of me! I will write to him — ay, write to him instanter and demand the truth!"

And I did. Many letters and messages passed before I was mollified, but before long I was incensed again. News was brought to me that the Londoners had crowded round Bridewell Palace shouting for Katherine and when they spied her, they would call out: *'Victory over your enemies!'* And that meant Anne Boleyn.

I would have had the lot hanged. What was old Katherine to them but a fat, ageing Spaniard who could not hold her husband's love and did nothing but tell her beads and pray? But the King was angered also. He forbade the folk to assemble around the palace and told the Lord Mayor that anyone who should speak ill of him, that person's head would be made to fly. This was good hearing and I was calmed for a space. Then all my peace was cut up when His Grace appeared at Hever, having taken a house some five miles off.

"Why are you here?" I cried brusquely, formalities and courtesy to a monarch quite forgot in my agitation. "Why are you not in London?"

"But darling!" he gasped, all amazed at such a rough welcome. "Are you not pleased to see me?"

"No, I am not!" I snapped, heedless of all but my worries. "You should be in London, urging our business on, not thinking to laze down here in the country! What chance do we have if you are not present to keep your hand on the matter? Do you really wish it to come about, or are you weary of me?"

"Anne, sweetheart! How can you speak so? You *know* that my heart is entirely yours. What more can I do to prove it?"

"You can prove it by returning at once to London!" I cried, stepping away from his embrace. "You can be of no help here."

"But my Councillors advised me to leave London," he said mildly, "and I do think, that for once, they may be right, lovedy. The townsfolk do not take kindly to the divorce and there is some unrest over it, which I like not. I have sent Katherine to Placentia to be out of the City and have travelled down here to be near you, sweetheart. My baggage-carts are all on the way."

"Oh, it is too bad! You do not think! We should not be together now. You do not consider my feelings! You must return!" Surely you realise it?"

He stared at me astounded. I had never

spoken to him in such fashion. "I thought you would be pleased to see me here," he said quietly, after a long moment, "but now I see that you — "

Swiftly I endeavoured to cover my mistake with kisses and loving words and, after a meal and some wine, I persuaded him to go back to London.

But all was to no avail, for shortly after this, Katherine showed Campeggio a copy of the papal dispensation writ years ago for her to wed the King. This damned document was set forth in such a way that the trial fell all to naught. No one knew she had it, the sly bitch. 'Twas complete and horrid surprise.

After this setback, there was no need for me to seclude myself at Hever. Of what point when all our plans were gone awry? So I agreed to go to Town, but this time on my own terms. "I do not wish to reside at Durham House," I told His Grace when he came to visit me. "To be kept so, in a separate establishment, will give others to think that I am your mistress rather than your future wife. I should have apartments at Bridewell Palace as benefits my standing. If this cannot be, I remain at Hever."

Well, he would do anything for me rather than lose me and I was given my own rooms at Bridewell, next to those of His Majesty, while Katherine was left at Placentia. That was at the beginning of December, but for Yuletide the King, the Court and I moved to Placentia also. It was not long before I had my own little court there, for my uncle, the Duke of Norfolk and the Duke of Suffolk, the King's brother-in-law, visited me constantly, though not out of love, for neither gent was fond of me, but to keep on the right side of His Majesty. My father would come, my dear brother and my cousins, Francis Bryan and Tom Wyatt, so I was not short of company. And yet, despite his vaunted love of me, the King kept the festival of Yuletide itself with old Katherine! I could not credit it. Although he had not mated with her for two years, still he shared her bed occasionally! For appearances only, he admitted sheepishly, when I took him to task over it. How could I tell that she would not win him to her side again? After all, he had not had my body and he must have been starved of love. 'Twas easy enough for Katherine to snare him between the sheets!

So I was in awkward quandary, having promised the King that I would share his bed upon my return to Court, thinking that all would be in train for us to wed, but now all was gone out of joint with the Secret Matter, it were better that I continue to hold him off.

But would he agree to this? I could not tell. For all I knew, he might grow impatient and rape me, then I would never be his wife; or he might grow weary of me and leave me. Nay! I thought, stiffening my back. He has not kept his promise to wed me, so I shall not keep mine to share his bed. If he wants me, he must wait for me.

So, all in all, I had enough to fret me and still more when I discovered that Cardinal Wolsey was attempting, behind my back, to discredit me with the King. 'Twas careless of me, but I had left my copy of an heretical Lutheran book lying on the window-seat in one of my rooms at Placentia. It was a copy of William Tyndale's *Obedience of a Christian Man* and forbidden in this country. One of my ladies, Anne Gainsford, had a sweetheart whose sympathies also followed Martin Luther's teachings, and he had picked up my book to read for himself.

Unluckily, while it was in his possession, it was seen by Dr. Sampson, Dean of the King's Chapel, a staunch Roman and right stiff-necked, withal. This officious priest, holy and horrified, snatched it from Anne's lover and bore it, burning with righteous indignation, to Cardinal Wolsey. The Cardinal, upon learning whose book it was and knowing well the King's hatred of heretics, took it straight to his royal master, so Lady Anne, in tears, told me. For a moment I was afeared, but for a moment only.

"Is it indeed so?" I cried angrily. "Well, it shall be the dearest book that ever the Dean or Cardinal took away!" And, running at once to His Grace, I fell on my knees before him, blurting out the whole sorry tale, at which, God be thanked, he smiled, forgave me and promised to read the book himself! So that danger was averted, but my kindness for the Cardinal underwent a mighty change, for now 'twas plain that despite his seeming affability to me, he meant to worst me if he could. Well, we should see who would win. For my part, it would not be His Eminence, Cardinal Wolsey!

* * *

All through 1529 the matter swung this way and that. I lived as one on a knife-edge, alternating 'twixt hope and despair. It was desperate strain and my natural tendency to bad temper began to assert itself all too often. I became nervous and excitable as well as cross-grained and the wonder is that His Grace suffered it. All wondered at his forbearance. Certainly my father did.

"Why do you not curb your vile temper?"

he bawled at me one chilly spring day, when he had been rowed down to Bridewell from Durham House. "Stupid jade, dost imagine His Majesty will endure your fiendish tongue for ever? How dare you speak to him as you do! He is the King, remember, and no one has treated him so in all his life. Dost wish to lose his love? Though why he should love a wench with such a curst tongue is past my understanding! I ask myself, what does he see in you? Moderate your temper, I say, or you will bring us all down!"

"And moderate yours!" I shrilled, glaring at him, sweeping my hand furiously over the cards laid out on the table for a game of Gleek, scattering them all to the floor, where they fell amongst the rushes. "Remember that I am to wed His Grace and will be Queen. You had best practise respect in your dealings with me, father!"

"And why should I?" he shouted. "You are neither wed, nor yet Queen and, by the way that things are turning out, do not look to be, Madam High-and-Mighty! Your temper could be the ruin of you *and* me!"

"Aha, you are still feared for your precious earldom, are you not?" I cried spitefully. "Well, I may not be Queen, but neither are you Earl of What-May-it-Be, and so remember *that*!"

"Bitch!" he roared, raising his hand to strike me, while I shrieked out that I would tell His Grace of such violence and *pouf*! Away would go that much-desired earldom. We made a great noise between us, but it resolved nothing, of course. I felt that nothing would ever be resolved, that the longer the business took to come to trial, the less likely I was to win; and I was right.

There was a second great trial held in June, set up by the King and Cardinal Wolsey, during which Katherine played upon her hearers' heartstrings and Campeggio played the coward. He adjourned the proceedings until October 'according to the practice of Rome', which meant that the trial would never re-open in England. Moreover, some weeks later, Pope Clement, the sly hypocrite, decided to try the case in Rome, thus ensuring an unfavourable verdict.

I had lost.

Two years! Two years of struggle and strain and all come to naught! I was further from Queenship now than ever before. I shrieked, I screamed, I wept. I was ready to murder Wolsey. "He is against me — you know it!" I railed to His Majesty. "He wishes me ill, he cares not for your desires, he works against me — you know it, you know it!"

And His Grace, who had ever defended the

Cardinal right stoutly, now turned against him for want of someone to blame for the failure of the trial and banished him from Court. It was only when we were at Grafton in Northamptonshire at the end of August, while His Majesty was on Progress, that Wolsey was again received, but not in the manner as formerly, nor was he given lodging in the house as he had been used to have. Nay, he had to find his own place, while Campeggio, who had accompanied him, was given apartments near the King's own. Yet, even so, when Wolsey came to the King, falling on his knees, right miserable and pathetic, His Grace went to him and lifted him up with both his arms, drawing him into the recess of the great central window of the gallery, listening to his pleas and explanations as kind as ever, while I ground my teeth with rage. And after dinner, they both went into the Privy Chamber and remained there, talking alone for the whole afternoon until darkness fell, when Wolsey was commanded to return the next morning 'to finish the conversation', so said the King, patting him on the back. I near burst with fury and mortification. Would I never be rid of Wolsey?

I decided that the projected 'conversation' would never finish and to that end made a plan to keep His Grace from the Cardinal. I

191

would go to the King, all smiles and sweetness, telling him of a notion that I had devised for his delight on the morrow, and I would go at once. Opening the door of the Privy Chamber, I peeped in, smiling roguishly. There sat His Grace in his carven chair alone, head on hand, a frown on his brow which vanished when he spied me.

"Ha, what would you, my love?" he called, rising in a swirl of yellow satin and cloth of silver to come to me. "Come in, come in, stay you not by the door," said he, taking my hand. "And what does my darling desire?" he asked, kissing me as though he had not seen me for days, and setting me on his knee.

"I have a notion for your pleasure," I replied, rubbing my cheek against his. "What think you of a visit to the place that you are considering for a new deer park? It will be a long ride, but the countryside is beautiful and what is more, we can be together, away from curious eyes. We may eat out of doors, too, if the day be fine enough, but we must leave betimes in order to accomplish the journey. What say you, Sire?"

His face lighted up. "Why, I say 'tis excellent notion. We shall do it!"

I clapped my hand to my mouth in feigned dismay. "Oh, I had forgot!" I exclaimed. "You have a meeting with the Cardinal tomorrow.

Oh, and my heart was so set upon the outing, Sire. Oh, do not disappoint me!"

He hesitated, but for a moment only. "Nay, you shall not be disappointed, sweetheart. Alone together — how can I resist? I shall have to talk with Wolsey upon our return. I feel for him, thou knowest. I shall come, fret not, dearest, and shall be ready as soon as I have broken my fast in the morning."

True to his word, he was ready, clad in a green satin cap and a short green gown for riding, when Cardinal Wolsey arrived just as we had mounted our horses and were about to leave. "Ha, Thomas!" called His Grace to the discomfited Cardinal. "I cannot stop now. I shall see you when I return. Until then!" And we galloped out of the courtyard, under the gatehouse and away.

I knew that Wolsey and Campeggio had to leave that day and so I made sure, with kisses and caresses, that the King did not get back to Grafton until after they had departed. His Grace was never to lay eyes on Wolsey again.

★ ★ ★

After that, the English Cardinal's downfall was swift. On the 9th of October he was charged with setting the Pope above the King and the penalty for this was the forfeiture of all the accused's goods and lands. In order to save his skin, Wolsey confessed to the crime and offered all his belongings to His Majesty, which His Majesty was delighted to accept. He had always longed to possess York Place, as well as Hampton Court, of which Wolsey had given him the lease two years earlier. Hampton was beautiful, but out of town, whereas York Place, so near Westminster, would be ideal as a palace. His Grace's pleasure in it was so great that he brought me and my mother secretly by boat from Hampton to inspect his new treasure from cellars to attics.

Ciel, what riches were there! We had seen naught like it; even His Grace was amazed at the gold and silver tapestries and hangings, the ecclesiastical copes covered with jewels and embroidery enough to dazzle the eye. In the Gilt Chamber there was a great cupboard filled with ewers, jugs, bowls and basins, all of gold and silver and studded with jewels. In the Council Chamber we gaped at plates made of fine pottery, such as we had never seen before, all glazed shining white and gilded in patterns, while in the Long Gallery there were laid out tables laden with rolls of velvet, silk, satin, sendal and fine wool, all in the most brilliant colours, as much as would fill a mercer's shop and leave some over. As I gazed, I bethought me that I had come a long way from the little maid whom Wolsey had termed 'that foolish girl yonder in the Court'! I might not yet be Queen, but I was up while Wolsey was well down, to descend still further, I hoped.

"I have many plans for the house," confided His Grace excitedly, pulling me behind a blue velvet curtain so that he might fondle me away from my mother's eyes. "I mean to use it as my London palace. Bridewell is too inconvenient and set so near to the noisome river Fleet as it is, the air of it stinketh even when the place is sweetened. I mean to make this the finest and richest of all my dwellings, with new galleries, a large park and two gatehouses of a grandeur to match the rest. Oh, darling, how I love thee, how I love thee! Hast bewitched me, pretty one?"

"And where," I enquired, leaning back in his arms and speaking with some reserve, "do you mean your wife to reside?"

"Katherine? Not here, for sure!" he replied with a laugh. "Nay, there will be much building and muddle while the work goes on and of course there will be no apartments fit enough for her — nor ever will be, indeed."

"What of me, then?" I asked. "Will there be rooms fit for me?"

"They shall be the first to be made ready, sweeting," he assured me fondly, "and they shall be the best in the land. What thinkest thou of my notion to whitewash the Great Hall? It will be a landmark thus, will it not?"

When this was done, the building stood out for a goodly distance round about and took its new name from this, being called White Hall ever after. It became my favourite residence, but despite all the rich gifts I was given and and the love and esteem in which I was held by the King, I grew depressed and despairing. As yet another Yuletide approached and I twenty-two years and still unwed, my heart was heavy indeed and my temper suffered for it. So, I feared did His Grace.

On the evening of St. Andrew's Day, he came to me wearing a glum visage. "Here is a thing," said he. "I quarrelled with Katherine right heartily this morning, for she took issue with me over the fact that I sleep with her no longer. 'Nay,' says I to her, 'I am no longer your husband and will not share your bed in sin.' '*Madre de Dios*,' cries she. 'For every canon law you may force to decide in your favour, I can find a thousand to declare our marriage good and indissoluble!' She will not yield an inch, Nan, so stubborn as she is. It is like beating upon a dungeon door — useless to make her give way."

I sprang to my feet, furious. "Did I not *tell* you that whenever you dispute with the Queen she will be sure to get the upper hand? I see that some fine morning you will succumb to her reasoning and cast me off! I have been waiting long and in the meantime might have had babes, which is the greatest consolation in the world. But alas! My time and youth are spent to no purpose and I am neither wife nor mother!" And I burst into wild sobs, full of bitterness and regret.

Swiftly, passionately, he seized me in his arms. "Dear heart, darling one, do not grieve so! Nay, I have a surprise for you, my love. 'Tis the last day of November today, is it not? Well, in a se'ennight, your father shall become Earl of Wiltshire and Ormond. What say you to that?"

And this, to my father's boundless joy and delight, took place in a great ceremony on the 8th of December at White Hall, with trumpets sounding and much pomp, followed by a wondrous banquet, during which I sat in the Queen's place at the King's right hand. So now I was the Lady Anne Boleyn, my beloved brother Viscount Rochford, my sister Lady Mary and my dear mother a Countess. It was very gratifying to us all.

After the banquet there was dancing,

197

drinking and laughter kept up until dawn. Needless to say, there were some discontented faces around the walls! His Grace's sister, the Princess Mary Rose, now Duchess of Suffolk, whose youngest lady I had been when she was Queen of France; the Duchess of Norfolk, mine uncle's wife, who detested me; they both wished me further and took no pains to hide it. They wished me dead and buried, I daresay. The fact that I was allowed to take precedence over them must have wrought like acid in their bellies. I cared not, why should I? So long as the King kept his promises to wed me, I felt I had naught to fear from those ladies. Besides, the King acted as though I were Queen already, paying for my underlinen, my shoes, gowns and headdresses. He bought me my bows and arrows and a richly embroidered shooting glove of Spanish leather; purple and crimson satin for kirtles and petticoats, furs for winter-time and gave me a leathern bag filled with gold coins to the value of £100[1] as a gift for New Year. Even when my great wolf-hound, Urian, killed a cow, in error, when I was out a-hunting, His Grace paid the farmer compensation for the animal and laughed about it. If I had been wed I would have been

[1] About £160,000

198

truly content, no matter what glares and whispers were directed at me. As it was, all believed me to be the King's mistress and treated me with as much open scorn as they dared, especially those who loved old Katherine.

Content was not to be my portion for, on the 7th of March 1530, Pope Clement issued a brief forbidding the King to wed before sentence was passed, saying that Katherine must be treated as his true wife. If this brief were not obeyed, His Majesty would be excommunicated and all England placed under an Interdict, whereby neither he, nor any English person would be allowed to attend a religious service, receive a Christian burial, nor children to be christened. It could be the beginning of a Holy War against England groaned the King, with Spain as the aggressor. There could be an invasion or, at the least, civil war caused by Katherine's many supporters. So I was faced with the undoubted fact that although King Henry desired to wed me, civil war was another matter entirely and I must understand that.

My future might hang in the balance, but Wolsey's was wellnigh certain, I thought. Although he had been pardoned, he left for York in April and I sat triumphant in the knowledge that he was out of York Place for good. He would trouble me no more. Judge of my feelings, then, when I heard that he was to be enthroned at York Minster as Archbishop of York! I near had an apoplexy. Should he be reinstated, I would be lost. Sobbing, gasping, weeping, I rushed through the galleries of White Hall, seeking His Majesty in his new-furnished Privy Chamber, where I found him in a window-seat, singing and playing the harp.

"Why do you allow Wolsey to take this Archbishopric?" I wailed, interrupting his song, shaking his arm so that the harp-strings fell a-jangling. "What mean you by it? Wolsey is my enemy! What of the years I have wasted? I grow old waiting for nothing — *nothing*! I shall leave you, Sire. I can endure this misery of uncertainty no longer. It is over between us. Over, I say!" I meant it.

He leaped to his feet, catching me and caressing me as I struggled in his arms. "Beloved, you would not! You must not leave me. Sure I could not live without you, darling Nan!"

"Let me go!" I wept. "If Wolsey be not arrested I will stay with you no longer. It is mine intent! My mind is set!"

A few days later, the Cardinal was arrested and charged with high treason at York, on the King's order, by the Earl of Northumberland, that same Harry Percy whom I had loved so long ago. That were Nemesis, indeed!

Yet still I had no rest, no peace. One day, after I had been out riding, the populace glowering and groaning at me as usual, I came withindoors to my apartment in glum enough mood, to find, on a stool in my bedchamber, a heavy, red, leather-bound book fastened with gilt clasps. 'Twas a book of prophecies, or so it was entitled. Taking it up, I opened it and turned the leaves, curious to learn its contents, for I greatly liked books and reading, and came upon a picture within it representing a king, a queen and a headless lady, her bloody head lying beside a block. The figures were marked thus: H, K and A. For a moment my heart near stopped with the shock of it. Then, affecting a bravado I did not feel, I called out to Anne Gainsford, who came running.

"Come hither, Annet!" I cried, "and see here a book of prophecy! This, he saith is the King, this the Queen, and this is myself with my head off. What say you to that?"

Annet turned pale and stared at me, large-eyed. "Sweet Christ!" she gasped, crossing herself. "If I thought it true, though he were Emperor of all the World, I would not myself marry him."

I shrugged, concealing my dismay under a show of disdain. "*Quelle absurdité: Pfui,* I

201

think the book a bauble. Yet, hearken to me, Annet," I went on, my eyes alight with determination. "I am resolved to have him, whatever might become of me. What, to retreat now and lose all? Not I!"

It was not all sweetness between His Majesty and me, neither. Nay, for my nerves were on edge and my temper grew worse, for I found any restraint on my feelings ever more difficult to maintain. I saw slights everywhere; I feared Katherine's influence upon him and that of their daughter, the fourteen year old Princess Mary, who did not attempt to conceal her dislike of me, showing me a contemptuous face and drawing her skirts aside, should she pass near me. Ah, I detested her as heartily as she loathed me and when I became Queen she should know it well, the haughty jade. I would teach her respect, by God!

Then, one day in the autumn of that year of 1530, my dear brother George took me well to task for my behaviour to His Grace. We two sat by the fire in my parlour at Placentia, the wind blustering outside and roaring in the chimneys like some wild bull, the trees in the park shaking their branches against a cloudy grey sky, tattered tawny leaves blowing like lost love-letters about the gardens. George gazed at me, his dark eyes earnest in his handsome, olive-skinned countenance, his blue velvet doublet taking a red glow from the flames in the hearth.

"Nan," he said, "you grow too tempersome. Your tongue darts like an adder, I swear. How long dost think His Grace will suffer your complaints? Art not grateful for what he has done for you? I tell you, he is offending everyone and making enemies everywhere for your sake. Do you realise that the wrath of the King is death?"

"Well then," I replied, half-laughing, "I am willing to face a thousand deaths for *his* sake. Now what do you say?"

"I say that you are a brave woman," he replied, "or a foolish one. But is it for his sake, or your own?"

"Ah, you have me there, George. For both our sakes, I dare say."

"Do you love him at all, Nan?"

"I do not know," I confessed. "At all events, I have told him I do so often, that perhaps I begin to believe it a little myself."

He smiled. "Well, for sure the King thinks so, or he would never allow your furies as he does."

"As to that, I do feel regret when I lose my temper with him," I admitted, "and constantly do I re-affirm my love so that he be not hurt."

"Then your heart has softened somewhat toward him," said George. "Doubtless he realises it and thus endures your outbursts. He must love you very greatly indeed, sister. Take care, then, that you keep his love."

"Oh, I will take care," I assured him. "None better, fear not."

Soon after this, Cardinal Wolsey went out like a spent candle and my oldest enemy was no more. He was arrested on the 4th of November and died of dysentery at Leicester on the 29th, whilst on his way to London, the Tower and the block. So I was one ill-wisher the less and thanked God for it, but I could trust no one, neither my own attendants, nor even His Majesty's agents oversea. As well as this, Katherine's ladies lost no chance to spite me in any way they could, twitting me on my still unwed state, on the fact of my curst sixth fingernail and upon my age, which was now full twenty-three years. It drove me wild and I persuaded the King to dismiss three of the hateful archwives. But he would not dismiss them all and they knew he would not and teased and baited me until I could have run mad.

"Oh Jesu!" I shrieked at one lady who had upset her wine a-purpose over my newest gown. "See what you have done, spiteful cat! I wish all Spaniards were at the bottom of the sea!"

"You should not speak so for the sake of the Queen's honour," bleated the mealy-mouthed offender, with an insolent smirk, "for she is Spanish as well as I. I'll wager she wishes *you* at the bottom of the sea, too!"

"I care nothing for the Queen nor for her ladies!" I screamed, jumping to my feet. "I had rather see her hanged than confess she is my mistress! So go and blab *that* to His Majesty, as no doubt you will!" And I ran from the room, sobbing. I hated everyone. All were against me, all.

Yet I was wrong, for there was one who was not my enemy at that time, one whose brilliant brain was ready to aid me, who believed that through me he might achieve his ambitions for himself. What matter the reason? The intention was enough for me. The man was Thomas Cromwell, low-born son of a Putney blacksmith and, one-time secretary to Cardinal Wolsey; short and fat, with a hard, coarse, square face and little brown eyes that held no warmth. Those eyes were like pieces of iron and in his breast there beat a heart to match, but I cared not, so long as it beat in my cause.

This Thomas Cromwell, in discussion with the King, put forward a notion to force the English clergy to proclaim His Majesty Head of the Church in England. "Then," said he, "Your Majesty need not look to Rome for a divorce."

"By God!" exclaimed the King, impressed. "But how? How to force the priests, Cromwell? They are everywhere, all over the country."

"There is the charge of *praemunire facias* which may be brought against clerics who have paid alliance to Rome, rather than to the King. Thus, they may be liable to forfeit their properties, as did Cardinal Wolsey, and to be imprisoned, Sire," replied Cromwell, smiling, though his eye remained cold.

"But against the whole of the clergy, Master Cromwell? Against every priest in the land?"

Cromwell's smile deepened. "Why not, Sire? There is no rule that says we may not. I doubt you will find them obstinate. They all be too afeared after Wolsey's fall."

"God's blood, the impudence of such a notion! I never heard the like!" The King burst into a roar of laughter, slapping his thigh. "You are a sly fox, Cromwell, by the Rood, you are! Bring the charge, if you think it will hold; bring it by all means. Those fat priests shall shiver in their shoes! And how shall we go on after that, eh?"

"Why," said Cromwell, "when they offer to

pay for their pardons, which they assuredly will, Your Grace must refuse to accept unless you are recognised as Supreme Head of the Church and Clergy of England, if the title appeals to Your Grace."

"Indeed it does." The King was delighted. "See to it at once, my friend."

So it was done, and on the 11th of February all turned out exact as Cromwell had predicted. Now I was sure, now I was certain, that I would be Queen. So excited was I that I cared little for what I said, or how arrogant I behaved. *Pourquoi pas?* I would be Queen soon enough and then none could say me nay. So I snapped my fingers at those who hated me, for they could not harm me now, save one, and that was the Princess Mary.

The King loved that wretched girl, babbling of her beauty and accomplishments as though she were some goddess, rather than a little pudding-faced gowk full of prayers and piety, with a ridiculous voice as deep as a man's. Nasty little masterpiece, I could not see why he should dote upon her so. She had her own household and her own houses, but His Grace would have her visit him with tiresome frequency and how did I know that she did not use these visits to champion her mother and turn the King against me? I'll wager she did her best! Ay, and how she would glare at me, toss her head and affect deafness if I addressed her. I was main afeared of her influence over the King and, to keep her away, I would fly into a rage whenever her name was so much as mentioned, screaming that I could not live in the same palace as the girl, thus putting my temper to work for me. And His Grace's love for me was such that, in the end, he acquiesced and the Princess's visits were discontinued. I felt great triumph at that. I felt that I could do as I would with His Majesty because of it. After all, 'twas no small thing to put his own child aside for me, and so I cared still less what I said and did, feeling powerful and secure as if naught could touch, nor hurt me.

And more triumph was to follow, for in July, wet, chilly and cheerless though it was, I went on Progress with the King, leaving Windsor Castle riding at his side, with a message left for Katherine that she was to remain behind, her presence not being desired. Two weeks later, His Grace wished to return to Windsor for hunting and sent a letter to Katherine, ordering her to take herself, her servants and her belongings to a house that had once belonged to Wolsey; the More, in Middlesex. She had no choice but to obey and, ha, ha! *I* had her room at Windsor!

"Go careful, Nan," warned my friends Marget Lee and Bridget Wingfield. "Take heed of His Majesty. Remember, he is all-powerful, a very lion in might, and his fancy falls where it will."

"He is but a lamb to me!" I laughed. "He does my least bidding, as anyone may see. Why should I take heed? He loves me."

They laughed, yet apprehension was in their eyes. I thought them fuss-budgets and ignored their warning. Why, the King was besotted with me. At Yuletide, which we spent at Placentia, he loaded me with gifts. There was a set of velvet hangings, all of light blue worked with silver, to cover the walls of my rooms, a beautiful, great bed covered with cloth of gold and crimson satin embroidered with roses in gold and silver, as well as a ransom in jewels, while the members of my family received rich gifts of gilt plate from His Majesty.

My family also had sumptuous apartments in each palace, with a special withdrawing room always for my mother, while my sister Mary was my closest companion at this time, for I favoured her much, being sorry for her. I did not heed her warning, neither. She had not known how to manage the King, so her advice was worth little, I thought, sweet though she was. Dear George was ever at the

King's side, laughing, jesting, joining him in games and sports of all kinds. They made a handsome pair; His Grace so ruddy and fair, broad and stately in build; George almost as tall, but slim, lithe and dark — dark as a blackamoor, some said. They said that of me, also. The King gave George a house of his own at Greenwich as well as using him as confidential messenger for state secrets.

Oh, high rode the Boleyn star and would ride higher yet if I could do aught to assist it. In fact, there was a fine manor house of good red brick a-building in the lush, green fields where the Hospital of St. James had once stood and this house was now to be called St. James's Palace. It had a great towered gatehouse, with a clock in the centre, and upon each side of it, carved in stone, were the King's initials and mine, plain for all to see, side by side, H and A. I thought it wonderful and near burst with pride until I heard sniggers from those who disliked me.

"Hast seen the work on the new gatehouse? It reads HA HA no less! Dost not think this a veritable laughing matter?" tittered one lady to another, giggling behind her hand, thinking me not by.

"Ay, 'tis right comical and the common folk think it so, too. They walk there to jeer and mock. They hate her."

"And I hate *you*!" I shouted, pouncing out upon them, my black satin skirts a-swish, eyes flashing, arm upraised to strike. "Shut your slanderous gobs, or I will shut them for you! Take that and that and *that*!" And I dealt them some ringing blows about the ears. They stood, pale and trembling before me, their cheeks red from the buffeting. "Shall I tell the King what you have said?" I cried. "He will show you little mercy, I promise you! Ah, you shake your heads, do you, miserable, tongue-wagging faint-hearts? You will speak of me with respect, or suffer for it — forget not my words. Now, get out!"

They ran off, quick enough, but for a moment my heart was heavy. The common folk surely did hate me. Truth to tell, I dared not show my face abroad in the City nowadays, for insults and worse were flung at me, so I had to travel there in a plain, closed litter for very safety. I knew that they called me the Night Crow, Black Nan, the Concubine, the Goggle-eyed Whore and sundry other sweet names. It made glum thinking, but I would not dwell on it. Once I was Queen, all would be changed, sure.

I bethought me of York Place, now White Hall, which was a-building for me as Queen. No one could laugh at that. There was a new gallery constructed near the orchard, all filled with paintings of His Grace, under a ceiling gilded and carved, while floor tiles of red, green and yellow, right elegant and pretty were being laid throughout the palace. As well as all this, many small, mean houses in Charing Village had been pulled down to clear the space for a handsome park beyond White Hall, dedicated to St. James, while the Tower of London was being refurbished within for my coronation when the time came. There was movement and change everywhere and all along of me, a woman.

So full of happiness was I at all this, that I allowed His Grace much greater intimacy with my body than hitherto, save for the act which makes a woman a wife or a whore. Our nights were exciting, but frustrating — for His Grace, anyhap. For myself, I quite enjoyed the love-play, but was not over-eager for the consummation. I felt it might give me too much into the King's power; that I would be mastered, overborne, captured and subdued. Moreover, I had but little taste for all the slobbering, grunting, pawing, handling and thrusting that seemed to be most of the accompaniment of bodily love, even that of a great King. He was such a big man; might he not hurt me, I asked him nervously.

"Hurt you, my treasure? Never would I!" he murmured hotly in my ear as we lay in my fine new bed, the curtains drawn, enclosing us in a warm, dark cavern of writhings and heavy breathings. "I would be gentle as silk with you. I would slip into you like a well-tempered sword into a jewelled scabbard, my precious one. May the time soon cometh!"

"Amen to that," I crooned against a rain of kisses and caresses. "Then our troubles will be behind us."

"And you will bear me fine sons," said he, tenderly stroking my breasts.

"Of a certainty I will," I breathed.

Ay, I was certain. Most women had at least one son, so why should not the Lady Anne Boleyn have several, she who had come so far and dared so much? I began to think that there was little I could not accomplish. Pride goeth before a fall, they say, but I would not fall, not I! Never would I fall. The King worshipped me. His love for me passed all bounds of reason; 'twas the talk of Europe.

Nay, I would not fall.

8

MY LADY MARQUIS

1532–1533

The early morning sun shone warm and golden through the many-paned windows of the Great Chamber at Windsor Castle upon Sunday the 1st of September 1532. King Henry of England, clad in glittering crimson and gold, sat stately in his great chair raised upon a dais at one end of the long, richly decorated room, gilding gleaming upon its panelled walls, bright paint vivid on the beams of the ceiling, his nobles and statesmen about him. There stood thin, dark, large-nosed Thomas Howard, Duke of Norfolk, and big, burly, fair-haired Charles Brandon, Duke of Suffolk. Nearby was Jean du Bellay, the French Ambassador, elegant and poised, sharp brown eyes missing nothing as the heavy door under the gallery opened and a page cried out: "The Lady Anne Boleyn de Rochford."

The King drew a deep breath as she came, his love, his adored one, beautiful as ever in a gown of ruby velvet bordered with ermine, her rich hair loose down her back, sparkling with jewels threaded through it. Before and behind her walked three officers-at-arms, while upon either hand she was escorted by Elizabeth, Countess of Rutland and Dorothy, Countess of Sussex, their faces blank and mask-like. Jealous as the devil! conjectured His Majesty, laughing inwardly. But they knew better than to show it — oh, well they knew! He stared long at the slender, willowy girl, moving so slowly and gracefully toward him and met the gaze of her great black eyes. In them he saw the hint of a smile, whilst the tiniest flicker caught the corner of her ripe, red mouth. His heart fairly fluttered with emotion as, reaching the dais, she fell on her knees, raven head humbly bowed.

Quickly stepping forward at an impatient snap of the King's fingers, Dr. Stephen Gardiner, now Bishop of Winchester, unrolled a scroll and in his harsh, deep voice, read aloud the patent of creation that was to make Anne Boleyn Marquis — not Marchioness — of Pembroke, a peer in her own right with precedence over any other marquis in the realm. Rising from his chair, the King placed the ermine-bordered crimson mantle of a marquis about the shoulders with careful hands and loving smiles. Then he lifted the golden coronet and placed it on her head, after which he handed her the patent and another document which granted her a thousand pounds[1] a year for life.

"I thank you, Your Grace," she said quietly. "You have done me great honour this day."

At once the sound of trumpets shrilled from the gallery, the new-made Lady Marquis kissed the King's hand and, with great dignity, left the Great Chamber, her attendants following in order of rank. After Mass, which was celebrated within the hour, the Court was alive with gossip and surmise; the courtiers gathering in chattering groups as they discussed the King's unprecedented action.

"Oh, it is disgraceful, Dorothy!" declared the Countess of Rutland. "To be forced to attend that *creature* at such a jumped-up ceremony! Who ever heard of a female Marquis? I begin to think His Grace means to make fools of us all."

"Hush, Bess, I pray you!" warned the Countess of Sussex. "You will be overheard if you speak so loud and then you will be in trouble, no force." She lowered her own voice. "I tell you, I had hard work to keep the indignation from my face, even as you did. It

---

[1] about £750,000

cut me to the heart to think that you and I entered the Great Chamber higher in rank than Black Nan and left it with her raised above us."

"Insupportable! And did you notice the words of the patent, Dorothy?" hissed Lady Rutland. "Did you note that the title was to be inherited by the male heirs of her body, but the words 'lawfully begotten' were left out?"

"No, indeed! I was too forstaught by the slight laid upon us. What could the King have meant by leaving out those words?"

"But one thing only!" whispered Lady Rutland, burning with virtuous indignation. "It means that if she should bear the King a bastard boy before she manages to wed him, she and the child will be secure. That is what His Grace means."

"Well, I suppose one cannot blame her for safeguarding the future of a child, but such goings-on are not what I am used to," remarked Lady Sussex in aggrieved tone. "Dost think she be virgin still? She prates of her virginity oft enough, God knows."

"God only knows in truth!" Lady Rutland was scornful. "But at the age of five-and-twenty, Dorothy? After six years of hot pursuit by a man as lusty as His Grace? Come, come, she must be his leman. If she is not, she is no ordinary female, but an icicle."

"Well — but — " Lady Sussex was hesitant, " — surely the wording of the patent seems to suggest that she and His Grace have not yet bedded? If she were already his mistress, surely such a safeguard would have been made long ago? Of course, I do not understand these things, but that is how it begins to appear to me. In which case, she *is* no ordinary female, Bess."

"She is certainly unlike anyone I have ever encountered. She is beyond words. A detestable woman. What the King sees in her I cannot imagine. Dark as a blackamoor, thin as a rail, the temper of a shrew, six fingernails on her right hand and a heart of stone. A veritable Helen of Troy, by my faith!"

At Lady Rutland's unflattering summing-up of the charms of the best hated lady in the land, the Countess of Sussex burst into a fit of giggles in which her friend joined with a will, and for some time the two ladies were bereft of speech.

If the new Marquis could have overheard the two Countesses, she would have shrugged and laughed, for she cared nothing for their disagreeable gossipping. Her wave was reaching its crest and naught else mattered to her. In her bedchamber, hung with bright tapestries depicting the story of Daphne and

218

Actaeon, she was seated upon a stool cushioned in pink velvet while Bridget Wingfield and Margaret Lee removed the jewels from her lustrous hair and a maid brought a bowl of scented water and linen cloths with which to wash her hands. As they laughed and chattered, a knock fell upon the door and the maid scurried to open it, revealing Jean du Bellay, the French Ambassador, Bishop of Bayonne upon the threshold.

"Ah, come in *Monsieur Jean!*" cried Anne from where she sat. "Hast come to congratulate me? *Qu'est ce que tu veut, mon cher?*"

"*Du vrai*, to congratulate," answered he, advancing with a smile. "Today you took my breath away, milady. There never was such a marquis, *ma foi*, never! And it is 'marquis', not 'marquise', I note. Does the King seek to make you a man, *hein?*"

She laughed. "Oh no, it is merely that he has given me a peerage like a man, *tu sais*. It is my own right, *comprends?* And women have nothing in their own right in this life, so it is quite extraordinary, *n'est ce pas?*"

"You are most fortunate, *ma belle*," he said. "Is it permitted that I seat myself? *Merci bien*. Now, about this visit to Calais that is projected for you and the King. May we be private?"

"*Mais oui,*" she replied at once, dismissing her ladies and the maid who left the room, casting inquisitive glances over their shoulders as they closed the door behind them. "Now, *mon cher,*" she said briskly, when she was sure that none could overhear. "What is all this about my visit to Calais?"

"I fear there may be some difficulties, Milady Anne," answered du Bellay unsmilingly. "There is no French royal lady who is willing to receive you, I regret to say."

"What?" Anne laughed high and long. "You jest with me! I am to accompany His Grace thither. Of course a suitable French lady will receive me. It is of a certainty, *mon ami!* Why, the King has made old Katherine disgorge all her jewels and has given them to me to wear for this very occasion!"

Du Bellay shook his head apologetically. "It will be of little use," he observed.

"But what mean you? I am to meet King François in state and be presented to him by his sister, Marguerite of Navarre! I know them both very well — very well indeed. It is all arranged!"

"I fear not," responded Jean du Bellay. "The Duchess Marguerite says she is too unwell to be present at the meeting."

"Too unwell?" queried Anne. "Ha, you mean too unwilling! Am I right? Give me the truth *Monsieur Jean.*"

"Ah — I think — that is to say — *hélas*, you are right, *ma chère*. She find herself too unwilling," admitted the French Ambassador unhappily. "She says she has no wish to greet you, your position being — " he hesitated delicately " — somewhat equivocal."

"Very politely put, my dear," said Anne, "but I'll wager her own words were not so polite! Did she term me 'the King's whore'? Ah, I see by your face that she did. And, do you know, *monsieur*, that I loved the Duchess Marguerite when I was a little girl in France? I loved and admired her, for she ever made much of me. Now she rejects me for something that is not true, for I am not the King's whore . . . Not yet, anyhap," she added after a moment.

"Not yet?" repeated du Bellay in a questioning tone. "You mean — ?"

"I mean that I have resolved to abandon my virgin state," she said with a half-laugh. "Ay, you may stare, sir. After all these years I have decided to yield myself to His Grace."

Du Bellay frowned. "It is a risk," he said.

"But a risk worth taking, *cher Monsieur Jean*. If I should fall pregnant that is all I need to be made Queen in a hurry. I am weary of waiting."

The Bishop pursed his lips, nodding as he

considered this. "What if you do not conceive?" he asked at last.

"Ah, there lies the risk. But I am still quite young — twenty-five is not ancient — and I am healthy, so the chances are good, are they not?"

"I thought you feared the act of love, *ma petite?*"

"Ay, that I do. And I realise full well that the whole business might prove a great disappointment to His Grace, for he has waited for me so long and sees me as the embodiment of physical love. I fear I may fall short of his expectations. It is *all* a risk and has been so from the very beginning, but I shall nor draw back. And I shall go to Calais, no matter what prevail."

"The Imperial Ambassador, Eustace Chapuys, fears that you will wed the King there. He is not your friend and will do all he can to keep you down," remarked du Bellay. "Shall you wed in Calais? It is an English possession."

"Oh, I trust not," she replied, "for I would rather marry in England, in the place where queens are always married and crowned. I should indeed prefer England if the choice be mine."

★ ★ ★

At the end of September, King Henry and the Lady Marquis of Pembroke came downriver from Windsor to Greenwich at the beginning of their journey to Calais. Many of their entourage had gone ahead to Dover to await their royal master's pleasure there. Meanwhile, their royal master was enjoying intense pleasure already, for while lying at Sir Thomas Cheyney's riverside house, the Lady Marquis had capitulated at last.

The King could not believe it. At forty-one years of age he felt like a young lad with his first love; unsure, uncertain, full of nervous excitement and wild desire, fearing that his manhood might not prove itself, that he might disappoint his lady. As he lay beside her in the candlelit shadows of the great, green-curtained bed, his heart beat so hard in his broad chest that he thought she must hear it. He was aware of her hair spread out on the white pillow, darker than the dusky shadows that enveloped them. Such hair! Lifting a strand, he kissed it, murmuring love-words. He saw the sparkle of her large eyes, liquid-seeming in the candle-glow, the curve of her naked shoulder like polished marble as she lay. Seizing her in his arms, he kissed her passionately and, despite all his efforts at restraint and tenderness, suddenly all was a whirl of frenzied activity, grunts, gasps and cries, as King Henry at last possessed the body of his long-desired love.

Afterwards, Anne raised herself on her elbow, gazing down at the sleeping face of her royal lover, listening to his loud and satisfied snores. So this was the great act of consummation over which so much ado and commotion was made! It was undignified, sweaty, painful, messy and unutterably tedious. She shrugged her shoulders in disillusionment. His Grace had obviously undergone a happy experience; a smile still lingered on his lips, whereas she had been thoroughly disgusted. She had felt no explosion of joy — no indeed! it was nothing but a cheat and altogether distasteful. Hateful, in fact, but she would have to endure it. She bit her lip, then smiled wryly. Hateful, ay, but worth enduring to reach her goal. She prayed that she would conceive quickly.

When the lovers reached Dover on the 11th of October, the King's besotted behaviour caused some raised eyebrows amongst the courtiers who had awaited his coming.

"*Mon Dieu*, he cannot leave her alone for an hour!" spat the Imperial Ambassador, Eustace Chapuys, revolted by such billing and cooing. "He is bewitched by the jade, I swear. I am sure that no good can come of

224

this business at Calais," he went on gloomily. "There is a plague in Kent, 'tis a wonder that none of us have caught it upon the journey. As for the crossing, why, I'll wager we may all be drowned! The sea is right chancy at this time of year. Hast heard of the comet that hath appeared in the north, with a tail five yards long, so it is reported? That bodes ill for sure."

"Oh, gramercy for your groanings, Messer Chapuys!" cried George Boleyn, laughing derisively. "You have forgot the great fish that has also appeared in the north. It was found dead on the beach, full ninety feet long, 'tis said and also augurs ill-fortune, I hear. So what of the fish, monsieur? Do not forget the fish!"

But fish and comets notwithstanding, the sea was calm, the weather mild and sunshiny, the port of Calais being reached in perfect safety. As she stepped ashore to the sound of gunfire, Anne's thoughts flew back to her arrival in France as a little girl of not seven years old, so long ago. Vastly different now, by God, and would be better yet! Against her own inclination, she had agreed to the King's persuasions that they be married in Calais, for she did not wish to argue with him now that the wedding seemed to be so near. It had been arranged for the 27th of October and

King François was to attend it in order to set the seal of approval upon the ceremony. The French King was to be escorted in state to the English possession of Calais by King Henry who would travel to Boulogne to fetch him.

The English King left for Boulogne on the 21st of October, with the sun blazing from the heavens as though it were still summer, and remained there for four days of public feasting and merriment. In private, the two rulers were not quite so merry, for King François had changed his mind and had decided not to attend the wedding for fear of offending the Emperor Charles V, Queen Katherine's powerful nephew, who had won a great battle against the Turks and was thus free to search for new conquests. However, François agreed to return to Calais with his good friend Henry and meet the Lady Anne again.

It would be decidedly titillating, he thought, to see what kind of woman the little Boleyn had become. She had certainly lived up to her promise of allure. To think that she was to be the next Queen of England! He laughed to himself. She was exciting, he remembered, but cold, he fancied. *Mais enfin*, she had courage, *la petite!* One was forced to admire her powers of enchantment —*merveilleuse, en effet! Quelle femme politique — tellement formidable!* He looked forward to the encounter with pleasurable anticipation.

On the evening of the 27th of October, the day that should have been a wedding day, the meeting took place at the house where King François had elected to stay whilst in Calais. The large upper room was candle-lit; dusky shadows stealing across the dark wooden panelling, candle flames glittering on the gold plate and on the gold and silver threads in the tapestries, while the two kings leaned back in their chairs, wine-cup in hand, smiling and replete after an excellent supper, chatting lazily, their attendants about them.

When the door opened, heads turned to see a bevy of eight masked ladies standing on the threshold as strains of music filled the air. Stepping in time to the beat of a tabor, the ladies advanced into the room, jewelled silver bodices gleaming, gold skirts, tinsel trimmed, a-sway, led by four more ladies in scarlet satin. Dancing forward, each lady chose a high-ranking French guest as a partner for a stately pavane; twisting, turning, bowing and curtseying up and down the room in dignified measure.

King Henry, resplendent in violet cloth of gold, a collar of pearls and diamonds about his sturdy neck, his strong hands blazing with rubies and diamonds, a huge carbuncle as big as a goose-egg hanging from a golden chain to rest upon his wide chest, smiled with satisfaction at the pretty sight, one of his hands beating out the rhythm on the arm of his chair. Suddenly, with a loud laugh, he rose, clapping his hands for the music to cease, and strode forward to where King François stood amongst the dancers.

"*Maintenant, mon frère!*" he cried. "Witness her who is your partner! Come, unmask, ladies all!" And he pulled aside the mask covering the face of the lady who had been dancing with the French King.

"Aha!" exclaimed François. "*C'est Miladi Anne!* Oh, well met, *chérie!* You have blossomed since last I laid eyes upon you."

"And are you pleased with what you see, Sire?" asked Anne, laughing. "Have I lived up to my youthful promise?"

"You have surpassed it," said he sincerely, his narrow, slanting, dark eyes alight with appreciation. *Doux Jésu*, but she was desirable! He would have her, cold or no, given the chance. What witchery, what appeal! He did not blame King Henry for his actions, now that he had set eyes upon this fascinating creature once more. However, he must control his ever-ready impulses and behave with her so *comme il faut. Hé, hé, c'est la vie, François,* one cannot win all games of chance! He schooled his long-nosed satyr's face into an expression of polite interest as he leaned toward her. "Ten years is a long time, *ma trés belle.*"

"Too long," she replied on a serious note. "I should have reached my goal long since."

"What then hinders you, *petite?* Is it in my power to aid you?"

"Indeed, I hope you may, Sire. It is the Pope who hinders me. He vacillates, deciding this way and that, in the hope that His Grace will tire of me before a judgment must be made. His Grace will not tire of me, Sire."

"He would be mad if he did," said François. "Why did I let you go? *Tiens,* it was I who was mad, *ma jolie,* quite, quite crazy, *tu sais!* Come, sit here with me and we shall talk of this so stupid Pope who spoils your plans, for he is like to spoil mine too, if he listens to the Emperor Charles who plagues him to decide for Queen Katherine. Me, I hope to remain friendly with England, yet at the same time, not to upset the Emperor, you understand?"

"Have you an idea in your mind, *Majesté?*"

A smile broadened his small, full-lipped mouth, making his long nose droop longer still. "I have many ideas in my mind for you, *chou-chou,* but one only for the Pope." He

229

stared meaningly at her, his eyes twinkling wickedly. "Ah, you are beautiful. How I wish — ! But to business. Here is my idea. What if I should send a Cardinal, perhaps two, to His Holiness, with the suggestion that if he should come to France and hold a divorce trial here in the spring of next year, *Le Roi Henri* will accept the verdict? This will give you and your party full time to arrange affairs in England; a good five months, *chérie*, and by the time the Holy Father has finished agitating himself about that — *pouf!* All will be accomplished."

"But will His Grace accept the verdict of the court, Sire?"

"*Ohé*, it will not come to that. I fancy it will be a *fait accompli, mignonne.* Have no fear."

★ ★ ★

King Henry was delighted with the result of his beloved's conversation with her old admirer. It was useful, he reflected, to have the French Fox on his side in the matter, although one could never trust the fellow completely, never be sure which way he might suddenly jump. But, for the present, it would do very well. "You are my little politician," he said proudly, stroking her smooth olive cheek and kissing her lovingly. "Now we must keep our wits about us. Our new Archbishop of Canterbury will be of inestimable use to us in all this when he arrives in England."

"The new Archbishop, Your Grace? Have you chosen him?" Anne was curious as to the choice of Primate of England.

"Chosen, ay, and summoned, before we left for Calais, darling. It is Dr. Thomas Cranmer; he who suggested I lay the business of divorce before the universities some time ago, dost recall? He has such a supple brain and sees matters clear. Clear enough to view the affair as we do, anyhap."

"Ah, yes," nodded Anne. "And you said that he had the right sow by the ear, did you not? I remember. While he was living with me and my parents at Durham House I came to know and like him well. But is he not with the Emperor Charles as resident Ambassador?" She yawned. "Lord, but I am weary."

"I gave Cranmer that post, certainly," said the King, "but now he must return. He is right clever, Nan, has such a good headpiece and, being Protestant, is eager to see you upon the throne." He shifted restlessly in his chair. "By god, I hope the wind will change soon and give us a calm sea. Calais is all very fine for a short stay, but I would be home in England. List to the storm, how it roars!

Come, sweetheart, let us to bed. I am sorry that you are weary, but I do not mean to let you sleep, my lovely one!"

On the 13th of November the wind dropped, the storms abated and the King and his company were able to set sail at last. For the first time in all her years of planning and waiting, Anne felt a deep inner confidence. Her ambition would be achieved, she was sure of it now. All that remained to do was to wait, and this, after so long, she found difficult. To ease her impatience, once they were home, the King took her downriver to the Tower of London to see the alterations he had made in preparation for her coronation. The winter sun shone sharply down upon the old stones, making their thin covering of frost sparkle like diamonded gauze. Anne cuddled closer into her magnificent cloak of sables, one slender ringed hand holding up her tawny velvet skirts as she climbed the steep steps of the landing stage, the other grasping the leash of her wolfhound, Urian, who had refused to leave her side since her return from Calais.

"Oh, you have had new windows put in the Queen's apartments!" she cried. "And a new roof, too. Very fine, Your Grace."

"But come and look within, darling," he urged her, seizing her arm and drawing her forward. "Inside there are new ceiling and floors. Also, I have had a new jakes installed so that close-stools be not needed and thus the rooms will not stink, I hope. Come and see, Anne. Oh, bring the damned dog if you must! See, the seat of the jakes[1] is of oak, neatly polished and turned. Right dainty for thy pretty bum, ha?" He pinched her bottom, laughing merrily "And the curtain may be drawn across all for privacy — so. Oh, and I have had a new way made for you into the Privy Garden and new steps to the river. What think you of it all, dear heart?"

"I think it excellent," she said, quite moved by his thought for her. She looked up into his face, smiling. "Is there nothing you would not do for me?"

He put his long arms about her and drew her close. "Nothing in the world, my love," he assured her fervently. "I adore you."

She sighed against his chest. "The people do not adore me," she murmured. "'Twas not so long ago that all the women banded together to kill me. Dost remember that, Sire?"

"I shall never forget it, darling! You, at Durham House, at the mercy of eight thousand women, twilight coming down and

---

[1] lavatory

233

I nowhere near! Sweet Jesu, my heart still fails when I think of it! It was thanks only to the quick wits of good Jean de Bellay that you escaped at all." He shook his head at the memory.

"Ay, he hurried me me into a boat and we were rowed swift across the river to the south bank in the falling dusk. So it all came to naught, thank God."

"I tell you, Nan, if I had had my way I would have hanged every one of those unnatural, murdering doxies, but Thomas Cranmer advised silence and diplomacy, so that — " He paused, not wishing to hurt her feelings.

"So that the news of my unpopularity would not be spread too much abroad," she finished for him. "Of course he was right. He always is, I think."

"So he is," agreed the King, breaking into a smile. "He should be with us soon and then we shall see happy doings, I make no doubt."

★   ★   ★

Some few weeks later, the Lady Marquis of Pembroke realised that certain suspicions she had been entertaining were suspicions no longer. From her luxurious cushioned day-bed in the bay of a long window in her apartments at White Hall, she stared dreamily out at the steel-grey Thames and the heavy snow-laden sky, at the dark clouds lowering above the trees of the market gardens beyond the wall of Lambeth Palace on the opposite bank. A few flakes of snow fluttered by the window. She shivered in her furs, despite the two braziers that burned so brightly in the cosy oak-panelled room. She must take great care of herself now, she mused. Her thoughts roved lazily back and forth. She was so near her long journey's end. The King would have to marry her now, no matter what befall. There could be no dilly-dallying now that she was pregnant with his child. He had flown high out of his senses with excitement and joy when she had told him the news. And he would lose no time in wedding her, that was sure. The haughty Princess Mary would have to lower her arrogant crest soon, by God! When this boy was born, she would be nothing. She could smirk on the other side of her goky, little, pushed-in face then, and Anne would see that she did! Prideful bitch, she would be well down, indeed.

Upon this pleasing thought, she stretched contentedly, sensuously. It seemed as though all were running right at last, for Cranmer himself had arrived but two days earlier and the King has already appointed him

Archbishop of Canterbury. Anne smiled to herself as she thought of that appointment. Who ever heard of a man being made Archbishop at a bear-baiting? Upon learning of the eagerly awaited arrival, His Grace had turned his back upon the bears and ban-dogs, rushed instantly to greet Dr. Cranmer and had created him Primate of England on the spot.

There had been many a disapproving head wagged at such impetuosity, but His Majesty was not one to care a jot for that. He did as he pleased, like it or no. One had to admire him, thought Anne and, although he was running a little to fat, being near to forty-two years, he was wearing better than King François, his contemporary, whose face had grown blotched and sallow, wrinkled and baggy as an elderly beagle, for all that folks still raved of his manly beauty. She gave a little snort as she visualised the French monarch. Manly beauty, fiddlesticks! He was nothing but a diseased old lecher and looked it. Nor would he ever have married her, not he! Ay, she had made much the best of any bargain, no force. Life was good and would be better yet, for her star was rising, soon to be heavens high, and then let the mockers mock! Much good might it do them!

9

MAN PROPOSES, GOD DISPOSES

January 1533–September 1533

The stars were paling against a dim, dawn sky on the 25th of January; the wind blew cold round rooftops and chimney, frost gleamed on gutter and window-sill in the silence of very early morning while London still slept within its stout walls. Beyond those walls, a mile or two to the west, a light shone in a window high up under the eaves of White Hall Palace, the only sign of life in the huge, dark mass of buildings. Within that attic room a secret wedding ceremony was taking place. After it was over, Anne Boleyn, Lady Marquis of Pembroke, had become the wife of Henry Tudor, King of England.

The embraces of her parents followed, with short, excited cries, quickly hushed, whispered congratulations, hissed warnings to be silent and make no noise.

A little later, as Anne's parents, the Earl and Countess of Wiltshire, stepped stealthily into their barge, waiting in the half-light to

237

convey then the short distance downstream to Durham House, Thomas the Earl took his seat under the canopy, pulled his fur-lined cloak about his shoulders and turned, with a shrug, to his wife.

"A poor enough show, i'faith," he remarked in a disparaging undertone. "I suppose it must be legal? One never knows with the Tudor."

"Of course, Tom! He would not play her false, surely? Not now that she is pregnant?" The Countess's words came in an agitated murmur.

"Well, all I can say is that I found it a very hole-and-corner affair. Of course, I realise that word must not get out until the Pope has confirmed Cranmer as Archbishop and he is regularly consecrated as such, or the marriage would certainly be considered illegal. It is sailing near enough to the wind as it is."

"Oh dear, you are sure it is not a *mock* marriage, husband? I could not endure that for my little Anna!"

"No, no," he muttered testily. "Take no heed o' me. I spoke hastily. The King is not a fool. He wants a legitimate son, so although he takes risks, he would not leave the child's legitimacy to chance. No, no, it is just that something might go wrong and things might fall awry. Antonio de Borgho, the Papal Nuncio, who has been pestering for weeks for an audience with the King, must not learn of this wedding, or he will go straight with the news to the Pope and all will be up then, you understand. Once the Papal Bulls arrive here, confirming Cranmer's Archbishopric, then we are off and away. Cranmer, Cromwell and His Majesty will do the rest. No need for you to fret."

"But it seems to be that, in a way, the King is still wed to Katherine, so how — ?" Lady Wiltshire's whisper was puzzled.

"Hush, wife, for God's sake! The oarsmen may be listening, ears a-flap, to blab all they might hear! I tell you that if the Pope sends the Bulls off *before* he learns the news of the wedding, all will be well. That is certain, so now let us leave the subject alone." He raised his voice. "See, here we are at Durham House! Come, let me help you out of the boat. Lord, but I am weary! Let us to our bed."

They walked arm-in-arm along the timbers of the landing-stage, through the shadowy, wintry garden and into the great, silent house.

★ ★ ★

239

But Anne, secretly married to the King and pregnant with his child, found the secret almost impossible to keep. She was thrilled and excited almost beyond bearing and, despite all warnings, all struggles for discretion, she could not prevent herself from making oblique references to her new state. One day, early in February, whilst playing her lute and singing with her friend, Bridget Wingfield, she suddenly burst into laughter and the music jangled to a stop.

"Oh, Bridget!" she cried. "I have just had a presentiment. Can you guess what it is? Nay? Well then, I am sure as death that the King will marry me shortly. What think you of that?"

"Why," answered Lady Wingfield, somewhat at a loss, "you should be right happy, if that be the case."

"Oh, I am, I am!" And she broke into laughter again on a high, excited note that made her friend glance at her curiously. "Come," she went on, "I have a desire for company. Let us go into the Great Hall and see who is there. Perhaps we might dance or play a game — come, Bridget!" Casting her lute down carelessly on a stool, she ran from the room, making for the Great Hall which was crowded with courtiers and friends of the King. Catching sight of her dour-visaged uncle, the Duke of Norfolk, she tripped up to him and engaged him in conversation.

"Hast heard any more of that priest who wished to enter my service, my lord uncle?" she asked him, smiling teasingly. "If you have news of him, you may tell him that he must wait a little, just a little, until I have celebrated my marriage."

"Oh ay?" The Duke glanced down at her from his heavy-lidded eyes, his straight gash of a mouth twisting unpleasantly. He had never forgiven his niece for ruining his high policy in Ireland so long ago, feeling that she had made a fool of him, and had disliked her heartily ever since. "And how long is a little while, niece? Another six years?"

"You are pleased to mock me, sir!" she laughed, ignoring his sarcasm. "I vow you will be surprised e're long. I tell you that if I find I am not with child, I shall go on pilgrimage straight after Easter!" Once more laughter bubbled out of her as she darted him a saucy, knowing look before dancing away, leaving raised eyebrows and mystified glances behind her.

Back in her room, readying herself for a banquet she was giving His Grace that evening, she could not forbear singing and tapping her feet as though unable to keep still. All her ill-temper, irritability and impatience seemed to have vanished as she turned this way and that while her maids laced her into a new black velvet gown trimmed with gold, pinned the full, cut-worked, furred sleeves in securely and fastened a diamond collar round her long, slender neck.

At the banquet, her royal husband ate heartily, scarcely vouchsafing a word or a glance that common courtesy demanded to the other guests, so occupied was he in laughing and whispering to his lovely lady. All were startled, therefore, when raising his head, he suddenly addressed the Dowager Duchess of Norfolk, Anne's step-grandmother.

"Good Agnes," said he, "is not my Nan a treasure? Is she not worthy of the very best?"

"Why, of a surety, Sire," replied the old Duchess, taken aback and wondering what these questions portended. "She is worthy of the best, indeed."

The King waved his hand toward Anne's sideboard and cupboard, filled and glittering with jewelled cups, golden plates and dishes. "See those," he said a barely-controlled grin upon his lips. "Has she not a great dowry and a rich marriage. All you see here belongs to her, as well as the dishes you are served from, Duchess — " He broke off, turning to Anne, who was shaking her head, eyes a-dance, and burst into a hastily-stifled crack of mirth. "Ah — ah — heed me not," he said with difficulty, after a moment. "I am flown with wine, I daresay, and my tongue outruns my wits."

All this secretive merriment did not go unnoticed and many suspicions were raised thereby, especially in the mind of Eustace Chapuys, the Imperial Ambassador, who wrote of them to his master, the Emperor Charles, warning him to prevent the Pope from issuing the Papal Bulls. His misgivings were not allayed at the end of February, when Anne, seemingly alight with joy and exhilaration, burst out of her chamber into a crowded gallery, seeking her friends for dancing, for games, for reading, for gossip — anything to serve her wild mood. Chapuys watched her with a jaundiced eye as she walked about the gallery, chatting vivaciously to this man or that.

Always the men, thought Chapuys sourly. She always seeks the men, light-minded hussy. And see how they crowd about her, like dogs round a bitch in heat! No behaviour for a Queen, should His Grace make the disastrous mistake of wedding the jade! He shook his head disapprovingly as he saw Sir Richard Page eagerly pushing his way through the small throng that surrounded her, a posy of snowdrops in his hand. Some men never learn, he thought. Born a fool, live like a fool. And there was Sir Henry Norreys, old enough to know better, fawning upon her words as though uttered by an oracle and laughing like a zany as though at pearls of wit! And her brother is no better, ever with her, his arm ever about her waist like a lover. A lover? The Ambassador frowned and dismissed the fancy. Nay, even George Boleyn would not be such a want-wit as to engage in such an unnatural practice! What was the woman saying now? Chapuys edged closer to hear Anne's words.

"Oh, Tom, Tom Wyatt!" she called across the room to Wyatt, her voice rising high above the bustle of movement and talk. "Hear thou this, Tom! Three days ago I had an inestimable desire to eat an apple and I have never liked apples before! Is that not strange? The King says it is a sign that I must be with child, but I tell him no. No, no, it cannot be!" With a peal of laughter, she ran from the room, leaving a buzz of curious and interested gossip, while Sir Richard Page's snowdrops fell unheeded from his hand to the floor.

* * *

On the 24th of February, the Papal Bulls were issued by the Pope and were immediately on their way to England, Chapuys' note of warning having reached the Emperor Charles V too late for him to inform His Holiness of King Henry's possible marriage. A week or two later the lords and ladies of the Court of England found themselves the recipients of two identical sermons, one from Anne's chaplain and one delivered by the King's priest. These clerics proclaimed from the pulpit that their King had discovered that he had been living in a sinful state of adultery with Katherine of Aragon and, since this was so, it was only natural that he should wish to wed another lady.

Within the same week, George Boleyn was sent to France on a secret mission to gain the support of King François for the match and to ask him to prevent any impediment to it, or to the succession which was undoubtedly to follow in the shape of a son. Amused, King François readily agreed to George's request and promised to induce the Pope to delay passing sentence.

When George returned with this satisfactory reply, King Henry waited no longer. In early April he informed a meeting of his Privy Councillors that he was married to Anne and that her coronation would take place after

Easter. As well as this, a deputation was sent to Queen Katherine, now residing ill and lonely in reduced circumstances at Ampthill in Hertfordshire, to tell her that she was no longer the King's wife and would henceforth be addressed as Princess Dowager. If she would agree to this, the members of the deputation were to assure her that the King would increase her now slender income and few comforts. But Katherine would not hear of it and insisted that her attendants continue to address her as Queen.

"For if I am not Queen," she said, "then my dear daughter is not Princess and cannot inherit the throne, should that come to pass. My marriage was a true one and I shall never repudiate it. My daughter is legitimate and I am Queen of England, no matter what is said or done."

In answer to this piece of defiance, King Henry sent her a sharp message to the effect that she would now be kept to the confines of house and garden and the Princess Mary would no longer be allowed to communicate with her in any way at all. Thereupon, Katherine ordered a new set of liveries for her servants embroidered with the initials H. and K.

"Would you believe it, Marget?" cried Anne to Margaret Lee. "The old besom will not give up! Why can she not accept the inevitable? If she would, she could have comforts, riches, jewels, houses, servants and, what she prizes above all, the company of that dwarfish daughter of hers. What can she hope to gain? I cannot understand it, except that she wishes to spite me and to appear to all as a martyr. Well, I mean to teach her a lesson!"

Margaret's eyes opened wide at this bold speech. None of the courtiers, except the members of the Privy Council knew of the marriage as yet, and she was amazed at Anne's hardihood.

"Meddle? I? Very fine, i' faith! You do not know to whom you speak, Marget. All I ever hear from you is, 'Nan, have a care, have a care, Nan!'! I have pursued my own course and you will soon discover where it has brought me, so be silent e'er you go too far with your 'Have a care.'!" Anne's black eyes flashed and she stamped her foot angrily. "Bring my chamberlain to me, Marget, and at once!" Snapping her jewelled fingers, she gestured imperiously toward the door and Margaret, big-eyed, hurried to do her bidding.

Her bidding resulted in the repainting of Katherine's former state barge with Anne's colours and Anne's new coat of arms. This did not meet with the King's approval, especially since it had been done without his knowledge and permission, but he defended Anne's precipitate action loyally to those of his Ministers who were inclined to view such haste as premature and in questionable taste. He defended it, but for the first time was conscious of a slight annoyance with his darling.

On the 12th of April, Anne went to Mass in the King's chapel at Placentia, blazing with gems and clad in a marvellous gown of cloth of gold, her long train being carried by her cousin, Lady Mary Howard, who was betrothed to the Duke of Richmond, the king's illegitimate son. It was Easter Eve and her first public appearance as Queen. There was a stunned silence as she appeared in the chapel, followed by sixty maids-of-honour, thirty more than Queen Katherine had ever had. Many eyes were round, many jaws dropped, but no protest was heard from the courtiers gathered there to worship. To press the point home, the officiating priest, Dr. Brown, prayed loudly for the health and long life of *Good Queen Anne*.

It was a wonder, thought many of the congregation, that God did not cause the roof to fall in at such prayers. *Certes*, the world was turning upon its head. As they knelt, heads bowed, murmuring the responses and

248

singing the hymns, they were amazed that swift retribution did not follow. But God moves in a mysterious way, they reminded themselves, and His mills grind slow, but exceeding small. Good Queen Anne! Whoever heard the like? Mayhap the Almighty would speed the mills just a little in this affair?

The service over, the King rose to his feet, his crimson cloth of gold doublet glowing in the light of the many candles. His voice echoed sonorously across the chapel.

"My lords and ladies," he said, "as you leave this place of prayer, I urge you, one and all, to bend the knee before my wife and Queen — " here, he broke off to, exchange smiles with Anne, " — and pay her the homage which is her due. Rise up, my lords and ladies and come now to swear allegiance to her who is to bear our Prince."

The news was out. If there were any gasps of dismay, they were stifled. If there were any hesitant members of that congregation, they remained unseen. Let discretion take the part of valour, they decided, even though one's knees felt struck with the rheumatism to have to bend before the Boleyn. Better to play safe now and see what would transpire later.

What transpired was that on the 3rd of May, Cranmer, now officially recognised by the Pope as Archbishop of Canterbury, gave judgment that the King's marriage to Katherine was not, and never had been; a true marriage; that he and she were henceforth forbidden to live together and were both free to remarry. Five days later, Cranmer spoke again. He pronounced His Majesty's marriage to the Lady Anne Boleyn both true and lawful. The Lady Anne Boleyn had won.

She had won, she was Queen, she was four months pregnant, her gowns were triumphantly too tight and extra material must be let in. She made no effort to hide her swelling figure from the disgruntled eyes of the Dukes of Norfolk and Suffolk who had tried hard to prevent her marriage, while her father professed himself as scandalised at such behaviour.

"You should keep yourself private and thank God for the state in which you find yourself and not parade your belly so brazenly before all!" he had ranted, eyeing her rounded stomach with disfavour.

"Ho, father!" she had cried tossing her head scornfully. "In this belly is your royal grandchild, and as for me, I am in far higher state than you and far better than you had dreamed of for me, so hold your tongue and remember that I am your Queen and you are Lord Privy Seal only because of me!"

Grinding his teeth, her father was silent. One did not argue with a Queen, even if the baggage were his insolent daughter. There was never sun without shade, curse it!"

Six days after this, on the afternoon of the 29th of May, the bright sun beat warmly down upon a flotilla of gaily painted boats making its way down the river Thames toward the palace of Placentia at Greenwich. There was a vessel containing a fearsome red dragon, seeming, to the awe-stricken rustics on the bank, to be alive, so restlessly did it move and belch fire from its open jaws. Behind this rocked another craft carrying a tree-stump painted gold, decorated with wired-on green velvet leaves and red and white silken roses, upon which perched the carved model of a white falcon, a crown upon its head, a sceptre in its raised claw.

"See the falcon there? That be the Night Crow's badge!" whispered the watchers. "She will come this way soon to her crowning." They glanced at one another furtively, one quickly spitting upon the ground, the others stealthily making the gesture warranted to ward off the Evil Eye, afraid to speak their thoughts upon the matter of the Night Crow and her crowning.

"Look!" cried another voice, breaking the uneasy silence on a note of relief. "There be the Lord Mayor of London! By the Cross, a brave sight he be. See his scarlet gown and golden chain! Long live the Lord Mayor, lads!"

"Long live the Lord Mayor!" echoed the shout across the shining water, half-drowned by the shrilling of trumpets, the beating of drums and the crack of gunfire as the boats dropped anchor in Greenwich harbour and various state barges of the high nobility tied up at the palace waterstairs to await the new Queen's appearance.

At three o'clock she came, a dazzling vision, dressed from head to toe in cloth of gold, brilliant with jewels, stepped into her barge and was borne upstream to the Tower of London, where her King and husband waited to greet her and lead her to her handsome, newly-decorated and refurbished apartments

Two days later, at five o'clock in the afternoon, along streets strewn with white sand, the houses hung with vivid tapestries, carpets, or lengths of silk and velvet, rode a great procession of gentlemen, squires, knights and judges in their robes of state, followed by Knights of the Bath clad in purple. Next came abbots and bishops in their many-hued copes all bright with gold embroidery, with barons, earls and marquises in their crimson velvet and ermine. There was the Lord Chancellor, brave in black and gold, there were the archbishops, their mitres like small steeples bobbing; dignified ambassadors, Garter-King-of-Arms and the Lord Mayor of London; a rainbow of colours, a continuous rattle of trotting hooves. In the centre of all this splendour shone Anne Boleyn, like a pearl in a golden shell as she sat in a litter draped in white cloth of gold, wearing a robe of white tissue trimmed with ermine. Her long, lustrous black hair, all threaded with pearls and rubies, hung down her back from a golden coif encircled with precious stones which sparkled as she bowed from side to side to the crowds assembled to watch her procession of recognition.

They watched, but there was no cheering. Not a sound. No tossing of hats in the air, no welcoming shouts, no throwing of flowers and posies. Nothing but sullen, scowling faces and a heavy, inimical silence.

At Westminster, after that glorious, but unnerving journey, Anne was glad enough to alight, go within, drink a restorative cup of wine, then slip through a back way, down to the water-stairs to her barge and be taken swift back to White Hall and her loving husband. She did her best to cut the disturbing experience from her mind, for she was to be crowned next morning.

And crowned she was, with solemn state and ritual, a ceremony made all the more complete to her by the satisfying spectacle of the Duke of Suffolk having to walk before her, bearing the crown. The Duke's face was a study in resentment and chagrin, enough to curdle new cream, thought Anne. Well he was one who had done all he could to hinder her success, had the King's precious brother-in-law, and was now forced to drop from his high horse — and not before time. She laughed inwardly. Who could harm her now? Let them but try.

So uplifted was she by her triumph that she scarcely felt the weight of the great crown of St. Edward as Cranmer placed it reverently upon her head, while her right hand clasped the sceptre without a tremor. She could rise no further. She had reached the summit. She was Queen.

★ ★ ★

Queen or no, in July her self-satisfaction received a rude jolt when the unwelcome news was brought of loyal scenes toward Katherine upon her move from Ampthill to the village of Buckden in Huntingdonshire.

"They shouted *what?*" cried Anne, unwilling to believe her ears.

"Majesty, the people shouted, *God save Queen Katherine! We are ready to die for you!* and other such phrases," blurted out the embarrassed messenger, cursing the mischance that had forced him to be the bearer of such a report.

"And did I understand you to say that the same happened with the Princess Mary when she was also moved to another house?" queried Anne incredulously. The messenger nodded, wishing himself elsewhere. "Good God!" exclaimed the new Queen bitterly. "They make such a fuss of those two women as if God had descended from the skies. It should be stopped!" She beat her hands on her knees as she sat. "How can it be stopped!" she cried wildly to the courtiers surrounding her, receiving only silence, blank looks and shrugged shoulders for her answer. She rose heavily from her chair, now seven months gone in her pregnancy, feeling ill and over-excited, turning angrily to the King who had entered the room.

"Am I not Queen?" she cried furiously. "How dare these treasonous rustics behave so. It makes me look a fool! Have I not given lavishly to charities and largesse to the poor of town and country? And have I received one word of thanks? No! They must be punished for their disrespect. And you must see to it yarely, husband, for all you do not care to bestir yourself in the matter!"

She began to sob hysterically and the King, his face an interesting medley of annoyance, discomposure and an almost unwilling sympathy, did his best to soothe her, finally promising that he would not go on Progress that year, but would stay with her and take short hunting trips only.

Really, pregnant women were the very devil, he reflected moodily. Anne was not taking the business very well; her temper, touchy enough in any circumstance, was wellnigh unbearable these days and her looks were suffering greatly. In fact, when he looked at her he was amazed how she had changed from a beautiful alluring creature into a pale, haggard, nerve-racked quarreller, ready to dispute with him about everything. His marriage was not bringing him the delight he had imagined. In truth, it was a damned disappointment. Mayhap she would recover her looks and charm after their son was born. Anyhap, looks or no, the boy would make up for all.

In August, the news came to Windsor that Pope Clement had at last moved himself to give a verdict, and unpleasant news it was, for His Holiness had declared the new marriage to be null and void, and any issue of it to be illegitimate, and King Henry himself excommunicated.

"Sweet Christ!" roared the King upon hearing of this. "The Queen must not be told. In her state, 'twill be enough to start a miscarriage! Here, Cromwell, instruct the Privy Councillors and doctors of canon law to assemble at Guildford and I will come there as fast as may be. I shall tell the Queen I am going hunting. Dear God, will this fuss ever be done? I am growing mighty weary of it, Cromwell, and weary of lack of love, too," he added irascibly. "Know you that I lived like a monk for six years and now that my wife is breeding, I live like a monk again, curse it! Women! They are naught but trouble, when all is said and done."

The new Lord Chancellor smiled. "Your Majesty could take a mistress," he suggested insinuatingly. "There are many lovely ladies who would be happy to accommodate Your Grace and to keep a still tongue the while."

"Well, a man must have some relief," replied the King in a pettish, grumbling tone. "But I am a law-abiding man at heart, Crum, and mindful of the laws of the Church. I do not like to stray. Yet, after all, 'tis not as though the Queen is able or willing to oblige me as a wife just now, and a wife must wink at a mistresses, as all the world knows. I will

257

consider it, Crum, my good friend."

His Grace did more than consider Cromwell's suggestion. He acted upon it with the connivance of several of his friends, some of whom disliked Anne sufficiently to let her know of the secret affair. The resultant explosions echoed all over Windsor Castle, 'making the rafter ring', as the Duke of Suffolk confided, sniggering, to the Duke of Norfolk.

Loud shrieked Anne, beside herself with outrage and distress. Louder still roared her husband, feeling at once guilty, misunderstood, righteous and wrathful.

"How could you? How *could* you? After all those years, when you have been true to me so long! I see 'tis one sort of behaviour to a sweetheart and another for a wife!" she had screamed, cut to the heart.

"Ay, you are right!" he had bellowed, heedless of listeners. "You *are* a wife and so must shut your eyes and endure as one who was better than yourself did! Do not yell at me, Madam!" he had shouted. "I would have you know, and know well, that I can, at any time I please, lower you as much as I have raised you. I advise you not to forget it!" And he had stamped out, leaving her shocked into silence, realising a little of what Katherine must have suffered as well as the horrid thought that her marriage was no sinecure.

After this incident, common-sense prevailed and the couple grew more friendly in time for Anne to prepare for her lying-in during the first days of September, when she took barge for Placentia for the ceremony of Taking the Chamber, when she was required by custom to remain in her room with her women until she had given birth to the confidently expected Prince of Wales. No man, even the King, would be allowed to enter.

All was in readiness. There stood the great cradle of state, large enough for a baby giant, and beside it a little, gilded wooden cradle for everyday use. Notices had been written to send out to all the English nobility and the King had already chosen Edward as the name for his son-to-be. He had also sent to France for special horses to be ridden in the grand tournament that was to be held as soon as the boy came into the world.

All was thus in readiness and, between three and four o'clock in the afternoon of the 7th of September, after a difficult and painful labour, Anne Boleyn's child by King Henry was born.

A servant hurried to the King's apartments, panting and breathless, and His Majesty leaped to his feet, his face blazing with excitement.

"How is the boy? How fares the little Prince?" he cried. "See that he is brought to me at once!"

After the short, horrified silence that followed the servant's reply, loud roars of rage and dismay were heard up and down the corridors, for the mills of God had begun to grind.

The little Prince was a little Princess.

10

THE MILLS OF GOD

September 1533–February 1536

After the first shock, with its accompanying feelings of failure, resentment and catastrophe, reason asserted itself and the King, with a flash of his better nature, tried to comfort his drained, exhausted, miserable wife.

"Come, Nan," he bade her robustly, "do not repine. We are not too old to have other babes who will be sons."

She was scarcely in a fit condition to appreciate this philosophy, her body and mind being in a state of weakness and confusion. No son! What had gone so terribly wrong? She had been so certain. How could she have failed? It was past understanding. Still, the little girl was very pretty — her very own child, her own daughter. But a girl, after all their hopes and expectations! What could God have been about to serve them so? Yet, the child, the tiny thing was so like His Grace that one could almost laugh if there were anything in this business to laugh about. The red down on the tiny head, the already imperious expression on the infant face — oh, it was a sweeting, a poppet! She would love this child for ever and protect her from disaster with her life, if need be . . . Disaster? Why, there would be no disaster! It was her low state that made her prey to such thoughts.

The baby was named Elizabeth after the King's mother, Elizabeth Plantagenet, eldest daughter of King Edward IV, and after Anne's mother, Lady Elizabeth Howard, in a magnificent ceremony, during which His Grace showed every evidence of pride and delight in his daughter, showing no apparent disappointment at her sex. His pride would not allow that. What, make himself an open laughing stock? Never! His real feelings must remain hidden.

At the same time, the King's messengers were riding to Beaulieu, at Newhall Boreham in Essex, where the seventeen year old Princess Mary dwelt in the comfort and splendour befitting her rank. When the messenger left, she was Princess no longer but, by her father's command, to be known as the Lady Mary only. Her badge was to be removed from her servants' liveries and replaced by that of the King and her household was to be subject to him alone.

In this way, the future of Anne's children as heirs to the throne would be secured, for next time, there would be a son, sure! Under the reassurance of this, Anne's health improved and her looks and spirits with it, so that the King was very pleased to bed with her. Her enchantment for him had not all vanished, which was a relief to them both.

"Darling," he said to her in all sincerity one day, "I would sooner beg alms from door to door than abandon or desert you whom I love more then ever."

A cold finger of doubt touched her heart. He had been considering such a move, then! She summoned up a saucy, rallying look and managed to laugh.

"What is this, Sire? Abandon? *Desert?* God's nails, I trust that such a thought never entered your mind?"

He kissed her. "Nay, I did but use those terms to show how deeply I still feel for you, dearest."

It was a warning, however oblique, and Anne's peace of mind, scarcely restored, was upset still further by the implacable stubbornness of the Lady Mary, who had refused to move from luxurious Newhall to the much smaller Hertford Castle and who had declined to put aside the title of Princess, to which she roundly asserted she had every right.

Here was defiance indeed. Anne was then horrified to learn that even though her husband's marriage to Katherine of Aragon had been declared null and void, many doctors of canon law still agreed and affirmed that Mary was the legal heir to the throne, for the marriage had been made in good faith. Desperate, Anne then persuaded the King to force Mary to live away from Court without any of her friends and servants and when Elizabeth would be given her own household, Mary was to become part of it and in a lesser rank and position than her baby half-sister.

It was real agony for Anne to have to part with her adored child only three months after her birth, but iron-bound convention decreed that the heir to the throne must have his or her separate palace and household, so the tiny Princess Elizabeth was conveyed in state to Hatfield Palace in Hertfordshire, leaving her mother sobbing her heart out.

The Lady Mary, upon her arrival at Hatfield, was also sobbing her heart out. She had been compelled to make the journey in an old leathern litter, with only two servants, escorted by the Duke of Norfolk, grim-faced and stern. At Hatfield, when she alighted from the litter, the Duke turned to her.

"My Lady," he said curtly, "it is required that you should go at once to pay your respects to the Princess Elizabeth." He saw Mary's eyes flash and her face flush and added, "It is of no use to rail at me. I do but carry out your father's orders, which must be obeyed."

"Princess indeed!" shouted Mary, unheeding, her face quivering with rage and misery. "I know of no other Princess in England but myself, sir! The child of Madame de Pembroke has no right to the title! Nay, I *will* speak — if only to say that since the King my father owns the babe as his, I shall call her 'Sister', as I call his illegitimate son of Richmond 'Brother.' Further than that I will not go, no matter how I am pressed!" And, weeping hysterically, she rushed to the rooms assigned to her.

When Anne was told this, she fairly shrieked with fury. That curst Mary! That rebellious bitch! It was plain that she still regarded her Queen as the King's mistress, marriage or no. She should learn her mistake, by God! Oh, well indeed should she learn it!

But no humiliation that Anne could devise for the obdurate Lady Mary would break the young girl's proud spirit. Stripped of her jewels, deprived of her privileges, the company of her servants and priests forbidden her, denied any communication with her beloved mother, she would not give in. As a last resort, Anne sent her aunt, Lady Shelton, to Hatfield to take charge of Mary and to bear with no nonsense from the girl.

"I order you, Aunt Shelton, to obey in this," she had directed, "and if the Lady Mary should persist in calling herself 'Princess', you are to slap her like the curst bastard she is! You understand me?" And Lady Shelton, although shocked, had promised to do her bidding, leaving feeling decidedly confused as to where her loyalties lay.

In the event, Lady Shelton found herself quite unable to comply with her niece's instructions. At last, finding her charge to remain wholly undeterred by reprimandings and upbraidings, the lady announced that, to her mind, instead of being ill-treated, the Lady Mary should be honoured and commended for her many virtues and the Queen could make what she liked of that.

Because of her fear and jealousy of the Lady Mary, the Queen was displeased with her aunt and said so roundly. Nor did she find the maintenance of Queenship to be as easy as she had imagined. Her great estates had to be properly administered, as well as her royal household and many royal dwellings. Also, she was responsible for her ladies, being required to see that they behaved in a moral and respectable fashion, which, being lively and flirtatious herself, she found somewhat ridiculous.

She did make it her business to pay much attention to her many charities, to which she gave with great generosity; generosity which availed her little, for it did not improve her standing with the people of the realm. They persisted in regarding her as a harlot and a witch who had practised her vile arts upon the King, causing him to break with the Church of their fathers in order to marry her, thus cutting them off from their God.

In spite of popular feeling, at the end of March 1534, King Henry agreed to an Act of Parliament which abolished the Pope's rule in England and settled the Succession upon the children of the much-hated Queen Anne. Any person, man or woman, who spoke against this would be found guilty of treason, with the penalties of imprisonment and forfeiture of property; moreover, the King required every adult to swear upon the Bible to uphold this Act in an Oath of Succession, under pain of death. In the same month, Anne attempted a policy of conciliation with the Lady Mary who was still at Hatfield.

In her relief at finding herself to be two months pregnant, Anne travelled to Hatfield herself to try to persuade the Lady Mary to return to Court promising that she, even though Queen, would not take precedence of Mary, but that they should walk side by side, even through doorways.

Mary would have none of this. She ran to her room, slammed the door and shouted: "Tell Madame de Pembroke that I acknowledge no other Queen than my beloved mother!"

Filled with anger and despair, Anne was forced to return and thereupon, to her dismay, suffered a miscarriage, brought on, it was thought, by the two journeys so early in her pregnancy and her feelings of fury and defeat. She took heart in April, finding herself to be with child again. All would be well now, surely! But another miscarriage followed and Anne was conscious of a deadly fear. What would become of her if she could carry no other child but Elizabeth? She would be another Katherine. Oh, God! Oh, God forfend! She felt ready to vomit at the very thought. What, after all, was a Queen but a child-bearer to a king — a wife to a husband? What would become of her?

In July, her fears were allayed, for it appeared that she was pregnant again. The King, who had been curt and angry with her, began to treat her more kindly and showed his pleasure in many little ways when they went on Progress together in August. But by that time she had discovered that she had made a mistake and was not pregnant at all. Terrified, she said nothing to her husband, finding it impossible to endure the thought of his fury at such news, realising that he would find it out for himself soon enough, which he did in the month of September.

After that, he changed toward her completely, avoiding her company and renewing his pursuit of the lady whom he had taken as a mistress a year earlier and who was no friend to the Queen. Anne ordered the lady to leave the Court. The King countermanded the order and sent her brother George to tell her so.

"But, George," she faltered, "what shall I do? How shall I bear such humiliation? What, exactly, did His Majesty say?"

"Nan, I do not like to tell you. I do not like to think of it myself."

"Tell me, brother. I must know." She gazed at him miserably.

"He said — oh God, he said you had best be content with all he had done for he would

269

not do it now, were it to begin again — ” He hesitated.

“There is more? Tell me.”

“You will not like it, Nan.”

“Tell me,” was all she said.

“Well then,” George continued haltingly, “His Grace said — he said you had best consider what you came from. An insult, Nan. I think it dangerous.”

She swallowed, wordless, and they stared at one another.”

“Oh, George!” she whispered. “Oh, dear God save me!”

“Amen to that, sister,” said George fervently. Then, suddenly, “And there is Mary pregnant.”

“What, Mary? The King’s daughter? Never!”

“No indeed. Our sister Mary.”

“You mean, she is pregnant, while I — ? Oh, George, I cannot endure it! And she is not wed, neither! What shame and disgrace she brings upon us!”

“Oh, but she is wed,” replied George. “She is wed to Sir William Stafford scarce three months agone, so it is no disgrace, Nan.”

“It *is* a disgrace!” exclaimed Anne. “As sister to the Queen, she has no right to throw herself away on a mere knight and without the King’s permission. He will be furious, for he could have wed her to some useful foreign prince. She has ill-served us. She shall leave Court. I order it."

"She said she loved him right well and he her," ventured George.

"Oh, she has no sense, no mother-wit. She shall leave Court, I say."

"You are jealous, my love," observed George sadly.

"I am jealous," she said and burst into tears.

★ ★ ★

Although the King had saved his subjects from the Pope's Interdict, instituting, by an Act of Supremacy, a separate Church in England, conferring upon himself the title of Supreme Head, his subjects were not grateful. Apart from a few Protestant, they preferred the Roman Church in which they had been raised and mutterings grew against the King. These mutterings became louder still and were only silenced by terror, for words were now enough to constitute a hanging matter. One dared not grumble to one's brother, or one's wife for fear of torture and even death. It did not increase His Grace's popularity, nor that of his black-eyed second Queen.

King Henry recognised the unwelcome

signs all too well. A monarch who was unpopular could not hope for a long reign, history proved that clearly enough, and King Henry intended to remain upon the throne until the last day of his natural life. None of this wretched state of affairs would have been if he had not insisted upon marrying Anne Boleyn. He must have been crazy! How could he have allowed himself to get into such a ridiculous state over an ill-tempered shrew who was losing her looks, was cold in bed and who, it appeared, could not bear him another living child, let alone a son? He must have been mad — or bewitched. What a dolt, what a fool he had been!

To dull her ever increasing apprehension, Anne danced, played and flirted ever more giddily amongst her little court of admirers. She had pleasant Sir Henry Norreys in her train, Sir Francis Weston, dashing and athletic, always at her hand; young William Brereton who made her laugh; her brother George, Lord Rochford, ever by her side, his arm around her waist, her hand on his arm, and there was Marc Smeaton, noticed only for his music, poor, low-born Marc, who played the lute with angel's fingers and thought her perfection. Many hard eyes watched her and her little court and many busy brains took note.

At Christmas, Anne discovered that her old friends, King François and Jean du Bellay were her friends no longer. After the death of Pope Clement that autumn, François had done his best to retain the friendship of both England and the new Pope Paul III, but because of England's break with Rome had been forced to choose between the two. He had chosen the Pope, while Jean du Bellay had been made a Cardinal by His Holiness, who therefore demanded his loyalty. It was a great shock to Anne. First, her husband had become hostile to her, now King François and dear Jean du Bellay. In desperation, she whispered to Madge Shelton, her pert and pretty cousin, that she must try to catch the King's fancy.

"But why should I do so, Nan?" asked Madge, puzzled. "What is in your mind?"

"A notion that you should become his mistress, cousin. 'Tis audacious measure, I know, but the bitch he lies with now hates me and speaks ill of me in his ear. You could speak kindly of me, could you not? Would you not? You may have what jewels you please if you will, Madge. Pray say you will."

Madge, warm-hearted, easy-going and sorry for Anne, laughed and shrugged. "I do not mind," she said. "I think His Grace is well enough, though running sadly to fat. But 'tis something to have a King as a lover and I do want to help you. Ay, I will do it, but only until you and he are reconciled."

The plan worked. Early in the year of 1535, Madge Shelton became the King's mistress and very soon after that, His Grace and Queen Anne were re-united, resulting in another pregnancy for Anne. But it was an unhappy time, for it was beginning to be borne upon the English people that some of the country's finest men were being sacrificed to the Oath of Succession and the new Act of Supremacy, causing more unrest. The King managed to persuade himself that Anne was to blame for this. If she had not bewitched him into marrying her, he would not have had to create such an Oath or an Act! He told her this at the top of his voice.

"Oh, how unjust!" she cried, outraged. "Why, you should be more bound to me than any man be to woman! Have I not extricated you from a state of sin? Have I not made you the richest prince that ever was in England and been the cause of reforming the Church? And this to your own great profit?"

He ground his teeth. She was right, damn her. As high-ranking monk and priest refused to take the Oath of Succession and were hanged and disembowelled for it, the wealth of their monasteries had flowed into his depleted treasury, bringing him untold riches. Oh, certainly she was right, damn her. It did not endear her to him.

Among the martyrs to the Act of Supremacy were John Fisher, Bishop of Rochester, and Sir Thomas More, one-time Lord Chancellor of England and the King's dear friend. They had refused to accept the Act and had been imprisoned in the Tower. In June, the King learned that the Pope had had the temerity to create Bishop Fisher a Cardinal and that became the death warrant for the two learned, saintly and stubborn Roman Catholic prisoners. Both were beheaded; Fisher on the 22nd of June and Sir Thomas on the 6th of July.

On that July night, word of Sir Thomas's death was brought to King Henry as he sat at the gaming table. Blue dusk had fallen outside and candles were being lit within. His Majesty's back sagged, his hand holding the dice-box stilled and he gave a great sigh. He had *loved* Thomas More — loved him like a brother — and now this! All was turning awry. And wherefore? He knew the answer to that. Swinging round to face his wife who was standing at his side and who had been watching the game, he shouted: "This is 'long of you! The honestest man in my Kingdom is dead! Your fault, your fault!"

He jumped up, half-sobbing, and marched out of the room, rubbing his eyes with his hand.

During that unhappy summer Anne suffered another miscarriage and, as a result, became totally unattractive in the eyes of the King who felt most hardly used by ill-fortune. Who would want such a wife? She was thin, worn-looking, pale, haggard, vile-tempered and *barren*. By God's Feet, he thought angrily, a haughty, capricious mistress is exciting, but a haughty, capricious, barren wife is nothing but an infuriating burden. He wished her further, he wished he had never met her, he wished to have no more to do with her. In fact, his heart was so turned against her that he was indeed unable to have aught to do with her, for he had become nigh useless in her bed! He, the lustiest lecher in the land, all but useless in her bed! It was her fault, the termagant! Everything was her fault. She had brought ill luck upon him and he would he were rid of her.

It was in this mood that he, with Anne and the Court, came to Wolf Hall in Wiltshire while on Progress, the house of Sir John Seymour, Groom of the Chamber to the King and Governor of Bristol Castle. It was at Wolf Hall that His Grace met Sir John's daughter Jane, pale, quiet and twenty-five years old. He

276

found her most appealing, with a serenity about her that charmed him. He suggested to Sir John that, after the Progress, his daughter should come to Court as one of the Queen's ladies.

* * *

After that meeting with the prim little Jane Seymour who had so strongly and strangely attracted him, King Henry experienced an upsurge of passion. Since Jane's virtue, on the advice of her brothers, would not be assailed, he turned again to his wife, who once more found herself with child by him. Any relief she had felt as a result of this pregnancy was wrecked in December when, upon suddenly entering a secluded room, she discovered the quiet, shy, self-effacing Jane Seymour seated upon His Grace's knee, their arms about one another, he fervently kissing the lady. This led to a great outburst of hurt rage on Anne's part and a chilly withdrawal on the part of the King.

As a consequence of this, the Christmas celebrations were over-merry and very strained, leaving everyone wearied and exhausted, but on the 7th of January Anne received a message that made her frightened heart lift with joy. Katherine of

Aragon was dead at last.

"*Ah, Dieu me sauve, c'est magnifique!*" she cried, heedless of diplomacy. "I am truly Queen at last — the *only* Queen! *Quelle joie! Comme je suis heureuse*. Here, take this, my good fellow, you deserve a rich reward!" And, snatching a bracelet from her arm and a ring from her finger, she handed them to the startled and grateful messenger.

After he had bowed himself out, a horrid thought struck her and her smile faded, leaving her face ashy-pale. The King wanted to be rid her, she knew, but that had been impossible while Katherine still lived. If he had divorced Anne, he would have been forced to take Katherine back and that he would never have done. She shivered. Now she stood alone. Now she realised that Katherine's life had protected her own. Now the King could divorce her and marry again. Oh, Jesu, what would become of her and little Elizabeth if so?

The King suffered no such heart-burnings. His delight was unfeigned. "By heaven, we are free!" he cried jubilantly. "Free from threats of war from the Emperor Charles over my treatment of his precious Aunt Katherine and free of the old incubus herself, for which God be praised."

That afternoon he danced and sang like a

young man, feeling a great weight raised from his mind. No dark mourning was to be worn, he instructed. Nay, he fancied something bright; something lively, such as a good, strong yellow should be the rule. Ay, all should wear yellow and dance for joy. And he would arrange a fine tournament to celebrate the happy occasion, ay, and would take part in it himself! Hey, all would go right now and mayhap the expected child would be a boy, if his useless wife managed to bring it to full term.

Jovial with happiness, he began to organise the tournament, which took place, as he had planned, on the 24th of January at Placentia, with himself riding in full armour with a surcoat of silver, attended by thirty gentlemen on foot, each clad in velvet and white satin. Confident as ever, he took his place in the lists and galloped, lance lowered, toward his opponent. He was aware of a crash, a frightful pain, a loud cry — and no more. To the horror of the watchers, he lay upon the ground unconscious, concussed, with a severe injury to his leg. So long did he lie, so long was he unconscious, that it was feared that he was dead . . .

Without waiting long enough to ascertain whether the King had indeed passed away, the Duke of Norfolk, whose dislike of Anne had grown ever stronger, fanned by her Lutheranism and her turbulent effect upon the country's policies, burst into her room, where she lay upon a couch by the fire.

"Niece!" he shouted brusquely. "Your royal husband lies for dead, so take heed of yourself if you wish to stay alive, for at Court and through the land your room be preferred to your company!"

"The King? Dead?" she cried, raising herself on her elbow. "No! It is not true! You seek to frighten me!" Struggling to her feet, she rushed to the door, encountering a messenger in the passage and seized him by the arm. "Tell me, how is the King?" she screamed in a frenzy of fear. "Tell me he is not dead!"

"Nay, Majesty, he lives and speaks, thank God," the messenger reassured her. "He is recovered, heaven be praised."

Staggering with relief, Anne echoed his words before fainting away.

She lost the baby. She miscarried of a little boy on the very day that Katherine, her unwilling rival, was buried. Trembling so that the bed shook, her hair heavy with sweat, her body still racked with pain, she heard her husband's heavy footsteps in the corridor, uneven because of the injury to his leg caused by his fall during the tournament. He stood by her bed, staring down at her, his eyes hard, his face grim.

"I see clearly that God does not wish to give me male children," he said through his teeth, as though barely able to speak to her.

"Nay, oh, nay!" she gasped. "Nay, Sire, I pray you. 'Tis not of God, nay. I was sore affrighted when mine uncle told me of your fall. He thought you to be dead and told me so. It was the shock — the great shock. And I have been much saddened, feeling that you love me no longer," she whispered, gazing up at him imploringly. He was silent, glaring at her, and she went on weakly, "Also, my heart broke when I saw you with others — " Her voice trailed away.

The King was not mollified by this speech. Was she daring to blame him for the miscarriage of their son? *Her* miscarriage of *his* son! How dare she so presume! "You will get no more sons o' me," he said in a low, menacing growl. "I will speak to you when you are more recovered."

He left the room, his head full of ways and means. He would be rid of her. He must be rid of her. But to find a good reason would need some heavy thinking — where was Cromwell?

11

THE HIGHER THE CLIMB,
THE FURTHER THE FALL

February 1536–May 1536

Her fall was far and swift. The King and
Thomas Cromwell, now knighted, Chief
Secretary and the second most powerful man
in the realm, put their heads together to bring
it about.

"By the Trinity, Crum," said His Grace,
"this is a right serious business. I see my
popularity flowing away like sewage down the
Thames. She must go, and soon." He paused.
"And I cannot divorce this one."

"Unfortunately, no, Sire. There are many
lawyers who still insist that you are not legally
wed to her, in which case, there can be no
divorce if there has been no marriage. On the
other hand, for you and I who believe — nay,
who *know* — " he corrected himself hastily,
" — that the marriage is true, there are — "

"No grounds," finished the King glumly.
"Jesus God, what a pickle I am in!"

Cromwell's face assumed a look of careful

blankness. "There are ways, Your Grace. Not obvious, perhaps, but ways, nevertheless."

"Oh, do you mean that we could use her pre-contract with James Butler as a reason? It was all arranged for her to wed him."

"Well, no, Sire, with all respect. I think it a poor enough reason, if you will forgive my presumption."

"Indeed? Ah yes, I believe I persuaded everyone that the pre-contract was not a true one. Good God, what a fool was I!" He stared at Cromwell, bewildered at his folly of nine years earlier. "Then what can I do?"

"Leave it with me, Sire, and I will put my mind to it. I am sure to think of something."

"By the Rood, you are a good fellow, Crum! Where is the Queen now? What is she about?"

"She has taken boat for White Hall, Sire, where the Princess Elizabeth now rests. She loves the child greatly, Your Grace."

"Well, naturally she does — she is its mother! And so do I love the babe; it is not so strange! Can the Queen not wait until the child comes here?"

"Apparently not, Sire. The Queen wishes to spend every moment possible with the Princess, especially as the babe is on a short visit only. She has made her many little caps and a silk fringe for her cradle. A devoted mother!"

The King frowned. "Are you then the Queen's friend, Sir Thomas Cromwell? Mayhap you do not mean to help me after all?"

Cromwell's pasty cheeks turned paler still. "Your Grace! How can you think it? I am entirely loyal to you; I am yours to command. Your lightest wish, Sire, is my — "

"Yes, yes," broke in the King testily. "I'll take your word for it — do not prate so, man. Keep your mind upon our problem and waste no time in solving it. You understand? Waste no time."

Cromwell understood very well. He returned to the City, to his handsome house in Throgmorton Street, the house that was filled with the priceless art treasures that he had collected during his rise to wealth and power, and bent his cunning brain to the task. He thought of the Queen. He had certainly aided her to her position, she had been friendly toward him and trusted him as a friend also, and he had been pleased to have it so. But sentiment had no place in his work. His mission was not to be kind or sympathetic, merely to keep the King's favour in any way he could and to feather his own nest accordingly.

The only way to be rid of the Queen was by her death, and the only way to bring about her death, without adverse murmurings against himself and the King, was by a charge of treason. His mouth widened in a slow smile. Yes, that was it — treason. Now, how to accomplish it? He called to mind a prophecy against the King's life of which he had heard. A charge of witchcraft? Would that hold? A possibility. There were many common folk who deemed her a witch for her seeming power over the King . . . Adultery? Better still. Oh, much better. Let the Queen be accused of that and the wheels would begin to turn. Ay, and her circle of admirers could be accused as well . . . And what of that poxy brother of hers? Surely something could be trumped up against him. Who would then plead for her? Her timeserver of a father? He doubted it. Aha, the pattern was forming. He must work out the details and perfect it . . .

For five days Cromwell worked hard on his plan. On the 23rd of April he emerged with a secret commission that authorised the most powerful nobles, together with the officers of the Household and nine judges, to enquire into various acts of treason 'by whomsoever committed' and to try the culprits. On the 24th the King signed the commission and Anne's days were numbered.

The sun glared down from a bowl of burning blue, turning the windows of Placentia into so many great diamonds set in cliffs of brick and stone. It was unseasonably hot for the end of April and Anne the Queen felt nervous and restless, with a strange sense of foreboding that hung over her like a grey shadow, in spite of the junketings of the Court and the brilliance of the weather. She turned to her chaplain, Dr. Matthew Parker, her face fraught with unease.

"Dr. Parker," she said suddenly, "if aught should happen to me in the future, may I ask you to take especial care for my loved daughter, the Princess Elizabeth? I feel much concern for her."

The tall, elegant Dr. Parker nodded gravely. He did not attempt to make little of her fears. "You may rely on me, Madam," he assured her. "I shall make the Princess my particular charge."

"She is not yet quite three years old, thou knowest," went on the Queen musingly, "and her governess, Lady Bryan, says that she is already possessed of a powerful brain and formidable will, but will always respond to kindness and reason." She sat quietly for a moment, then threw up her hands with the air of one who casts care aside. "Oh me, I fall into a doleful dump, sir, and that will not do. I must away now," she cried, her voice hard with false gaiety, "for I am to play in a masque and must rehearse my part. And there is the May Day Tournament to which we all look forward, so I will think no more glum thoughts Dr. Parker, for what there is of life must be lived, *n'est-ce-pas?*" And she ran off, singing, though her heart shook in her breast.

The weather continued fine for the tournament. King Henry and Queen Anne watched the jousting from a gallery hung with scarlet, gold and silver tapestries and lengths of silk; bright armour flashed in the sun, trumpets shrilled, drums tapped, horses stamped and tossed their heads, harness a-rattle; the air buzzed with talk and laughter. All Anne's favourites, including her beloved brother, were to take part and she felt joyous for the first time for many weeks, chattering merrily with the rest, as she watched the contestants in their mock battles.

"Oh, see, Sire!" she cried suddenly, turning to His Majesty. "There is Harry Norreys looking hot as fire! He fought right bravely, did he not? Well done, Harry, well done!" she called. "Here, wipe your brow with this!" Down fluttered her handkerchief to fall at Sir

Henry's feet as he was helped out of his armour.

The King compressed his lips in swift annoyance, but continued to smile and nod to his friends. "Ay," he replied, "but I'll wager that he would not have won had I not lent him one of my horses."

"That was kind of you," answered Anne appreciatively. "And you lent my brother George one also, did you not? You are right fond of him, I know."

"*And so are you*," said the King in a tone of extraordinary emphasis that contrasted oddly with his jovial expression.

Anne's heart gave a jump. How strangely he spoke! What could he have meant? Could he have meant anything at all, or was it merely her imagination that his voice sounded unpleasant? I must calm myself, she thought. I see demons where none exist. Anyhap the jousting is ended and it is time to go in.

She turned, hearing a slight bustle beside her, to see the King rise from his chair and, without a word to her, march away, calling to Sir Henry Norreys and some others of his gentlemen to accompany him at once to London. Bewildered and humiliated by her husband's lack of courtesy to her as his wife and consort, she sought her rooms and with

288

two of her ladies remained there, fidgeting restlessly and chattering nervously, full of a horrid sense of impending disaster.

At noon of the next day, the 2nd of May, the door of her Privy Chamber was flung open unceremoniously by her uncle, the Duke of Norfolk, who marched into the room, followed by Chief Secretary Cromwell and the members of the Privy Council.

Anne sprang to her feet. "How is this, gentlemen?" she cried indignantly. "Do you not knock? Do you not request the Queen's permission to enter? I will not suffer such disrespect!"

"What you will or will not suffer is of no importance to me, niece," replied the Duke insolently. "You have no power to command now, for you be accused of treason."

She stared at him, dumbfounded. Had he gone mad? "What mean you?" she faltered at last. "I do not understand."

"No?" sneered her uncle. "Then I must explain. Your lovers are taken, Madam."

"My — lovers?" she repeated, stunned. "I do not understand."

" 'Fore God, you are dull this day, niece! Your lovers, Sir Henry Norreys and the musician Marc Smeaton, are taken and are even now in the Tower. They have confessed to adulterous relations with you."

At this monstrous speech, she found herself bereft of breath. Sure, her uncle had taken leave of his senses! She stared round at the ring of hostile faces surrounding her. Had they all gone crazy? What in the world was happening? Could it be a joke — a cruel joke?

"But what you say is nonsense!" she cried. "You know it is untrue! I am clean from the touch of any man, except for His Majesty and I am the King's true wedded wife! Do you jest, gentlemen? You cannot be in earnest!"

"Oh, tut, tut, tut! Come now!" The Duke's tone was mocking, as was his derisive grin. "Smeaton and Norreys have already confessed their guilt, so pray end this unedifying game of innocence!"

"How could they confess to what never took place?" Her breath caught. "Ah, — they have been tortured!"

"Naturally. What do you expect? A little torture works wonders, even on the most obdurate. Now you must come with us."

In a terrified daze, she found herself seated in the state barge, escorted by the Lord Chancellor, the Duke of Norfolk, Sir Thomas Cromwell and Sir William Kingston, Constable of the Tower of London, being rowed quietly and swiftly upstream to the Tower. With her also were four dour-faced ladies;

Lady Kingston, Lady Boleyn, her aunt-by-marriage, Mistress Coffyn and Mistress Stoner. When the barge drew up at the Tower stairs, no word having been spoken on the journey, Anne alighted and began to follow Sir William Kingston. Suddenly her feet refused to move, her legs trembled and she fell upon her knees on the sun-warmed stones.

"Oh, I am not guilty of this accusation!" she cried on a high, wailing not. "Oh, I beg you to beseech the King's Grace to be good unto me!"

She received no answer to her plea, and the men who had escorted her, embarrassed at this painful scene, hastily turned away to re-embark on the barge and be carried back to Placentia. Wide-eyed and disbelieving, Anne watched the barge cast off; saw the oars flash up and down as the vessel moved slowly away across the shining water. She was abandoned, falsely accused, left at this place — palace once, prison now — with the four unfriendly ladies who had accompanied her hither. Her breath came in uneven gasps, her head spun.

"Prithee, Sir William," she gasped in a small, shaky voice, "shall I go into a dungeon?"

"Nay, Madam," he replied gravely, "you

291

shall go into your lodging that you lay in at your coronation."

The relief of this, coming upon her terror, was too much for her self-command. She began to laugh, to weep, to scream, as her horrified ladies attempted to calm her. When she was a little recovered, Sir William Kingston led her to the familiar and comfortable Queen's Apartments and left her with her four attendants. She was to be told nothing, Cromwell had instructed Sir William Kingston, nothing at all.

"Leave her to silence," Cromwell had ordered. "Uncertainty she cannot endure. Silence and ignorance of what is taking place will break her spirit and loosen her tongue as nothing else will. I know her ways."

Cromwell knew her ways indeed. She learnt nothing of what had become of the members of her family, receiving only bland, non-committal answers to her agitated, tearful questions. All that night, sleepless, she chattered; excitedly, nervously, indiscreetly, endeavouring to prove her innocence of the charge of treasonous adultery that had been laid against her. There was no actual evidence to be obtained from her hurried, terrified flow of words, realised her worn-out, disappointed ladies, but she had said much that could be twisted and misinterpreted, either by chance

292

or design, and this they did not fail to do, reporting all to the ready ear of Sir Thomas Cromwell.

She did not know that her brother had been arrested, nor that he had denied all the disgraceful charges; she did not know that her uncle had lied to her about the confession of Sir Henry Norreys, who also continued to protest his innocence in no uncertain terms, torture notwithstanding. She could not believe that Marc Smeaton had actually confessed, under torture, to an utter false-hood, nor would have credited Cromwell's delight at this. She did not know that her hysterical attempts to clear herself had been very useful as evidence against her, after a certain amount of skilful editing, nor that this had come at a time when any evidence at all was proving difficult to find. She begged, weeping, for news and at last Sir William informed her of her brother's arrest.

"No!" she cried, as if struck. Then, with a pathetic effort at bravado: "Why then, I am very glad that we both be so nigh together!"

"Indeed? Then perhaps you will be equally glad to learn that Sir Francis Weston, Sir William Brereton, Sir Thomas Wyatt and Sir Richard Page are also in the Tower," remarked Sir William drily, watching her face keenly for a reaction of guilt.

But he was disappointed, for this brought no such result. "Nay, but my brother? And the rest of my family, what of them? Pray, pray tell me, sir. If nothing else, I beg you to tell me of my brother!" she pleaded.

"You will find out in time," was all he would say.

★ ★ ★

Although Queen Anne lay in terror and misery, such was not the case with her spouse. For diplomacy's sake, he remained withdrawn from the public eye during the day, but in the evenings the sounds of music stole out across the water from the boat in which His Majesty was rowed up-river to the house of Sir Nicholas Carew where Mistress Jane Seymour was residing, virgin still, a state which excited the King almost beyond endurance.

On the 4th of May, enough suitably incriminating evidence having been invented, Sir Henry Norreys, Sir Francis Weston, Sir William Brereton and Marc Smeaton were marched, under heavy guard, to Westminster Hall and tried there for treason before the King's Commissioners. One of these Commissioners was, unbelievably, Thomas Boleyn, Earl of Wiltshire, father of the Queen, dead to love, to family ties, to honour and self-respect, so eager was he to retain the favour of his King.

The verdict was a foregone conclusion. The four accused men were found guilty of conspiring to bring about the death of the King, of having had carnal knowledge of the Queen and of therefore having committed treason against the King and Queen's heirs. It was of no avail to the accused that they had pleaded not guilty; of no avail to Marc Smeaton that he had lied only under torture. As all knew in those days, that one who was accused of a crime was presumed guilty until proven innocent, so the fate of these unhappy men was sealed. They were marched back to the Tower, the drums of the guards beating their heavy rat-a-tat-tat, the executioner's axe, its edge turned toward them as a symbol of their condemnation, their minds in a bewilderment of horror and despair.

On the 15th of May, Anne herself stood accused. Elegant in black satin, pale and tense, she glanced anxiously about the hall, seeking a friendly face among the hard, hostile countenances before her. The Duke of Norfolk, as High Steward of England and the representative of His Majesty, was seated under a cloth of state, his craggy, dark features grim, yet subtly triumphant. The

Lord Chancellor sat on his right, the Duke of Suffolk, the King's brother-in-law, on his left. There was no subtlety in Suffolk's triumph; his eyes fairly glittered with it. *We have you now*, said those eyes. All the leading nobles of the land were present, including the miserable Henry Percy, now Earl of Northumberland, whose stricken visage was plainly visible to Anne.

How could he, Harry Percy, of all men, be there? For a moment, her mind rejected the horrid realisation that his presence must have been enforced by the order of her own husband. Oh, Harry, Harry Percy, could you not have resisted? she wondered sorrowfully. Then, remembering; no, you could not, poor Harry. Nay, for he had always yielded to a stronger will, even in the days of their young love so long ago. He was a leaf who would sway with every wind. And where was her father? Not here, thank God. Her four ladies had told her, with eager malice, that he had taken his place at the trial of Sir Henry Norreys and the others, and had actually begged to take part in hers! That news had almost broken her. She could not have endured such a thing.

She started. Someone was speaking — what was he saying? He was accusing her of inciting Sir Henry Norreys to — *what?* She must have misheard, for it was crazy, or she must be dreaming!

The deep voice rolled on, " . . . *and that she did procure Sir Henry Norreys to violate and carnally know her, by reason thereof the same Henry Norreys on the 12th of October, violated, stained and carnally knew her . . . ."*

But that was insane! She had but just borne her daughter Elizabeth and was still too weak to walk, let alone have any man, even the King, in her bed! And why should she lie with another man, when to do so would endanger her very life? No, no, it was ridiculous. This was evil — a nightmare . . . Wait! She had caught the name of her brother. George? How could he be involved in this madness? She must pay attention and not allow her mind to wander.

"On the 2nd of November 1535," boomed the accusing voice, *"the Queen did procure her own brother, George Boleyn, Lord Rochford,"* — the voice paused as an incredulous murmur arose from the court and then continued expressionlessly " — *her own brother, Lord Rochford, with the Queen's tongue in the mouth of the said George, with kisses with open mouth, by reason thereof Lord George Rochford, despite all the precepts of Almighty God and every law of human nature, on the fifth day of*

November did violate and carnally know his own sister."

Anne gasped, stupefied with horror. Who had devised such filth? Whose mind could be so evil, so twisted, as to think such things, let alone have them roared out in public for all to hear? Ah, she understood it now. She was to be put out of the way, and by any means, no matter how foul the lies, how wicked the betrayal. There was to be no divorce for her. She was to be removed — thoroughly, quickly and for ever. She was to die. Oh God, she was to die! And dear George, beloved George, there would be no mercy for him, neither, of that she was sure.

Now she was hearing names and dates. Names? *Dates?* Impossible! She forced herself to listen. " . . . *With William Brereton on the 8th of December 1533; with Francis Weston on the 20th of May 1534 . . . ."* Why, she had done no more than to smile and exchange jests with Weston! " . . . *With Marc Smeaton . . .* " Marc Smeaton? Anne's mouth fell open in disbelief. " . . . *on the 12th of April 1535, and not once but many times."*

Sweet Christ, she would have to be a succubus, a monster of lust to have — what was this? She was being accused also, of conspiring with all five men to murder the King! This was lunacy. This was lunacy, for

298

sure. But lunacy with a purpose and that purpose was clear.

But there must be witnesses to speak for her, she reminded herself, for the charges were so horridly absurd that all must know them to be false. Looking about the court, she waited for her witnesses to come forward.

There were none. Cromwell had seen to that. She was to have no chance of survival.

So she spoke in her own defence and spoke well. If the verdict had been left to the people of England, Queen Anne, unpopular or no, would have gone free. But the people of England, the stout English folk who hated unfair dealings, were allowed no word in their Queen's fate. That was the business of the nobles who, one after the other, pronounced the dreaded word, "*Guilty!*"

The quavering voice of Harry Percy of Northumberland, gasping and cracked with emotion, was audible amongst the rest and the Duke of Norfolk rose to pronounce sentence. Dislike his niece though he did, even he found some difficulty in speaking the words he must utter.

"*Thy judgment is this. That thou shalt be burnt here, within the Tower of London on the Green, or else to have thy head smitten off as the King's pleasure be further known.*"

"Oh God!" cried Queen Anne in tones that

those who heard her never forgot. "Oh, dear my God, Thou knowest if I have merited this death!" Then, composing herself, she faced the nobles who had accused her. "I think you know well," she said, her voice low and trembling, "the reason why you have condemned me to be other than I am. My only sin has been my jealousy and lack of humility. But I have prepared myself to die. What I regret most deeply is that men who were innocent and loyal to the King must lose their lives because of me."

There was a short bustle and confusion as she finished speaking. Lord Northumberland, utterly overcome, had collapsed and was being carried from the courtroom.

★ ★ ★

Once his sister had been taken away under guard, George, Lord Rochford, took her place. Slim, dark, tall and handsome, he had a debonair appeal that nothing could destroy, a gaiety of spirit that nothing could quench.

No, he had never had incestuous relations with his sister; the notion was preposterous and no, he had never plotted against the King. Why should he for God's sake? The King was his bread and butter!

"There is another charge," continued the

Duke of Norfolk in his quiet, grating voice, "but it is a charge of such disgraceful nature that I cannot bring myself to speak of it aloud. So it is written down. Clerk of the Court hand this paper to the prisoner. He may read what it contains, but must keep silent as to its meaning."

George took the paper, read it and burst into a loud laugh. What ludicrous rubbish was written there! He would read it out. What had he to lose by so doing? He was condemned anyway, he understood that. Ay, he would read it out and serve His Majesty right. Let the Royal Murderer cringe!

"Why, here is written that my wife, Lady Jane Rochford, hath told me that the Queen had said that the King be impotent!" chuckled George, showing every sign of extreme amusement. "And what if she did? Is the King's cock so sacred that it must not be spoke of? He has used it oft enough the Lord knows. Mayhap it is wore out!"

In the uproar that followed, George was swiftly found guilty and sentenced to be hanged, drawn and quartered as a traitor at the King's pleasure.

But all was not over yet. King Henry desired the Princess Elizabeth to be bastardised in order to make way for any child he might have by Jane Seymour. This would need some doing, since Cranmer had pronounced his marriage to Katherine null and void only three years earlier. So, after a talk with Cromwell, the invaluable, His Grace felt it only right that Cranmer should be the man to pronounce the same sentence upon his marriage to Anne. It seemed to round things off very neatly.

So, after a difficult interview with His Majesty, the very reluctant Cranmer visited Anne in the Tower. It was to be a secret interview and remained secret, without word or document ever being heard or read. What passed between them was never known, but at nine o'clock in the morning of the 17th of May, Cranmer, his lips trembling, his throat dry, his heart heavy, pronounced Anne's marriage to the King null and void, doing his spirit a grave injury.

The King, pleased, and seeing himself as a merciful monarch, chose that Anne should not be burnt but beheaded. Not by an axe, for there were often bungles with an axe, but by a sword wielded by a well-known and skilled swordsman from Calais who could be relied upon to do the business cleanly and in one swift stroke.

"I have gone to considerable trouble and expense to effect this for her," he told Cranmer, "for as you know, I have a magnanimous heart. Besides, the lower the scaffold, the quicker the stroke, the less seen and the less likelihood of crowd sympathy. You know well how the mood of a mob can swing."

On the afternoon of the same day, Anne was taken from her chamber to a room in the Devlin Tower on the eastern side of the Tower of London and made to stand at a window that looked across the moat to the rise of Tower Hill. There stood a scaffold, built very high so that as many of the populace as possible were able to obtain an excellent view of the fate of a traitor. It would serve as a reminder. Stunned with a silent horror that almost turned her reason, Anne was forced to watch the hideous spectacle of her brother and her friends being done to death. Only Marc Smeaton was to be disembowelled at Tyburn. For the others, as nobles, the King had exercised his dubious mercy and the sentence had been changed to beheading. She could not watch. Half-fainting, she closed her eyes against the terrible sight. But she heard.

She heard enough to make her heave and retch and tremble. The drums, the sudden silence, the heavy thud, the low roaring murmur of the crowd as each ghastly, dripping, bloody head was held up by its hair.

Her very brain shook. Oh George, oh my brother! Oh, my innocent friends! Oh, my sweet baby daughter, soon to be motherless . . . Oh, my God . . . Help me . . . Help me . . .

Someone had thrust her head between her knees. Someone was holding her own little vinaigrette, taken from its small leather toilet case, under her nose and the swirling black mist that surrounded her was fading away . . . Someone was saying, "It is her turn tomorrow morning. She had best prepare."

"Ay," said another voice. "Now that her marriage to the King is pronounced null and void, there is nothing for which to wait."

But the execution was delayed until the afternoon, for neither the sword, nor the headsman who was to wield it, had yet arrived from Calais.

"Oh, Sir William," said Anne despairingly to the Constable of the Tower, "I hear say I shall not die afore noon and I am very sorry therefore, for I had thought to be dead by this time and past my pain."

Sir William, although he had never been her friend, now felt great pity for her and could not but admire her courage in these desperate hours. He tried to comfort her as best he might. "Madam," he said compassionately, "I must tell you that it is no pain. It is so subtle that you will feel no pain."

She stared at him. How did he know? He had never been beheaded! She put her hand about her neck and gave a sudden wild, hysterical laugh. "Oh, I have heard say that the headsman is very good, sir, and see — I have but a little neck — a very little neck!" Her laughter rose to a shriek and she clapped a hand over her mouth to stifle it as Sir William patted her shoulder in a clumsy effort at comfort.

The afternoon came and went and still Cromwell delayed as he sought for the easiest way to accomplish the Queen's execution without incurring any sympathetic demonstration, disloyal to the King, from the crowds that would come to watch her die. A low scaffold, certainly, and all foreigners must be excluded, so that no report of any show of pity from the mob could find its way to Europe. He also mounted an extra heavy guard to keep strong order.

Anne, in her prison, turned to Lady Kingston. "Prithee," she said, "wilt sit in my chair and feel that you are the Lady Mary Tudor?"

Lady Kingston laughed. "If you wish," she said. "I am well used to masques and mummery."

"This is no mummery," said Anne quietly.

"See, I kneel before you so, my Lady Mary, whom I have wronged. I beg your forgiveness from my deepest heart. I beg that you will try to look kindly upon my little Elizabeth, for she is but a baby and no longer a Princess."

Lady Kingston's laugh was silenced at these words. "Oh, Madam!" she cried, much moved. "Oh, I will indeed see that the Lady Mary hears this. I promise you, Madam!" She kept her promise.

Anne did not sleep that night, but she spent the hours in prayer. She thought of her adored little daughter; she thought of Katherine and Katherine's daughter, the Lady Mary. How cruel she had been to both of those poor women! She understood their stubbornness and their misery now. She prayed for forgiveness, struggling to raise her spirit to a trancelike state of unawareness and by dawntime had almost achieved this. At nine o'clock in the morning of the 19th of May, Sir William Kingston came to her door to escort her to the scaffold.

"Here," she said to her aunt-by-marriage, Lady Boleyn, "take these little gauds. They were gifts to me from the King and are all I have left." She handed her aunt the red toilet case and the scented locket, sparkling on its golden chain. "I shall need these no longer where I am going. I charge you to give them

306

to my sister Mary, Lady Stafford, who will weep for me. It is my last wish."

Then, with a steady step, accompanied by her four ladies, she walked to Tower Green where a large crowd had assembled, despite Cromwell's efforts. There, also, were the King's illegitimate son, the young Duke of Richmond, the Duke of Suffolk, the members of the Privy Council, the Lord Mayor of London and Chief Secretary Sir Thomas Cromwell himself.

On the low wooden scaffold stood the French headsman, his face covered by a black mask, a great two-handed sword near him in readiness.

She mounted the wooden steps. She had striven for all and had gained it. Now she had nothing. No rank, no reputation, no love. Her husband had condemned her, her father had accused her. Her brother lay dead, her baby daughter was declared bastard. All was lost except for life and in a few minutes that would be lost also.

She stood and faced the crowd gathered there, her grey damask gown falling in heavy folds about her, the low bodice leaving her neck bare, her hair dressed high under a fashionable French coif. She spoke a few short, careful, low-toned sentences, then stepped back, her feet rustling in the straw.

She removed her headdress herself and handed it to one of her ladies. She knelt quietly before the block. An attendant came forward, trembling and pale, to tie a kerchief over the large black eyes. The executioner raised his sword, the drums rolled like threatening thunder.

The thud of the sword on her neck sounded like a crash in her shocked, frightened brain. She was whirling, flying, spinning . . . spinning . . . spinning . . . where? . . . how? . . . dark . . . dark . . . a-a-a-ah . . .

"A-a-a-ah!" groaned the watchers as her head and body fell and blood soaked the straw on the scaffold.

First the silence, then the gunfire.

The show was over, the spectacle ended, the murder done. The watchers, chattering now, began to disperse and turn away, for life must go on, work must be done, boots mended, clothes washed, dinners cooked. And the sun still shone from a blue sky, the leaves still fluttered on the green trees, birds still sang; the river Thames rushed its way, as ever, under London Bridge, thereafter flowing lazily to the sea; apprentices cried their wares and the world continued its turning without the person of Anne Boleyn who had, for a short time, been England's Queen.

Hearing the gunfire and receiving the

welcome message that all was over, King Henry, dressed all in white for Court mourning, walked on to the landing stage to be rowed upstream to a riverside house where the plain and biddable Jane Seymour awaited him. He was free, heaven be praised, free of the witch, and the world was a lovely place. Humming softly, he stepped into his barge.

* * *

And there his dead wife lay on the scaffold. Aghast, the attendant ladies and nobles realised that there was no coffin present, as was usual on such occasions; no one to pick up the body — nowhere to put it. Horrified and bewildered, they could not think what to do, for no instructions for the burial had been given. The ladies sobbed and shuddered, the young Duke of Richmond fainted and the confusion of voices grew. What to do?

At last, it was decided to do nothing and to await the King's order, for fear of mistaking His Majesty's wishes by being too precipitate. No orders came. Eventually, some courtiers left, shocked; some waited awhile, but as darkness drew on, there was nothing for it but to return to home or to Court.

And so she lay, all that bright day. Lay until black night fell, when two figures climbed silently up to the scaffold, into the blood-sodden straw and gathered up the mutilated remains of the woman who had once been so beautiful and so beloved. An old arrow-chest lay empty and they stuffed her head and body into that.

Where to bury her? They did not know . . .

Author's Note

1. In accordance with her last wishes, Anne Boleyn's little red leather toilet case and black enamelled pomander locket were given by Lady Boleyn, after the execution, to Sir William Stafford, second husband of Anne's sister Mary Boleyn. They were then given to Mary and thereafter handed down through the family, finally coming into the possession of the Pennington-Mellor-Munthe Charity Trust, Southside House, London.
2. Anne Boleyn's place of burial is unknown. It has never been discovered.
3. Sir Thomas Wyatt and Sir Richard Page were released from the Tower for lack of even the most trumped-up evidence. Wyatt had kept well away from Anne after her marriage and his return from Italy and all were aware of that.
4. King Henry's illegitimate son, Henry Fitzroy, Duke of Richmond, died of consumption on the 22nd of July 1536, never having recovered, it is said, from the shock of witnessing the execution of Anne Boleyn some months earlier.

5. Jane Seymour married Henry VIII on the 30th of May 1536, eleven days after her predecessor's execution, and bore him a son on the 12th of October 1537, herself dying of puerperal fever twelve days later. The boy subsequently became King Edward VI.

6. Thomas Cromwell was executed on the 28th of July 1540 for allegedly 'misleading' King Henry over the looks and suitability of his fourth wife, the Princess Anne of Cleves.

7. King Henry died on the 28th of January 1547 aged 56 years.

8. The excerpts from some of the King's letters are authentic, as is some of the dialogue.